THE FIST of GOD

By

A.T. NICHOLAS

Thirty Pedal Rose Publishers 1998, First Edition: October 1998.
Published by TPR Publishers, all rights reserved by TPR and Nicholas Triantafilledes.
The Fist of God, Copyright 1997 by TPR and Nicholas Triantafilledes. Registration Number Txu 813-565, United States Copyright Office. ISBN number, 0-9666807-0-7.
Printed by Automated Graphic Systems, Inc. 4590 Graphics Drive, White Plains, Maryland 20695.
Cover Design by Automated Graphic Imaging. 1090 Vermont Ave., NW, Washington, DC, 20005, and Nicholas Triantafilledes.
Photograph on back cover by Ken Wilson Photography, Annapolis, MD, 1-800- 915-0041. E-Mail kenwilsonphotograghy@erol.com.

Special Thanks to;   My Lord and Savior, Jesus Christ, who always had good advice. My wife, Anita, for her patience, understanding, encouragement, and help during the entire writing process. And, G. Ronald Murphy for his insightful editing and constructive counsel.

Special Note; To my parents. Thank you for always being there for me, and for aways being a great example throughout my life. Your words taught me well, but your actions and the way you lived your lives was the greatest teacher; and it made all the difference. I love you both very much.

To my brother, Bill; No one could have a better brother, friend, and the occasional substitute father when Dad was hard at work. I want you to know , I'm grateful for the sacrifices you made for me, and that I love you. Thank you.

Others to Thank; My family and friends that helped and encouraged me. Ken Wilson at Ken Wilson Photography, Sonny Barranca, Mike Wilson, Lou Martini., Scott MacDonald, Danny at Three Brothers., Linda Wilson for her help with the proof reading, Louise Peters at Brock Gannon Literary Agency, Greg Carlucci and the staff at Automated Graphic Systems, and Jeff Klavon at Automated Graphic Imaging for his great work on the cover design. And last, but far from least, the reader. Thanks!

Dedicated to Alexander.
One first born to another.

"Hear my words.
When the unholy takes flight,
He will send One,
and thou will feel the Fist of God . . ."

Chapter 1

Washington, D.C., Autumn, 1999

A beautiful, young girl walks slowly and seductively along a sidewalk. She's dressed as if it were a hot, midsummer night. She's new to the game; no one has taught her the rules. She approaches a dark alley and notices someone standing in the shadows. She's startled, but she waits. A warm, soothing voice asks, "How much?"

She steps closer and blunders, "That depends on what you want." She moves a little closer, now an arm's reach away. A few moments pass with silence. "So, what do you want?"

The warm, comforting voice turns raspy. "Your soul," he says as he reaches out with serpent like speed and pulls her into the shadows without a sound.

The winds of change are in the air tonight and they blow a sinister stench over the city. The neon lights flash late into the night, warming the city streets. Between dusk and dawn, morals die and the beast claims another victim.

*

A priest dressed in a tattered, black robe stands on the steps of a federal building fervently preaching a sermon. Across the street a political dinner party is being held. The priest stands inflexibly on the steps with his long, stringy, gray hair flowing in the autumn breeze. The bags under his eyes suggest that he hasn't slept in days, and the lines on his face, worn by sixty years of life, are prominent. His sky-blue eyes pierce the small crowd gathered in front of him. His words roll overhead like a tempest and come crashing down like almighty hail. Poised as if he were standing at a pulpit, his voice resounds with eternal divinity.

"If thou shalt confess with thy mouth the Lord Jesus and shalt believe in thine heart that God hath raised Him from the dead, thou shalt be saved. For with the heart man believeth unto righteousness, and with the mouth confession is made unto salvation. For the Scripture saith whoever believeth in Him shall not be ashamed. For there is no difference between the Jew and the Greek, for the same Lord over all is rich unto all that call upon Him. For whosoever shall call upon the name of the Lord shall be saved."

The priest stops speaking as an entourage leaving the political dinner party draws his attention. He focuses on a tall, lean man with white-gray hair in the center of the group.

"Mr. Malefic, Mr. Malefic, are you thinking about running for office," a reporter shouts.

Charles Malefic continues to walk toward his waiting limousine, closely surrounded by his bodyguards. One question after another is thrown at him, always coming back to the same one. "Mr. Malefic, are you gonna run for office?"

Malefic stops in front of the open limousine door and turns to face the mob of reporters. He waves his hand to quiet them. The sound of flashing cameras fills the air. The reporters stretch with their microphones and tape recorders to get close to him. Malefic's icy-blue eyes stare sternly into the crowd.

At an early age Malefic developed a telecommunications system for the federal government, which launched his first corporation. He made his fortune by being a cold, calculating man. He has an acute ability to find the meek and vulnerable, and seize the opportunity. Charles Malefic became a national hero when he planned and built youth centers and health clinics across the country, but his biggest headlines were attributed to what he called, "Reclaiming America." When he invented a strategy to buy out foreign-owned properties and corporations in the United States, Malefic became "Mr. America." Some say, however, that laced with the charity and patriotic deeds are hidden motives and a heart of stone.

"I started reclaiming America and I plan to finish it. The time has come to rid the poisons that plague our country."

As Malefic begins to enter the limousine, he overhears one reporter saying to another, "That, sir, is our next president."

Malefic stops, turns to the two reporters, looks them straight in the eyes, and says, "You can bet your souls on it."

Malefic turns and sees the priest across the street staring at him. Their eyes lock for a moment. Malefic sends the priest a cynical smile before he ducks into the limousine. The priest's eyes follow the limousine taillights as they fade into the city night. He turns back to his small gathering, "Hear my words. When the unholy takes flight, He will send One, and thou will feel the Fist of God."

Chapter 2

A cool, blue blanket of moonlight covers the Israeli desert sand. Winds whisper secrets two thousand years old. Shadows conceal the ruins that have been pried from the grip of the desert in an archaeological dig. One of the desert's darkest secrets is silently screaming to be heard.

The ground begins to shake, and the ancient ruins slowly begin to crumble. Temple stones totter and fall from their foundations, crashing into the cool sand. Pillars of marble sway and tumble to the ground. Centuries of architectural brilliance are brought down to random stones within seconds. The trembling stops as suddenly as it began. The dust settles and the hissing sound of sand pouring into the crevices fills the air. A crater forms in the center of what is left of the hoary temples, releasing air that has been trapped for centuries. The clouds above begin to form an angry storm. Falling rain pounds the sand and the winds blast the site. The rain becomes burning balls of hail, crashing into the desert sand. Flashes of lightning illuminate the sky and the fallen ruins. Bursts of thunder tremble across the land as a single immense lightning bolt splits the sky. The lightning bolt strikes directly into the crater, causing a sparking blue glimmer. A sudden sizzle of electricity intensifies, then explodes within the crater, echoing over the desert, followed by a calm silence. The residue from the explosion drifts quietly to earth, burning with an orange glow on its way down. Tranquility falls over the desert night, and the clouds slowly part for the moon. The fires subside, leaving their scars on the desert sand.

A fog crawls slowly out of the abyss, spreading itself across the desert sand. The fog resembles a sea tide of blue moving under the moonlight. A sparkling black mist follows the fog out of the crater. The vaporish mist begins to swirl and forms a human like figure. The figure stands over six feet tall and appears to weigh over two hundred pounds. The black figure possesses the perfect physique of a chiseled Greek statue. The black mist gathers behind the figure, transforming into wings. The wings reach fifteen feet across and are the color of a raven's. They attach themselves to the wide shoulders, becoming one with the newly formed figure. The black wings gleam in the moonlight. They fold down, disappearing into the figure's body. The creature's skin begins to harden into a lustrous, black surface. Suddenly, he falls to his knees in anguish. His skin, though flesh like, has become a smooth, black, mirror like shell. Standing before this creature, one would see his reflection perfectly. If one were to look close enough, one would see two thousand years of history floating within. This creature has been born from the past to preserve the future. The figure conceived on this night is not of this world, but his eyes and soul are human. His eyes appear suspended in the infinite darkness of his face. Staring into the eyes of this creature, one would behold the reflection of human suffering and guilt peering back at him.

Chapter 3

Washington, D.C.

James Rood wakes screaming, soaked in his own sweat. Another dream turned nightmare, a man haunted by his own mind. James was once a man that had it all: a beautiful wife, a baby on the way, a nice home in the suburbs, and a job he loved. Then one rainy night the dream died. The car spun out of control, hitting the guardrail and flipping into the trees. James laid bleeding, bruised and trapped beneath the collapsed driver-side roof. A few feet away in the passenger seat lay his pregnant wife. James watched helplessly as his wife and unborn baby bled to death that night. He blames himself because he was driving the car, but in his mind there is another who should share the blame.

"Hello," a voice on the receiving end of James' call says in a slumbering tone.

"I need to see you." James' voice is faint and forlorn.

The voice on the receiving end belongs to Dr. Stanley Leanman, the psychiatrist assigned to James after the death of his wife and unborn child. Dr. Leanman recognizes James' voice immediately.

"Come over, James, right now," Dr. Leanman says urgently.

It's three a.m. and Dr. Leanman is aware of it, but when it comes to the healing of the mind, time is meaningless.

James stands on the sidewalk struggling with his thoughts, remembering when his wife was his psychiatrist. James is a homicide detective and the things he sees sometimes leave him with a poor opinion of the world. She was an incredibly patient listener, and she always restored his faith in the human race. Now, he stands in front of a shrink's house talking to himself. He realizes he should go to the door, thinking that if a black man were seen in this neighborhood at this time of night, the entire police force would be dispatched.

James walks directly to Dr. Leanman's office and sits in a black leather chair that faces the doctor's desk. Behind the desk is a large bay window framing a view of the Chesapeake Bay. The moon reflects off the calm water, and the grasses sway gently in the breeze, a view familiar to James. Dr. Leanman sits in a similar chair that also faces his desk, but they are separated by a small lamp table. None of the lights are on; the full moon is the only source of light. James stares out the window, watching the small disturbances on the surface of the bay. Dr. Leanman always waits for James to begin the conversation.

The doctor begins to remember the pain James has fought through to simply go on existing. He recalls the anguish in James' voice as he spoke about the death of his wife and unborn child. He thinks of all the phone calls in the middle of the night, because the horrible memory of watching them die tormented him. Dr. Leanman remembers how they put the pieces of James' life back together and silenced the screams in his mind. The screams are back.

James mumbles a question that brings Dr. Leanman sharply out of his thoughts. "Do you believe in God?"

Dr. Leanman is surprised by the question, because it's the first time anything relating to God has ever been mentioned during a session.

James sits in the chair, leaning forward with his elbows on his knees and his head in his hands, staring at the wooden floor. Glancing up at Dr. Leanman, James asks again, "Do you believe in God?"

"It doesn't matter what I believe. Do you believe there is a God?" the doctor responds quietly.

After a few moments of silence, James asks in a quiet and calm voice, "What was the purpose?"

Dr. Leanman stares, sensing the calm before the storm.

"So, what's the master plan?" James' voice has become deep and sarcastic. "Why the fuck would He give me it all, and then take it away?" he says with his teeth clenched together, and his fingertips nearly piercing the leather armrests of the chair from his grip.

"James, James, let me ask you something." Dr. Leanman attempts to get his mind off the anger that's heading for rage. "You were doing fine, what caused the relapse?"

"Dreams," James says as if it hurts to say it.

"But you have had these dreams before."

"I can feel my dreams," he says, staring up at the star-filled sky through the skylights.

"I don't understand."

"I wake up with the wounds I suffered in the accident."

James pulls off his trench coat and shirt. Dr. Leanman turns on the lamp and sees bruises across his chest and ribs. They surround the hideous scars left from that rainy night in the emergency room.

"When I have these dreams, this is how I look in the morning."

Dr. Leanman's eyes see, but his brain can't comprehend.

"There's more," James says in a wearisome tone.

Dr. Leanman's eyes pull away from James' badly bruised body to make eye contact.

"In my dreams I see and feel the same pain I had in the accident, exactly the way it happened. But a few months ago the dreams went further than the accident."

"What do you mean?"

"A warm, bright light shined on us in the car. Then, Faith and I were standing outside of the car. Faith looked different; she had a transparent glow. She wasn't physical anymore. I felt as if I could reach right through her, but her eyes looked the same. We turned and started walking toward the light. It seemed like twilight, but different. It was as if the sun were setting in every direction. I couldn't feel the ground, but it was there. We were walking in a garden along the shore of a sparkling sea. There were trees and flowers; everything had a golden glow. We were happy and full of peace, a peace I have never felt before. As we were walking toward the light, a large silhouette came forward toward us. I remember hearing music, but the instruments and voices were different, indescribable. It was beautiful. We stood at a stream watching the sun set. The stream started to turn into an ocean. As the figure drew nearer, the water beneath its feet would freeze instantly. It wasn't long before the silhouette was directly in front of us. It was a large figure, human like, but it was no human. I wasn't able to see any details on the figure, because the sun behind it became incredibly bright. It motioned with its hand for us to move forward. Faith was allowed to go by, but it wouldn't let me follow her. I reached out and that's when I realized I didn't look like Faith. I was still physically the same. They turned and began to walk away. Then, the warm light began to grow cold and the pain increased by the second. The figure opened what resembled a cape, a starry cape. It kept growing until it consumed everything. Then, I'm back in the car lying beside Faith's body and a rescue team is pulling on me."

Dr. Leanman's mind searches for answers, unable to comprehend the thought of a dream causing physical wounds. He tugs on his beard as he collects his thoughts.

"Do you walk in your sleep?" he asks.

"What? Do you think I'm doing this to myself?" James asks, irritated, but somewhat amused by the question.

"Either you're doing it to yourself or someone is doing it to you."

"Brilliant," James says sarcastically.

"Or your mind is causing the symptoms," he says in a manner that suggests he doesn't believe the theory, "which isn't unheard of. The mind is an incredible device. But mind you, it would be idiosyncratic."

"Great! I'm beating the shit out of myself! Call Ripley's!"

"I can't see any other explanation."

"That's why the Department pays you the big bucks. Well, I guess I'm all better now. All I need is a lifetime supply of Ben-Gay. Thanks, Doc."

"James, do you think the dream is real? Do you believe the figure in your dream is causing your wounds? Tell me what you believe is happening to you."

"I don't know what I believe."

"You must believe something."

"I believe the feeling is real, the pain is real, the wounds are real . . . "

"So, the dream must be real." Dr. Leanman completes the thought.

"As real as my torment," James says in a dark and despondent tone.

"Why do you think this is happening to you?"

"I don't know . . . because I'm crazy?," he asks despairingly.

"If you keep thinking like that, you will drive yourself crazy."

"Well, that's why I'm here, isn't it?"

"You're not crazy, and you and I both know that."

"Well, something crazy is going on, Doc, because I'm not doing this shit to myself. It's coming from somewhere, something, or someone."

Dr. Leanman begins to rub his eyes, while he evaluates the situation. "Look, if you believe all this has something to do with some supernatural being or power, I may not be the person you should be talking to. We are stepping out of my realm. I specialize in the reality of the mind. I'm not sure if I even believe in a Creator or intervening angels the way most people do. I know a man; he's a theologian. He has a great understanding of the relationship between man and God. Would you be willing to see him?"

James puts his shirt back on. A few moments pass

quietly in the moonlit room.

"Is your friend going to tell me why God fucked my life up?" James asks in a deep and hurting tone.

"I don't know what he will tell you, but he may be able to help you understand what is happening to you."

"Sure, Doc," James says as he leans back into the chair and closes his eyes. "We'll see."

Chapter 4

The desert sun begins to climb into the eastern sky. A vehicle approaches from the distance, leaving a cloud of dust in its wake. As the vehicle nears, the passenger's posture suggests that he is anxious to arrive at the archaeological site. The jeep comes to a skidding halt and Professor Samuel Phault, the head archaeologist of the site, leaps out. He slowly pulls his sunglasses off, revealing an astounded stare. An Israeli man has started to trot over from the dig site.

"What in God's name happened?" Phault asks with a slight French accent.

The worker begins to explain. "Professor, there was an earthquake," he attempts to catch his breath, "and a thunderstorm."

"An earthquake?" Phault asks quietly. "A thunderstorm? Here?" he adds with a skeptical expression.

"Yes, Professor." The worker wipes his forehead with his dusty hand and glances back at the dig site.

They begin to walk toward the site. Phault observes the burn marks on the sand. He stops and kneels down to examine the marks. He takes his tan, leather hat off and looks up at the worker. "Tell me, Amsad, what would cause such a thing?"

Amsad stares at Phault and in a low voice says, "Burning hail."

Phault stands with a fist full of sand. "Burning hail?" He smiles as the grains of sand pour through his fingers. "Amsad, my friend, you need a day off."

Phault smacks his hat against his side to knock the dust off before he returns it to his balding head. He walks over to the crater and stands at the edge, staring down at the tomb that has been split down the middle. "Has anyone gone down there?"

"No, sir," Amsad shakes his head fearfully.

"What's wrong with you?"

Amsad hesitates, "The men, sir."

"What is it?"

"They're afraid."

"Afraid of what?"

Amsad stares with apprehension. "God," he whispers.

Phault glances at the group of men gathered at the far end of the dig site, obviously avoiding the crater with the tomb. "What did they see?" he asks.

"They saw . . . ," he looks at his men and back at Phault, "They saw the Angel of Death."

*

Deep in the middle of the tropical rain forest in South America sits an agricultural miracle. Charles Malefic and his partner, Luke DeMynn, have independently financed and introduced western-style, high-output farming. They've done what some have said could not be done, taken the low nutrient soil of the rain forest and developed a productive farming enterprise, without destroying the natural environment and exhausting the soil. They have turned a profit annually and have become very popular with the citizens of the world and the environmentalists. They have been credited with personally halting the destruction of the tropical rain forest.

Deeper in the rain forest, in a restricted area, is a more important project. No one knows what is produced there except a select few, handpicked by DeMynn himself. Trespassing results in disappearance.

"You heard?" a man asks nervously.

"Heard what?" one of the three men responds.

"DeMynn's coming down."

The look on the second man's face shows the same anxiety as the man who brought the news.

"What's his problem?" the third and newest man to the project asks.

The other two men glance at one another and look around to see if anyone is listening.

"DeMynn is one of the men you work for. This is his personal project."

"Yeah, so he's coming down to straighten out the labor problem we're having," the new man says as he flicks a large beetle like insect off his arm.

"That's right. He came down a few months ago to straighten out a labor problem. A couple of the local natives working in the warehouse were stealing some of the product and DeMynn found out. The morning DeMynn caught a flight back north, he left his solution to the problem at the security desk."

"What? What was it?"

"On the check-in desk, where all the employees pass through security, DeMynn left his solution for all to see. There were two decapitated heads sitting on the desk with the top of their skulls sawed off and hollowed out."

A rare breeze rustles the tropical foliage around the three men, causing them to glance around nervously.

"Their heads were filled with the product and a sign hung over them that read, 'Let him who stole, steal no more.' It was written in the native language. That was DeMynn's solution to the problem."

"Unfucking believable!" says the new man.

"Yeah, I know, and he's coming back."

Chapter 5

James steps out of the taxicab. He glances down at the small piece of paper in his hand, checking the address. He stares at the enormous church. His mind flashes to his wedding day. That was the last time he was at a church, and that was many years ago. A disconcerting feeling races through his body. He glances over his shoulder, but the taxicab has left.

As James steps inside the church, he spots a slightly heavyset man with thinning gray hair combed straight back. He looks to be in his late fifties. James approaches the man and says in a questioning tone, "Excuse me, I'm looking for Professor Gregory Orfordis."

"Follow me." The elderly man with a slight limp leads James to a long corridor. The only source of light comes from the stained-glass windows high above, which provide a brilliant display of colors to the cobblestone hallway floor. Each stained-glass window portrays a biblical event, reflected on the pavement on which they are walking.

James follows a short distance behind the man, occasionally glancing up at the windows. At the end of the corridor are two large wooden doors. They are open, allowing the morning light to brighten the end of the corridor. The doors lead to a beautiful garden. James and the man walk without speaking a word. The corridor is cool and damp, but James can't help experiencing a warm and peaceful feeling.

Halfway through the corridor, a silhouette of a person emerges, wearing what appears to be a cape or cloak. The person is walking toward them. James senses the peace within him being constricted by a familiar feeling. Flashbacks shoot through his mind, throwing James into a dream state. The corridor becomes a throbbing tunnel, and the cobblestone floor begins to glow like hot coals. The silhouette draws near. The flashes from his dreams begin to consume and strangle all sense of reality. James physically keeps his composure, but mentally he's in a chaotic struggle. James begins to reach out toward the elderly man's shoulder. The silhouette is upon him, and a voice from the figure quietly says, "Good morning."

"Good morning, Judge," the elderly man with James responds, as the man passes them.

James sighs quietly and thinks to himself, "I'm losing my damn mind."

They reach the end of the corridor and walk into the garden. The garden is glorious. The trees are displaying their full autumn splendor of colors, occasionally surrendering leaves to the breeze. The garden appears to be acres in size. Large Chinese dogwoods and Japanese maples line the main square. The ten-foot walls that surround the garden are entirely engulfed by ivy. The sidewalk is flanked by purple and white strawflowers and snapdragons. Marble religious statues are embraced by thousands of yellow and ruby mums and asters that linger past the summer season.

"Beautiful day, isn't it?" the elderly man asks as he looks up at the trees."

James is still thinking about the corridor and the man that passed them. He knows that the man was Judge Russell, someone he visits frequently for official business. He wonders why the judge was here.

"What?" James asks, half dazed.

"Isn't it a beautiful day?"

"Yes, it is," James says, glancing around the garden.

The elderly man and James are now walking side by side around the garden. James begins to feel some peace within himself again as they walk and take in the beauty of the place.

"It's amazing a place like this exists in the middle of the city," James says with surprise.

"Is it?" the elderly man asks, glancing up at James.

"Right outside those walls is a decaying world full of murderers, prostitutes, drug dealers and addicts, and racists."

"Sounds like a world I wouldn't want to live in," the man says quietly.

"I clean it up some, and it gets dirtier. I clean a little more, but it just keeps getting dirtier." James stares down at the ground. "It's like sweeping a dirt floor." Hopelessness is revealed in his voice.

"A long time ago there once stood a nice little house here. A man and his wife and their infant son lived in it. They had a small garden with a swing in it very similar to that one over there." The elderly man points toward an old swing under an oak tree. "They would rock in that swing on days like this one until sunset, talking about their son's future and their wonderful plans. One night after they went to bed, a fire broke out. The old wooden home was a roaring blaze within minutes. The man managed to carry his wife and child to a window, but there was an explosion that catapulted the man out the window, which was two stories above the ground. The man was badly burned and had broken bones, but he attempted to crawl back to the house. But there was nothing to crawl to. His wife and son were gone. Everything he lived for burned into the night, leaving him with many scars. For many years that old house remained exactly the way it looked after that night, an ugly scar on the landscape surrounded by dirt and weeds. One day the man came back and donated the land to the church next door and helped raise the money to build what you are standing in today."

"Why did you tell me that story?"

"I thought you might want to know the history of the piece of land you are walking on."

"Or . . . ," James says, sensing another reason the old man told him the story.

"Or you might benefit by knowing that something like this garden and the council clinic can come out of a tragic occurrence."

"Professor Orfordis?" James asks, realizing the conversation is beginning to sound like therapy.

"Please, call me Greg."

"I thought so. Am I supposed to find some good in my situation? Is that it?"

"Come, sit here with me, James. My neck is beginning to hurt from looking up at you." They sit on a stone bench under a large oak tree. "Yes, I do believe something good can prevail from your situation, or that there may be a reason for the dramatic change in your life."

"Something good, I doubt, but a reason would be nice."

"You find yourself asking, 'Why?' often, don't you, James?"

James stares out into the garden, watching the autumn breeze pluck brightly colored leaves off the surrounding trees.

"You have been thinking about God frequently over the past year, haven't you?"

James continues to stare, but there's something beginning to boil in his mind. "I'm sick of thinking about God, as sick of it as I was growing up as a kid. That's all my grandmother ever did. God this, God that, 'Jesus loves you, James,' 'I'll pray for you, James.' 'Jesus is the only way to . . . '." James stops before he finishes his sentence. His expression can only be described as a look of enlightenment.

"What is it?" Greg asks.

"Did Leanman tell you about my dreams?"

"Yes, of course."

"I wasn't allowed to pass; I couldn't go with my wife."

"Do you think it's because you didn't believe as she did?" Greg asks.

James stares down for a moment at his wedding band on his finger. "But why?" he quietly asks under his breath.

"Why what?"

"The doctors said I should have died in that accident. Why the second chance?" James leans forward, putting his face in his hands. "Why did He take my wife and baby and give someone like me a second chance?" His eyes become glassy and red.

"If you had died in that accident, you would not be with your family," Greg explains.

"Oh, so He kept me alive to become a religious freak and then die and be with them? Is that it?"

"I don't know about the religious freak part, but I do know that your grandmother was right."

James stands and stares out into the garden. "Right about what?"

"Jesus is the only way."

Chapter 6

"Page Rood," Captain Ross urgently commands the dispatcher.

"What's up?" one of the homicide detectives asks.

"A body was found, and it has the markings."

There's an eerie silence in the room. Everyone is aware of what that means. He has killed again, "he" being the serial killer. He has claimed four victims a year for the past six years. Over this time span, a number of clues have been left behind with the victims. The clues consist of notes and carved numerals and markings on the bodies. The clues have been analyzed a million times, resulting in no leads. They have been fed through the department's computer another million times, leading only to more dead ends. What is known is that he kills once in each season, and he starts in the north part of the city during the summer, then south, next east, and ends the cycle in the west section of the city in the spring. His victims are confined to prostitutes, pimps, and drug dealers, but he has no preference for race or gender. To the media he is notoriously known as the "Garbage Man," because he's "cleaning" the city's streets. To the department, he is known as the "Evil Dog," because they found on his first victim's body carved markings that appeared to spell out the words.

James walks into the office looking as bad as he feels.

"I got your page. What's up?" he asks, struggling to keep his eyes open.

"Your friend went to work last night," the captain says.

James has suddenly become alert. "South side?"

"It's their turn."

They assemble the homicide team and proceed to the site of the murder. It's your typical ghetto, but worse. You couldn't even say this was a nice neighborhood twenty years ago. Drug dealers replace the newsstands; the prostitutes infest the streets; and the addicts pour out of the alleys. A murder here is not unusual, but this one is "his" and therefore becomes headline news, making the site a media frenzy.

The dark blue police cruiser pulls up to the murder scene. James steps out to a restless mob of reporters and citizens standing behind a yellow strip of tape. The flashing lights rhythmically cast blue and red onto the surrounding buildings. The clamor of voices seems to increase as James nears the site. As James draws closer to the crowd of spectators, he senses everything slowing down and becoming a sluggish and hazy motion. James begins to walk toward the entrance of the building. He attempts to block out the sounds around him, but the harder he tries, the more he hears.

"Why haven't you caught this guy yet?" a man yells from the crowd.

A woman standing in front of the police barricade says, "Maybe they don't want to catch him." She didn't say it loud, but to James it's as if she screamed it into his ear.

A reporter stands at the side of the doors. "Well, well, if it isn't the head of the buzzard bunch," the reporter says, grinning.

"What do you want, Johnson?" one of the detectives blurts out.

"I got this theory," the reporter says as he cleans the lenses of his glasses. "You have the best homicide detective in the city working on a case for six years with no results. The word is that the detective isn't as good as everyone thought." He slides his glasses back on. "I don't buy that for a minute. I think this psycho is still on the street because that's where you guys want him to be."

"That's your theory?" a detective asks with an entertained expression on his face.

"Sure," the reporter grins. "All street crimes have declined over the last six years because of this nut. Hell, he's doing your job for you."

James stares at the reporter, giving the impression that there could be another homicide.

"What do you think of my theory, Detective Rood?" the reporter asks.

There's a sudden tension in the air. James continues to stare. "I'm impressed, Johnson," he says quietly.

The shocked reporter appears to be happy with himself.

"But there is one thing," James says, acting confused. "Where's Watson?" he asks as he turns and walks away.

The other detectives follow with parting grins. One of the detectives says, "See ya, Sherlock" as they disappear into the building.

James slowly climbs the dark stairwell. The broken glass grinds beneath every step. The sun has set, and the cold wind rushes throughout the old abandoned apartment building, but there's no relief from the stench of urine. James discovers an inhabitant on the steps, an old man who appears to have lived on the streets forever. He smells of cheap wine and his own waste. He begins to laugh as James steps over him. The old man mumbles something under his breath.

"What did you say?" James turns and asks.

The old man uses his finger to signify that James should come closer. James leans down from a couple of steps above, and the other officers wait for the old man to speak. He begins to giggle and mutter again.

"Say what you have to say, old man," James says.

The old man stops snickering. With a sudden serious expression and tone he says, "You'll never catch him."

"Who?" James asks.

"You know damn well who," the old man says in a sinister voice.

"What did you see, old man?"

The wino begins to laugh again. James starts up the stairs, feeling he's wasting his time.

"You wanna know what I saw?" the old man asks, becoming serious once more.

James turns and waits, now at the top of the stairwell.

"The Angel of Death," the old man whispers loud enough for James to hear.

James shakes his head and begins to walk up the next set of stairs.

"You can't catch the Angel of Death," the old man shouts. The old man's laughter echoes through the stairwell.

In the apartment James finds himself staring at a familiar scene, a naked dead body lying face up, arms extended, and legs crossed at the ankles. The first thing he notices is the pale white body framed by dark red blood. The victim is female and young, nineteen tops. Her clothes are piled neatly beneath her head like a pillow. James leans down to examine the markings on her abdomen. He doesn't search for cause of death, knowing there's a puncture wound in her back that struck her in the heart. The identical wound has been found on each of his victims. The abdomen is where he leaves his clues. Sometimes it's a note, but this time it was carved into her stomach with some sort of razor device. The first marking appears to be a half-drawn heart. Beside that are the words, "Warm Water," and below them are the markings, "XVIIIt0."

James stares at the markings as if somehow they are going to mean something to him or indicate anything that would point him in a direction. He walks to the window that has been shattered out and watches the traffic below. He scans the streets, working his way to the building across the street.

"Did anyone see anything?" he asks.

"Old lady across the street saw someone walking down the alley," a young officer answers.

James immediately goes across the street. He knocks on a door, thinking this may be the break he has been waiting for.

"Go away," an old woman's voice filters through the door.

"Ma'am, it's the police," James says.

"Sure you are," she says.

James' face strikes a humorous expression. "No, really, I am."

"Where's your uniform?" she asks, obviously peering at him through the peephole in the door.

"I'm a homicide detective; I don't wear a uniform," James explains.

"Ohhhh, why didn't you say so?"

"May I ask you a few questions?" James asks.

"Where's your badge?" she asks, still reluctant to open the door.

The humorous expression returns to James' face. He puts his badge up to the peephole as he rolls his eyes.

"That's not real," she says.

"I'll tell you what," James says, "I'll ask the questions from out here."

The door begins to click. It clicks half a dozen times before the door opens, still secured by a chain lock. A little old black lady peeks through the crack of the door.

James begins to ask a question, but the door shuts in midsentence. He shakes his head and begins to walk away. Then the door opens and the little old lady pokes her head out into the hallway.

"You may come in, young man," she says.

James walks into the apartment and is astonished. The old woman's home is beautiful. It's furnished with Victorian cherry furniture and religious pictures and statues. It reminds him of his grandmother's house. He begins to sense a warm, comfortable feeling in himself. He stares at a portrait of the crucifixion of Jesus hanging on her wall. It has two large candles burning on each side of it.

"Do you like it?" the old woman asks, coming out of the kitchen with a tray in her hands.

"Yeah, it's nice." He can't remember her going into the kitchen. He begins to wonder how long he has been standing there. He glances down at his hands and notices they have blisters and splinters.

"Would you like a cup of tea?" the old woman asks.

"Sure, thank you."

The elderly woman smiles. "Has anyone ever told you that you look like Denzel Washington?"

James smiles and nods his head with an expression on his face which implies that he hears that frequently.

"So, what would you like to ask me, young man?"

"Exactly what did you see across the street this evening?" he asks as he pulls a splinter out of his hand.

"I saw a big person wearing a long, black coat, like the one you're wearing," she says.

"Could you see the color of his skin or hair?" James asks, picking another splinter out of his palm.

"His back was turned to me, and he was wearing a black hat." She sips her tea. "I can tell you this, he was a big fella."

"Thank you for the tea and your time, ma'am," he says, getting up.

"Please, sit and finish your tea."

"I really must go."

"May I ask you something, young man?"

"Sure."

"Did he really write 'evil dog' on one of his victims with a knife?"

James stands speechless for a moment. "Where did you hear that?"

"I saw it on TV some time ago. It was all over the front pages, too. Didn't you see it?" she asks.

"I don't watch TV or read the paper."

"That's good, because they're not very nice to you guys."

"I should be going," he says.

"The man you are looking for is a religious man," she says casually.

"Why do you say that?" James asks, staring in interest.

"Look carefully at what he has written. Open your eyes and your mind. You must look at it from all perspectives," she tells him.

James stands with a blank stare in the doorway. "Thank you for the advice and tea, ma'am. Good night."

Chapter 7

"What the hell?" Malefic wakes abruptly and tries to focus his eyes. He thinks he sees someone. "Who's there?"

There appears to be an outline of a figure in the corner of the room. Malefic activates an alarm beside his bed. The corner is cluttered with tropical plants, and the only source of light comes from the three-hundred gallon aquarium.

"Who's there?" Malefic asks again in a sharp, demanding tone. His heart skips a beat when he realizes there is a pair of eyes staring out at him from the corner. He leans toward the lamp. After a half dozen clicks, it's clear to him that the light doesn't work. He opens the drawer and pulls out a .357 Magnum.

"Show yourself or I'm gonna blow your fucking head off." He points the gun directly at the two eyes peering out of the dark corner. He cocks the hammer back on the gun. "You're a dead man."

Malefic fires two shots into the corner of the room. He stares and waits, but it's quiet and dark. The smoke from the gunpowder begins to clear.

Suddenly, a voice whispers into his ear. "You can't kill the dead."

Malefic turns and finds himself eye to eye with the intruder. He blinks once, and he is alone in the room. Five heavily armed men break through Malefic's bedroom doors.

"Where the hell were you?!" Malefic screams.
"We heard the gunshots and came up right away!"
"Someone broke into my room!"
"None of the signals went off."
"I set off the alarm."
"It never came on downstairs."
"What the hell is going on? This guy was in my face!"
"Where did he come in?" one of the bodyguards asks.
"I suggest you find out and fix the fucking problem!"

Chapter 8

The Israeli desert begins to heat up, and the archaeological site appears deserted. Near the crater, where the tomb rests, stands a lone tent. Amsad squats at the edge of the crater, clutching the top of a ladder. He nervously watches Professor Phault examine the tomb fifteen feet below. Phault carefully maneuvers to a position that will improve his view of the tomb. The sunlight begins to pour over the edges of the crater. Dust particles float lethargically in the streaking rays of the sun. Phault directs his flashlight into the tomb. He stares at the silhouette the body has left behind over its hundreds of years at rest. He begins to explore the rest of the tomb with his flashlight. The light glides over a dark item that causes him to jerk back toward the object. He steadies the flashlight and focuses on the dark cylinder. He wipes the perspiration from his eyes with a bandanna. His heart begins to race and his eyes expand in excitement. He realizes he's staring at ancient scrolls. The thought of someone stealing a worthless body and forsaking valuable scrolls puzzles him. He yells up at Amsad to bring him the equipment needed to remove the fragile find. Amsad runs to the tent to retrieve the equipment. Phault is left alone with his thoughts and the ancient writings.

*

A tropical rain forest in South America

"Buck, come here," Len, one of the warehouse workers, whispers.
"What are you doing in the bushes?"
"Keep your voice down. Get down here and look."
"Where?" Buck asks.
"Over there."
"Oh shit! Is that who I think it is?"
"Yeah, and he's talking to the elder tribesman," Len nervously tells him.
"What's with all the hand gestures?"
"It's part of their language, dummy."
"How in the hell does he know their language so well?" Buck asks.
"Why don't ya ask him?"
"Fuck that, I'm getting outta here."

"Wait. Look," Len says, "the old man's drawing in the dirt."

"DeMynn doesn't look happy."

They watch DeMynn pick up a handful of dirt. He holds his hand out in front of the tribesman.

"Oh shit! The dirt caught on fire, right in his hand!" Len exclaims.

"Man, this is getting weird," Buck says, shaking his head.

"Look at the old man. He didn't even blink."

The two men in the bushes are startled by a clap of thunder. The leaves begin to make a tapping sound from the falling rain. DeMynn and the elder tribesman go their separate ways. The two men hurry over to where DeMynn and the tribesman were.

"Is that what I think it is?" Buck asks in wonderment.

Len stares at the ground until the rain washes the picture away. "I don't think it could be anything else."

Chapter 9

James sits at his desk, staring at a pile of computer printouts and unpleasant photos. He keeps repeating the markings over and over in his mind: Z, 3, V, I, 1, D, O, 6. He keeps asking himself what it means. "Sick son of a bitch, that's what it means," he says under his breath.

He picks up a photo of the first victim. On her abdomen were the words "EVIL DOG," which has a strong resemblance to the markings he read to himself. He holds a plastic bag containing a note left behind with a butchered drug dealer. It says, "BESIDE THE GREEK GODDESS AN OLD CITY OF ANCIENT GREECE 1 tOXV."

He can't help wondering if the clues mean nothing. They're simply left behind to keep the department occupied. He pulls the latest victim's file and stares at the close-up photo of the markings on the abdomen, a half-drawn heart and the words "Warm Water" next to it. Beneath those markings are the symbols "XVIIItO." Hours have passed and he begins to lose his concentration.

"Hey James, did you get my message?" a coworker asks.

"What message?"

"Some guy named Derrick Moore called. It's there on your desk."

He reads the message. Derrick Moore is his brother-in-law, and he wants to meet him at the bar down the street. They haven't seen one another since the funeral.

*

"Derrick, what's up?" James pulls a stool up next to his brother-in-law.

"James, how have you been?"

"Can't complain."

"No one listens anyway," Derrick says with a smile.

"The usual, James?" the bartender asks.

"First name basis with the bartender?" Derrick raises his brows.

"A man has to have his friends," James says.

"She's cute."

"I use her for her cooking abilities. She makes a mean 'Jack on the Rocks.'"

"The two of you an item?" Derrick asks.

"Nope."

"Seeing anyone?"

"Nope. What about you? Any kids yet?" James asks.

"One on the way," Derrick proudly tells him.

"Congratulations!"

"I have some more good news. I'm running for office."

"Aren't you a senator?" James asks.

"Sure, for a while now."

"So, what are you running for now?"

"The presidency."

James' mouth drops open.

"Here, let me help you pull the splinters out of your chin," Derrick laughs.

"Why?" James asks.

"I can help this country," Derrick says with sincerity.

"Derrick, let me tell you something very important." James signals to Derrick to come closer as if he doesn't want anyone to hear what he's about to say. James whispers in his ear, "You're black."

"Very funny," Derrick says.

"A black man will never be elected president in this country, period."

"It's the twenty-first century, James."

"I have a hundred that says it won't happen."

"I don't want to take your money," Derrick tells him.

"Who's your vice president?"

"Shelly Deanstor."

"A black president and a woman vice president, make it two hundred." James begins to laugh uncontrollably, as Derrick shakes his head smiling slightly. "I'm sorry, Derrick," James says, wiping the tears from his eyes. "I just can't see it happening."

"We have been testing the field and doing a little inside research. I'm two percent behind the leading candidate in the polls."

"Are you serious?" James asks, surprised by the number.

"I do have a chance, James."

"Well then, Mr. President, let me buy you a drink."

"Thank you. There is something else. Would you check into this death threat for me? I was told it's nothing, but I got a funny feeling about it."

"Sure, I'll look into it. All kidding aside, Derrick, you will be receiving shit like this throughout your campaign. More so than others, if you know what I mean."

"I figured as much, but something about this one shook me up a little."

28

"I'll take care of it."

"Oh, I almost forgot. I have some personal belongings of Faith's. Her work sent them to me, and I was out of town at the time. They got stored away until a few weeks ago. I was searching for something and ran across them."

"I'll get them on the way out."

Chapter 10

An old man chisels late into the night. He has been commissioned by the church to make a sculpture of the crucifixion of Christ on a large marble wall. The church is warmly lit by many candles. The old man's black skin and gray hair have a golden glow from the shimmering candlelight as he works on the wall. Every strike of the chisel echoes through the church. The echoes float upward to the bell tower.

There in the darkness sits the newly formed creature of the Israeli desert. It is there he feels he belongs. The sound of the hammer striking the head of the chisel invades the creature's dream. The sound of metal on metal brings back a haunting memory. The creature wakes, screaming a horrible, hair-rising "No!" The creature is not human, but the memories are, memories that pierce his very soul.

The old man stops chiseling as the last echo of the scream rings through the corridors of the church. He puts down his tools and begins to walk up the stairs that lead to the bell tower. Slowly, he creeps up the spiral staircase, keeping his eyes fixed above. He climbs a weak, wooden ladder and lifts the creaking hatch door. He pulls himself into the bell tower and begins to brush himself off. A bat swoops down near his head, causing him to lose his balance and fall backward onto his rear. He begins to laugh and mumbles to himself, "Just a bat, old fool." He's not aware of the pair of eyes directly behind him. He begins to sit up when it appears he's being helped to his feet, but he can't feel anything touching him.

"Hey, who's there?" he asks.

It remains silent and dark.

"I know there's someone here," the old man says, a tinge of fear in his voice.

His head pivots side to side, waiting for the silence to be broken. Then, he sees them, the eyes staring at him. The hint of fear is gone. Now, he's just plain scared.

"You're, you're . . . not, not . . . supposed to be here," he stammers.

"I was told to come here. I have no other place to go," a low, comforting voice says from the dark.

"They have shelters and centers for people like you. You can go there."

The eyes stare out from the dark in silence.

"You can't stay here. The church won't like it."

"Why are you here?" the voice from the dark asks quietly.

"I work for the church."

"I also work for the church."

"Oh, why didn't you say so? Are you the new janitor?" the old man asks.

"Janitor?"

"Yeah, you know, the guy who cleans and repairs the church."

"Yes, I clean and repair the church," the voice says.

"Are you hurt? I heard you scream."

"No," the voice says softly. "What is it that you do here?"

"The church hired me to chisel a marble frieze," the old man says proudly.

"What will it be?" the voice asks.

"The crucifixion of Christ."

There is silence for a moment, then heavy breathing. "Oh Father, why have thou brought your servant to this place? The echoing sounds of torment are here, Lord. Allow me to dwell elsewhere." The eyes fade into the shadows.

"Where'd you go? Are you all right?"

The eyes reappear and begin to move upward. The old man follows them. "You're a big fella, aren't you?" he says.

Glittering stars begin to materialize around and beneath the eyes. An outline of a figure begins to emerge and come into focus. The newly formed physique steps out into what little light there is, becoming visible.

"Oh my God." The old man is a couple beats away from cardiac arrest. "You're no janitor."

"You have no reason to fear me," the creature says, as little flickering flashes of light drift about him.

"That's easy for you to say," the old man says, his eyes twice their normal size. He stares at the large figure draped with a black, hooded trench coat. He can see around the figure's face and neck the black bandages that appear to continue downward around his entire body. "Who are you? What are you?"

There is no response. The stars begin to fade, leaving a vaporish mist behind. The eyes are the last to evanesce into the dark.

*

The glittering mist reappears across town, reforming into its massive figure.

"Malefic," a voice whispers from behind him as the lights go out in his office. "I need to speak to you."

"What do you want?" Malefic asks, inconspicuously reaching under his desk and pushing the alarm.

"No one will come," the voice tells him.

"Do you have any idea who you're fucking with?" He spins his leather chair around to confront the source of the voice. He discovers an enormous silhouette gazing at him. The city lights filter through the blinds, revealing a clear outline of the figure. "Who the hell are you?"

The figure steps forward and leans down, putting his gloved hands on the arms of the chair. His eyes glare out from the black bandages. Staring directly into Malefic's eyes, he says "Redemption."

Three heavily armed men abruptly burst through the doors. Malefic spins the chair around and dives to the floor. The intruder stands watching the armed men adjust to the darker room.

"What the fuck is that?" one of the three men blurts out. They stand staring in astonishment.

"Shoot, you idiots," Malefic screams.

The bullets spray out of their automatic weapons. The clamor of bullet shells hitting the floor rings throughout the room. Glass shatters in every direction, leaving no surface uncovered. Wood chips splinter the air, falling twenty stories to the sidewalk followed by additional debris. Malefic's head remains buried in his arms as pieces of his office fall about him. The roar of the guns comes to a halt. The smell of gunpowder and the sound of bullet shells rolling about the wooden floor linger. The smoke slowly begins to clear, replaced by the cold night air.

"I can't fuckin' believe it!" Malefic looks at his bodyguards. "You fucking missed!"

The bodyguards look at one another and their weapons. "We unloaded over a hundred rounds in him."

"I can see that by the way he's standing there!" Malefic shouts.

The tiny flickers of light begin to sparkle. Beacons of light come streaking out of the creature, apparently where the bullets struck his body. The men stop reloading to gaze at the phenomenon. The beams of light ricochet off the walls and everything in their paths. The streaking rays of light strike the men, causing sharp pains within them, immediately followed by a warm, serene feeling.

The figure begins to speak in a deep, dark tone. "Be warned. Attempt to harm me once more and vengeance will be mine."

The figure begins to fade. The streaks of light come to an end and all that remains is a smoldering residue, floating in the air. Malefic and his men stare at where the figure once stood. The silence is broken by a familiar voice.

"You gents must learn the art of conversation."

"DeMynn, where in the hell have you been?" Malefic says scornfully.

"Missing all the fun by the looks of your office."

DeMynn is of average height and solid in build. He has slicked back, jet-black hair and cool, blue eyes. He is a handsome man and carries himself with utmost confidence.

The three men begin to reenact what happened at the same time, making it difficult to understand any of them.

"Shut up and get out!" Malefic barks as he cleans the debris off himself.

"What happened here, Charles?" DeMynn asks calmly.

"Well, some guy about seven feet high and three hundred pounds with beams of light shooting out of his body broke into my office. And oh, I almost forgot, we put a hundred rounds of lead in him and he just stood there."

"Seven feet tall?" DeMynn asks as he casually walks around the room, picking up pieces of the office.

"Yes, seven feet."

"Three hundred pounds?" he asks, looking out what once was a window.

"That's right, three hundred pounds! I saw him with my own eyes!"

"I believe you, Charles, but you must confess it is an odd occurrence. A man weighing three hundred pounds and standing seven feet tall breaks into your office, which happens to be on the twentieth floor of a highly secured building."

"I'm pretty damn sure that thing broke into my house, too," Malefic says, still worked up from the incident.

"Really? Maybe you've got a new admirer."

"That's not amusing. You're awful nonchalant about this whole thing."

"Well, I'm not certain what he wants, but I believe he doesn't want to harm you, not physically anyhow."

"What does that mean?"

"He's had two opportunities to knock you off and didn't. Let me guess, he was standing right here."

"How did you know?" Malefic asks.

"Besides the fact that this side of your office looks like Swiss cheese, there are about eighty slugs right here."

"So, we did hit him," Malefic says.

"You definitely hit something. All the bullets look like little accordions." DeMynn bends down and runs his finger across the wooden floor. "What do we have here?"

"What is it?"

"Blood."

Malefic appears relieved. "If he bleeds, he can be killed."

"Don't get your hopes up, Charlie."

"Why not?"

"He bleeds, but it's not from your guns." DeMynn stares out into the city as he turns a bullet between his fingers. "He bleeds from an ancient wound."

"Am I supposed to understand that?" Malefic asks.

"No, you're not."

Chapter 11

James sits staring at a box in the middle of his small, unfurnished livingroom. The box contains a million memories and just as many heartbreaks. He takes a sip of whiskey and remembers the days that followed the funeral, days of numbness, with no feelings, no thoughts, and no questions. If it could have stayed that way, life would be uncomplicated for James. Going through life would be a lot easier numb, simply waiting for his time to expire. But it isn't that way for James. He's tormented by questions and has a soul consumed with guilt and anger.

He pulls the box closer and opens the flaps. A framed photograph of Faith and himself in Greece stares back at him. His mind flashes back to a walk on the beach with Faith under a star-filled sky in the Greek Islands. He recalls the soft breeze on his skin and the Mediterranean Sea washing up around his feet. Then he remembers the first moped they rented and how they nearly crashed it on a curve. The memory provokes a smile. He sets the picture aside. A black leather briefcase is the next item that confronts him, the briefcase that he gave her. He lays the briefcase in his lap and the anguish begins to burn throughout his body, but the pain is repressed by the memory of the day he gave it to her. It wasn't a birthday present or a Christmas gift. It was a spontaneous gift on an ordinary day, a perfect spring day, not a cloud in the sky. He remembers every detail. Faith was wearing a pink buttoned-up blouse and cut-off jean shorts. She was working in the garden in the backyard. "Smoke Gets In Your Eyes" by the Platters was playing on the radio. She was so overjoyed when she saw the gift, she nearly knocked him over with her hug. James smiles as the memory consumes him. His mind is at peace for the moment. He's standing in the middle of the garden embracing Faith with the Platters on the radio in the background. He can smell Faith's perfume in the spring air, mixed with the scent of flowers.

The memories begin to fade and a tightness forms in his throat. He opens the briefcase and finds a sealed folder with an envelope attached to it. The envelope has Faith's name written on it. Her name is written in blood. A few moments pass, but it seems like a lifetime for James, before he opens the letter. The lump in his throat grows as he reads the letter, making it difficult to swallow. The letter begins as if an obsessed lover had written it. His mind is swarming with thoughts and memories, making it impossible to think clearly. His eyes begin to tear with each line, putting him into a deeper depression.

Suddenly his dismal feeling turns to anger and his grip on the letter begins to crumple its outer edges. The letter has revealed disturbing information. He slowly discovers that the accident wasn't an accident at all but a professional hit. The letter is a death threat.

He stares at the sealed folder on his lap. The realization that he has what appear to be the answers sends a shiver through his body. His life has been dedicated to serving justice; he believes in it now more than ever. But there's a powerful and ugly beast overshadowing his sense of justice. This beast goes by the name of Revenge.

Chapter 12

"We need to talk," DeMynn says as he adjusts his tie in the mirror.

"Sounds serious," Malefic says with a distant demeanor, flipping through papers on his desk.

"We lost ninety percent of our labor force on the RF2 project," DeMynn says calmly.

"How in the hell did that happen?" Malefic's attitude and focus turn instantly.

DeMynn wipes a few pieces of lint off his suit. "Our native friends found religion."

"What?"

"Religion."

"What the fuck does that mean?" Malefic demands.

DeMynn glances over his shoulder. "It means that they refuse to work."

"They already had religion! I've seen them all painted up and dancing around, beating the crap out of drums to some wooden god."

"It appears that behavior will not be occurring anymore," DeMynn says, grinning.

"Are we talking about that born-again shit?" Malefic asks.

"That's what we're talking about," DeMynn says, noticing that one of the chess pieces on the chessboard has been moved, as if a game had begun. He walks over to the chessboard.

Malefic walks to the bar and fixes himself a drink.

DeMynn stares at the crystal chess set resting on an antique oak stand. The chess pieces are magnificently chiseled and polished to a detailed brilliance. The clear pieces warmly capture the light, while the tinted pieces, equally beautiful, reflect the light. The chessboard itself is also made of clear and tinted crystal. DeMynn reaches out and moves the tinted knight, his first move.

"How the hell did a bunch of heathens deep in the bush find religion?" Malefic asks, staring out the office window.

DeMynn slowly walks over from the chessboard and sits in a black leather chair. "Visions," he says quietly.

Malefic turns around. "What kind of visions?"

"The villagers saw the night sky come down and engulf the entire village. They told me that they were temporarily blinded, but the darkness gave way to a brilliant light." DeMynn slides a gold metal object from his suit coat. "The townspeople say their village became a beautiful garden. They were walking among trees, plants, and animals that they had never encountered before." He begins to file his fingernails. "They went on to explain that the rarest of fragrances and sounds filled the air. They say it was very intoxicating. Then a man appeared before them, a man that no one could describe to me, nor could they recall what he had said; but, whatever he looked like, or whatever he said, left an extraordinary impression on them."

"Sounds like they've been dipping into the product," Malefic says.

"The entire village?"

"Anything else?" Malefic asks.

"The head elder had a vision also."

"What did he see?" he asks, anticipating more bad news.

"A woman giving birth in a small room, warmly lit by candles. He watched the child become a man. He witnessed the healing power of this man and heard the healing words come from his mouth. He witnessed the man being nailed to a wooden cross." DeMynn has nearly filed his fingernails to sharp points. "The elder said he remembered weeping like a child, but he quickly clarified that they were not tears of sorrow, but tears of joy. Then he went on to say that he watched an earthquake destroy a large cave. The man appeared once more to him. He described him as a brilliant floating light. He said the man glowed as if he were the sun. I asked if the man said anything to him."

"Did he?" Malefic asks curiously.

"One thing."

"What?"

"This I do for you, receive my gift through me."

"What did the elder do?" Malefic asks.

"He fell to his knees and worshiped Him."

"Shit! They have some crazy dreams and all of a sudden develop morals."

"Damn shame, isn't it?"

"Yes, it is."

Chapter 13

It's a cold day and there are more to come, but this day has a unique glow to it. It isn't everyday a good man sells his soul. There's a man kneeling by a grave in a cemetery, with a spiritual "For Sale" sign hanging on him. The man had a wife and a soul that he could call his own once, but his wife belongs to a higher power now, and his soul sits at the bottom of a bottle.

"Faith, why didn't you tell me?" he says with tears streaming down his face, nearly freezing in their tracks. "You could have told me. I could have been ready. I could have protected you." He stares up at the cold, blue sky. "Why didn't you tell me? Goddamn it!" He claws the frozen ground in front of Faith's tombstone.

*

"Beer, James?" the bartender asks routinely.

"J.D.," he says with an emptiness in his voice.

"Are you all right, James?"

James stares at Anna for a moment as his drink is being handed to him. "All right? Yeah, I'll be all right as soon as I do a little swimming," he says as he shoots his drink down.

"You want another?"

James pushes his empty glass toward her. The second one went down as easy as water. The empty glass heads back toward Anna. She hesitates for a second. He pushes the glass a little closer, explaining that he has to work on his backstroke.

"Are you going for the gold?" a woman's voice comes from a couple of stools over.

James looks over to locate the source. A young woman, maybe in her thirties, with a slim build, straight auburn hair, light green eyes, and golden brown skin is looking over at him.

"Excuse me?" he asks.

"Are you going for the gold? You know, like a gold medal."

He stares at her for a moment and observes a tape recorder in her hand. She has reporter written all over her. "What do you want?"

"Be nice, James," Anna says, smiling slightly. She knows he has a history of throwing reporters out the door.

"To ask you some questions," the young woman says.

"Sure, why not?" He slides his glass to Anna, who has an astounded expression on her face.

"Why haven't you caught the Garbage Man?" the young woman spurts out.

James stares into the mirror behind the bar. A few moments pass with silence.

"Well?" she asks.

"Well, what?" he asks as he glances over at her.

"Why haven't you caught him?"

"I said you could ask your questions, but I don't remember saying I would answer them." He throws a twenty on the bar and thanks Anna for the drinks.

"Wait a minute, I . . ."

"No, you wait a minute. I don't know you; I don't want to know you; and I don't want to talk to you."

"My name is Hope Naples."

"Goodbye, Hope Naples," James says as he walks out the door.

She turns to Anna and asks, "Is he always that nice?"

"I think he likes you," Anna says, smiling.

*

Jack Daniels'- old number seven brand- quality Tennessee sour mash- whiskey- alcohol 43% by volume 90 proof- distilled and bottled by Jack Daniel Distillery . . . That's the only thing James has been reading lately. He sits in his chair with the sealed envelope on his lap and the letter crumbled in his hand. He begins to think about the letter, and the pain starts to flow through his body. He slowly opens the sealed folder and slides the contents out. There are photographs, clippings of articles, receipts, and notes. He thumbs through the contents, expressions of disbelief and anger cross his face. He stares at the evidence, knowing he's looking at the information that is going to provide him with a face and a name. The information he has in his hands is going to provide him with his wife's murderer.

A knock on the door disrupts the flow of anger. He opens the door to find no one there. A plain brown-wrapped box, the size of a shoebox, sits at his feet. He wonders if it's a bomb. If it is, he doesn't care. He tears the wrapping off and waits. He thinks of his father for a moment and then opens the box. It's a Bible. Someone left a Bible at his door. He thinks of Greg, and then sees a

marker sticking out of the book. He opens the book to the marker and finds something written on it, "Romans 12:19." He begins to read the passage to himself.
> Beloved, do not avenge yourselves, but rather give place to wrath; for it is written 'Vengeance is mine, I will repay, says the lord'.

He slams the Bible shut. "Not if I get to him first."

Chapter 14

"What are our options?" Malefic asks in a frustrated tone.

"There are two avenues we may be able to explore. We can either filter men down south slowly without drawing attention to ourselves, or we can recruit more of the natives. Either way, the project is at a standstill," DeMynn explains.

"Shit, I can't believe this! They have a little hallucination and a multimillion-dollar business comes to a halt."

"They must have been some powerful visions." DeMynn sits on the leather couch, crosses his legs and extends his arms, resting them on the top of the couch. "Very realistic," he adds, grinning.

"What are you trying to say, that this shit is real?"

DeMynn's eyebrows rise. "Don't forget our seven-foot, three-hundred pound friend," he remarks, smiling.

Malefic stares out for a moment, contemplating a thought. "You think he's connected with the natives?"

DeMynn nods his head.

"Why? What the hell is going on?"

"Someone is attempting to destroy the RF2 project."

"Wait a minute, you think that bulletproof magician is trying to destroy the Rain Forest Project?"

"But who is he?" DeMynn asks, talking to himself. He rubs his chin in thought. "It appears he has a plan, an agenda."

"Whoever he is, he's beginning to annoy me. I have approximately one year to convince this country that I'm the man that should be elected president. I don't need this freak screwing it up," Malefic growls, irritated.

"Who do you think he is? Who do you think sent him?" DeMynn asks.

"I don't know! I'm still trying to figure out how the hell he got into my house and office."

"Do you believe in God?" DeMynn asks.

"I guess so," Malefic replies, not giving it much thought. "What the hell is this, DeMynn?" He stands and pours himself a drink. "Don't turn this into one of your deep, spiritual discourses. You know I hate that bullshit."

"Don't get excited," DeMynn says calmly. "I'll take care of it."

Malefic shoots his drink down and begins to fix

another. "What about the RF2 project?"

"I'll see to that also, but I believe that, because of the visions, it's going to be very difficult to recommence operations."

"What exactly did they see?" Malefic asks, annoyed.

DeMynn's expression appears solemn along with his tone, "Jesus Christ."

Malefic shakes his head with skepticism.

"Do you not believe?" DeMynn asks in an investigative tone.

"I wasn't brought up that way. My parents didn't have a religion, except for the worship of money. In fact, I didn't hear about Jesus Christ until college. I still don't know a thing about it." His voice reveals his ignorance of the subject. "When you were talking about the natives' dreams and visions, I didn't understand anything you said. The elder's vision and what it had to do with religion made no sense to me. I was going along with you, trusting you knew what you were talking about. I'm oblivious to this kind of thing, and I guess I count on that." Malefic stands and stares out his office window. "Like the natives, they were fine until the visions."

"What do you mean?" DeMynn asks.

"What you don't know can't hurt you." He observes the people below on the streets.

"Oh no, Charlie, it doesn't work that way."

"No?" Malefic turns back around to face DeMynn.

"You believe that because those natives had never heard of Christ, they would be excused?"

"Sure."

"Let me clear something up for you. Every person on this planet has a code of ethics or a moral standard that they live by. However high or low it may be, they know when it is violated. There is an awareness throughout the universe that there is a Creator or at least something above them. No culture, no one, not even the heathen, is excused." DeMynn stands and puts his coat on. "But don't fret, Charlie, you will receive a fair trial like everyone else."

"You seem to be quite knowledgeable on the subject."

DeMynn stops at the door. "Experience is the greatest teacher." The door slowly closes behind him.

Chapter 15

"I'm looking for Professor Gregory Orfordis."

"Down the hall and on the right, he's in the basement," the janitor points in the general direction.

James arrives at a staircase and stands at the top of it for a moment. The stairs appear to lead nowhere. They disappear into the darkness. He begins to walk down them slowly. He nears the bottom and sees a flickering light coming from somewhere in the cellar. He has to maneuver through boxes full of books and religious, artifacts making his way toward the light. He stumbles over some boxes and loses his balance. James quickly reaches out and grasps a large object in the dark. His hand clutches firmly while he regains his balance. He glances at what he is holding on to. It's a hand. His eyes follow the arm to a shoulder, then to the neck. Eventually, he finds himself staring up into the eyes of the owner of the hand. A lifesized replica of Jesus for a cross stares back at James. James continues to stare into eyes of the lifelike Jesus for a few moments. James glances back at his hand as he pulls it away and back to his side. He looks up and quietly says, "Thanks." He proceeds to walk toward the light and sees a man slumped over a desk in the corner with a dozen candles burning around him.

"Greg, are you all right? Greg . . . are you all right?"

"James, is that you?"

"Yeah, Greg, are you feeling OK?"

"I must have fallen asleep."

"You scared me."

"Don't worry, it's not my time."

"Remember the first day I came here?"

"Yes, I do," Greg says, looking over a scroll.

"Remember that man in the corridor?"

"Yes . . . Judge Russell."

"Yeah, does he come here often?"

"Sometimes," Greg looks up from his work. "Do you know the judge?"

"Yes, I do," James says quietly. "How do you know him?"

"He once came to me for help, and we continued to have conversations as the years passed. We have become good friends over the years. He helps us with all the charity functions and the inner-city children's programs that we have here at the church." Greg begins to look through the scrolls again. "Sometimes he simply comes by to sit in the garden."

"Strange," James says softly.

"Not really," Greg says, looking up. "The garden is a very peaceful place. It is a way to strengthen one's soul and reflect on life."

"And escape reality," James says quietly.

"There is no escaping that, James," Greg says, staring at him, "not even in death."

"What are you doing down here?" James asks, changing the subject.

"Researching scrolls."

"Like the Dead Sea Scrolls?" James lifts a section of scroll and curiously examines the writing.

"Yes, some of them."

"I saw a special on them once on the Discovery Channel."

"Good channel," Greg says.

"These aren't originals, are they?"

"No, they're duplicates. The university asked me to write a paper on one of the segments."

"What are these?" James picks up a tinted, air sealed glass casing with two fragments that are distinctly different from the others.

"The Scrolls of Mount Sinai."

"They're in pretty bad shape."

"Yes they are, but they're readable."

"Now these look like originals."

"They are."

"Really?" James carefully places the glass casing back on the desk and cautiously pulls his hands away. "How old are they?"

"The test were inconclusive, but I believe they are nearly thirty five hundred years old."

"Now that's old."

"Yes, it is."

"Wouldn't that make them some of the oldest writings known to exist?"

"Yes, it would."

"It must have caused a big stir in the media when they found them."

"Only a few people know about them," Greg says quietly.

"What?"

"Counting you, six people know about these scrolls."

"Why? How?" James asks in disbelief.

"I was part of an archaeological group that discovered them in the Sinai Peninsula on the banks of the Red Sea. But a middle east government that was overseeing the dig attempted to suppress the find. We smuggled some of the scrolls to the United States."

"Are you going to release them to the public now?" James asks.

"No."

"Why not? What are you going to do with them?"

"I'm going to use them to help you."

"What?" James asks curiously.

"I believe what is happening to you is in these scrolls."

"You've been in this cellar too long."

"Look at this." Greg points to a section of the scroll. "'Without faith in Him, there is no path. No man may enter the Kingdom of God without the Truth,'" Greg reads.

James stares at what appears to be scribble to him. "I don't get it."

"It says that the plan will be revealed in dreams . . . physical dreams."

"What plan?"

Greg begins to arrange the fragments of scrolls as if he were putting a jigsaw puzzle together. "I want you to listen very carefully to what I'm about to tell you. This piece says that an Agent of God will not pass to the Kingdom on his first journey, not until he gains the righteousness of justice. He must first deliver a man of God to the people. The Agent of God, also referred to as the Guide, will be in alliance with the Fist of God."

"The Agent of God, man of God, a Guide . . . the Fist of God?" James shakes his head in confusion. "This makes no sense to me."

"Let me explain it to you."

"Please."

"There is a story written in the scrolls. This story is about how throughout history the scales of good and evil are tilted to one side or the other. Throughout human existence, some are born with a sphere. This sphere is a great source of energy that grows from within, toward either a bright holiness or a dark force. It depends on the chosen path of the possessor of the sphere. The sphere feeds on the decisions made by the possessor and inclines toward one side or the other of the soul-spectrum. The person or persons possessing the sphere have the ability to lead people."

"How would a person know?" James asks to humor Greg.

"I'm not certain, but there is a part of the scrolls that speaks about a period in time when there will be one death and one birth. The possessors at that time will realize their gift."

"One death and one birth?"

"Yes."

"What does that mean?" James asks merely to indulge Greg.

"I don't know."

James pushes pieces of the scroll casually with his finger. He stares at them indulgently. "So because I'm having these dreams, you believe I'm one of the players?"

"I believe you may be the Agent of God, the Guide."

"I believe you need to see our friend Dr. Leanman."

"Believe it or not, James, I don't think you have a choice."

"Oh, really?" James says defiantly.

"You have to sleep sometime."

"I have to go." James begins to walk away.

"I also believe your brother-in-law may be the man of God that you must deliver to the people."

James stops at the foot of the steps and stares back at Greg, thinking that if any of this is true, it would put Derrick's life in jeopardy. He continues up the stairs without saying a word.

Chapter 16

"Good morning, the judge in?"

"Good morning, Detective Rood. You can go in, he'll be with you in a moment. He's finishing up with some youths in the counseling room."

James stands waiting, looking around the office. He sees a portrait of Judge Russell's family, which he hadn't noticed before. He begins to see many things he hadn't seen before. There's a reflection that draws his attention. It's a large gold-plated plaque hanging on the wall beside many diplomas and certificates. The plaque has the words "God Lives" inscribed on it.

"Good morning, James." A large man enters the room. He's losing his hair, but what he's lacking on his head is made up for with the beard he wears. "What can I do for you this morning?"

"I need some papers signed, your Honor."

"How have you been?" Judge Russell asks, as he glances through the file.

"All right. You know, Judge, I never realized you had a daughter."

"I don't anymore," he says casually, reading over the documents. "I lost her seven years ago."

"I'm sorry," James says, feeling a little awkward.

"Here you go, James, signed and ready for the street," the judge says in an unaffected tone.

"Thank you."

"You have a good day, son. Take care of yourself."

"You too, your Honor."

Staring down at the documents, James slowly walks over to the receptionist. "Sherry, do you know what happened to the judge's daughter?"

"I started working here after she died. But I do remember when his wife died. I had just started at that time."

"His wife died?"

"About a year after his daughter."

A familiar feeling comes over James.

"She committed suicide."

Suddenly feeling a little nauseated, James stares quietly at the door of the judge's office. The receptionist brings him out of his thoughts.

"I don't see how he lives with it," she says.

"That makes two of us," he says under his breath.

*

    James sits at his desk, organizing the documents. He's preparing the strategy for the bust later today. He begins to think about the judge. As his thoughts linger, he slowly slips into a daydream.
    "James, James, can I go today?"
    James flinches as he comes out of his trance. There's a young detective standing in front of him. "No," he says firmly.
    "Please, James."
    "I've got enough guys."
    "Al's sick. He called in this morning," Billy says eagerly.
    James throws his pencil on the desk and shakes his head. "All right, rookie," he says reluctantly. "You can go."
    "Yes!" He dashes down the hall and practically runs over a coworker.
    "Hey, Billy, congratulations on your baby boy," the coworker that was nearly knocked down says.
    "Thanks! I'll see you later. I have to call my wife." He hurries down the hall and disappears around the corner.
    The co-worker approaches James' desk, but James doesn't notice him standing there. "Here you go, James. I got those blueprints of the apartment building you wanted."
    James pulls his eyes away from the computer screen. "Thanks, Phil."
    "You know, James, staring at a blank computer screen will get you thrown back into that shrink's office."
    James stares at Phil for a moment. "I miss that comfortable couch," he says with a slender grin.
    "I'll see you later." Phil turns and walks away with a smile.
    James directs his attention back to the screen. He types the name "Martin T. Russell" and the computer begins a search. In the few seconds it takes for the computer to bring up the information, James has a hundred thoughts and memories cross his mind. "KATHERINE RUSSELL, FORTY-FOUR, FOUND DEAD IN HER HOME," the cold screen displays. "SUICIDE. SHE TOOK A RAZOR TO HER WRIST." James searches farther back. "MARY ANN RUSSELL, NINETEEN, FOUND DEAD ON THE 1400TH BLOCK OF THE NORTHEAST SECTION. OVERDOSE." He stares at the computer screen as the words slowly begin to blur. 'How does a man go on existing after something like

this?' His mind runs the thought over and over again. 'Could there be a chance for him to live a sane life?'

*

Six men wearing black trench coats turn the corner and walk quickly along the sidewalk. They approach what appears to be an abandoned apartment building.

"This guy is a psychopath, and he isn't going to go down quietly," James says as they close in on the building. "Watch your ass and everyone else's."

They begin to separate. Bob and Harris head for the back to position themselves at the fire escape. The remaining four men enter the building. Billy and Andy break away and proceed to the left stairwell. James gives Andy a parting look, that tells him to watch over Billy. James and Tony slowly work their way up the dark and damp stairwell on the right.

"Oh shit," Tony says as quietly as he can.

"What?" James whispers.

"Rats." Tony's phobia is apparent by the expression on his face.

Hundreds of rats are overrunning the stairs. James tries to clear a path for Tony, but the rats continue to crawl around their feet. When they reach the top of the stairs, they find that the hallway floor has disappeared beneath the rats.

"You stay here." James begins to walk through the rats, glancing at the doors as he proceeds down the hallway. He searches for apartment number 9, but all the doors are missing the numerals. He locates a door with a number, the number 6. He begins to walk, but then stops suddenly. James backs up and places his finger on the rusty numeral. He flips the 6 around to make it a 9. He stands and listens, but there's no indication of movement. He takes one step back, then forward, and kicks in the door, quickly placing his back to the hallway wall. He takes a quick glance into the apartment, but sees nothing. He begins to slide along the wall in the apartment with a flashlight in one hand, gun in the other. He comes to a black curtain. He pulls it back and discovers what appears to be some sort of shrine. Hundreds of candles burn about the room, but the majority of them encircle the shrine. As James nears the shrine, he discovers an enormous amount of animal parts on a stone block. The stone is doused with red, and the blood slowly crawls over its edges. The organs are arranged, spelling out the words, "I Am God." There's a large wooden cross hanging on the wall behind the shrine. A Bible rests on a shelf beneath the cross, a steel dagger lies on the book. A thought crosses James' mind. After six years he can end the killing. He begins to think no one is there. Then he hears the hammer of a gun being cocked back. He hits the floor simultaneously with the gun shot. Tony comes running down the hallway. James spots a figure running toward the door and fires two shots at it. Tony runs directly into the suspect. A shot goes off and Tony falls to the ground. The rats begin to crawl over and around him. The fleeing figure heads toward Andy and Billy's position. James gets to Tony.

"Tony, are you all right?"

"I got it in the leg."

"You're gonna be all right, man. Hang in there."

James pursues the running man. As he nears the top of the stairwell, a dozen shots ring out. He sees Andy lying at the bottom of the stairs holding his shoulder.

"He went out the doors," Andy says painfully.

"Where's Billy?" James asks.

"He went after him."

James busts through the doors in a full sprint, but he doesn't have to run far. He sees Billy lying on the ground. He's covered in blood. A few yards away lies the body of the man they had come to apprehend.

"Billy, are you hit?"

"I got him, James. I got him," he says grinning painfully with blood seeping from his lips.

"Yeah, you did."

"James . . . James, tell my wife I love her. Please tell her I love her."

"You're not going to die," James says defiantly.

"Tell her I . . ."

James holds Billy's head in his hands. Bob stands staring down at them.

"He just had a baby boy," James mumbles under his breath.

Andy joins them with blood flowing through the fingers of the hand holding his shoulder. Harris aids Tony down the stairs.

"I didn't see him coming," Andy says in a tone filled with guilt.

*

"Hey, James."
"What's up, Anna?"
"You want a drink?"
"Ice water."
"Excuse me?"
"Ice water," James repeats.
"What's going on?" she asks.
"I have to tell someone that her husband is dead."
"Oh no, who?"
"Billy Wilson."
"The rookie?"
"Yeah."
"Didn't his wife just have a baby?" Anna asks.
"Yeah."
"I'm sorry, James."
"Me, too."

James stands for a moment out in the street, staring at Billy's house. He gathers his thoughts and walks to the front door. He softly knocks.

"Ms. Wilson?"
"Yes," a pretty, young lady says, standing at the door with an infant in her arms.
"I'm Detective Rood."
"Oh yes, Billy's boss. How are you?"
"I'm all . . ." James begins to answer, then looks down.
"What's wrong, Detective Rood?" she asks.
"It's Billy."
"Oh God, no." The tears begin to swell in her eyes.
"I'm sorry," James says.
"No, no! Why God? Why?" She falls to her knees. James takes the baby in one of his arms and Ms. Wilson in the other. They kneel in the doorway, holding one another. He feels her pain soaking through his body, saturating his soul. He fights the tears as they begin to burn in his eyes. His chest is drenched with her tears. There's a warmth radiating from James. He begins to illuminate and sparkle. She lifts her head and sees James glowing. Her eyes become large and fixate on him. He raises his hands to his face and marvels at the miraculous sight. Ms. Wilson's eyes begin to stare above James. She smiles with a contented gaze. James turns to see what is behind him. He's knocked backward into Ms. Wilson by what he sees. It's her husband, Billy. He's levitating, and his body is encircled in a bright white brilliance. There is also light radiating from behind Billy. James reaches outward, placing

his hand in the golden beam coming out toward him. He realizes there's someone standing behind Billy.

Billy floats closer and begins to speak, "You must live for me and William. I will be fine. I love you, Nancy. Goodbye."

Two large arms embrace Billy and the glow begins to diminish.

"James, James, are you all right?" Tony asks, pushing on James' shoulder.

"Yeah, yeah, I'm okay. I must have dozed off."

"Go home and get some sleep."

"I have to go see Billy's wife."

"Man, I don't think you're up to it. Let me go."

"I'll be all right, Tony. I'll see you later."

*

James slowly walks up to the front door of the Wilsons' house. He stands for a few moments staring down at the welcome mat. James eventually knocks on the door and waits. The door slowly opens.

"Ms. Wilson?"

"Yes."

"I'm Detective Rood."

"Yes, I know," she says with a strange expression on her face. "You were here earlier."

"Excuse me?"

"You were here about an hour ago. Are you all right, James?"

He stands with a blank expression, staring at Ms. Wilson. He's thinking he has never laid eyes on this woman before, but she looks precisely the way she did in what he thought was a dream. He attempts to think back. Is it possible that he has seen a photograph of her at the office? There's no recollection that he has, and it makes him uncomfortable.

"James?" She brings him out of his thoughts.

"I'm sorry, did you say I was here earlier?" he asks.

"Yes. You told me about Billy. Are you all right?"

"I'm just tired," he says, rubbing the bridge of his nose, "real tired."

"You look like you could use some sleep."

"Yeah, I believe you're right." He begins to think he did come over and did tell her about her husband. Then, he went back to the department, fell asleep, and dreamed the rest of the bizarre incident. "Are you going to be all right, Ms. Wilson? If there's anything I or the department can do, please don't hesitate to ask." He realizes that she doesn't appear to be a woman who lost her husband a few hours ago. Her face reflects peace and contentment. His mind flashes back to the extraordinary vision. Was it real?

"Ms. Wilson, did you see . . ." James hesitates for a moment. He shakes his head. "Never mind." He turns and begins to walk away in a daze.

"James."

He slowly turns to face Ms. Wilson.

"Thank you and God bless you."

*

The day struggles by and the night comes, but it doesn't bring rest for all.

The sirens of a fire truck wake James. The room is completely dark. He stands and begins to wipe off his body. He feels something crawling on him. He feels thousands of things crawling on him. He reaches outward with his hands, searching through the dark. A small fire appears in front of him. It grows until it reaches a few feet in height. The fire casts shadows onto the walls, creating deformed figures all around him. A man sitting on a stone throne appears on the other side of the fire. His face is concealed by the shadows, but his eyes pierce the dark. His hands and feet are in the fire's light. His skin appears to be burning like hot coals. James steps closer and realizes the floor, ceiling, and the walls seem to be moving in a crawling motion. He focuses in front of his feet. There are millions of insects covering every inch of the floor. But there is one insect that outnumbers the rest . . . ticks. He frantically begins to brush and pick the ticks off his body. The figure on the throne speaks to James in a whispering tone, "If you want to catch me, you must become me."

The fire dies and the room becomes totally dark again. James wakes and sits on the side of the bed with his head in his hands. He can feel his skin itching. The heat radiates from his body. He suddenly thinks of something his grandmother used to say, 'God heals all illnesses with death.' She would call it 'divine healing.' He sits on the edge of his bed thinking how he would like to be healed.

Chapter 17

"Congratulations," Captain Ross says standing at James' desk.

"For what?" James asks, looking and talking like a man that hasn't slept in days.

"It's over, James."

James stares at the murder evidence spread across his desk. "It isn't over," he says in a quiet and weary voice.

"What are you talking about?" the captain asks.

James glances up with a daunted expression. "It wasn't him."

"How do you know?"

James looks at Captain Ross as if he were staring through him. His mind flashes back to the dream he had the night before. "I just know."

"Damn," Captain Ross says under his breath. "The department released a statement to the media."

"I suggest you prepare another statement for when he kills again." James stares at the evidence for a moment. He looks up at the captain and says with certainty in his voice, "And he will kill again."

*

The glass skyscraper stands superior to the other buildings. It appears warm in the setting winter sun, but its upper floor is a cold, dark place.

"What can I do for you, Mr. Sims?"

"I have an update for you."

"What is it?"

"As of yesterday, there seems to be one competitor."

"I have competition?" Malefic says, grinning and reading the latest article about himself in the paper.

"Early reports indicate that a young congressman from Virginia is going to give you a run."

"The black religious guy?"

"That's the one."

"How close is he?"

"One point."

Malefic stands and gazes out the window from his newly redecorated office, looking over the city's horizon the way a predator looks over his territory.

"What would you like me to do?" Mr. Sims asks.

Malefic's eyes remain focused on the horizon. He

quietly says, "I'll contact you." He continues to stare, as his mind drifts into deep thought.

Chapter 18

The old man lays his hammer and chisel down. He strikes a match and lights another candle. The additional light brings a large figure into focus. "Oh man, you scared the you-know-what out of me," the old man says, holding his chest.

"Your frieze is beautiful," the figure says, staring out from the darkness.

"Thank you. It still needs a little work."

The figure stands staring, tightly wrapped in his trench coat with a hood over his head.

"Where have you been?" the old man asks.

"I don't know."

"Mind if I ask you something?" The old man's voice suggests he may be getting too personal. "What happened to you? I mean, did you get burned in a fire or something?" he asks, looking at the black bandages on the figure's face and neck.

"Yes . . . I was in a fire," he says quietly from the dark.

"I'm sorry." The old man kneels down and begins to search through his toolbox. "That was a pretty neat trick up there in the bell tower. Do you do that often?" It remains silent. He glances up, and it appears the figure has vanished. "I guess so," he says to himself. He stands with his polishing cloth and turns to discover the figure behind him, staring at the marble frieze. The old man gasps. "You're going to kill me."

"I will not kill you," the figure says softly.

"Yes you will, if you keep appearing and vanishing like that." The old man begins to polish the marble. The figure is silent for a few moments. "You must've got burned really bad," he says curiously, "the way you try so hard to hide your face and body."

There's no response. The old man turns, thinking the figure has vanished again. The figure is still standing behind him, staring. "Listen, I'm sorry. Sometimes I don't know when to leave well enough alone."

The figure pulls its gloved hands out from the pockets of the trench coat and removes the hood, revealing the black bandages around its head and face. The old man nervously watches the figure as it begins to unravel the bandages from its head. The old chiseler's eyes grow wider with every inch of the figure's exposed face. He stares in disbelief at the glossy, black face and what appears to be an array of stars drifting within his face. The figure opens the trench coat to bare more of the same. The old man's arms dangle lifeless by his side; his jaw hangs, and his head tilts in astonishment. He stares, speechless at his own reflection floating among the cosmos. The old man looks up into the figure's eyes and asks in wonderment, "What are you?"

The figure quietly says, "Someone's hell." He replaces the bandages and pulls the hood back over its head. The figure begins to stare at the marble frieze as if his thoughts have taken him somewhere else.

"Whatta ya thinking?" the old man asks, sensing that the subject needs to be changed.

"About the day," the figure says quietly.

"What about it?"

"It was a cool and overcast afternoon. The clouds moved majestically across the sky." The figure continues to stare at the frieze without blinking. "The murmur of the crowd filled the air. The town below appeared abandoned and peaceful. The clouds above darkened and began to move swiftly across the sky. It was as if the heavens above were preparing for an extraordinary arrival."

The old man listens attentively to the creature and glances over at the marble frieze. He rubs his eyes, not believing what he is witnessing. The frieze has come alive, moving before his eyes. His jaw drops in awe and his eyebrows lift in amazement.

"Suddenly, day became night," the figure says. It glances at the old man's hammer and chisel and squints its eyes in anguish.

The old man looks at his chiseled work, which has become flesh and blood. He turns to speak to the figure, but it has vanished. He turns back to the frieze and it has returned to its original cold, marble state.

*

"Malefic," a voice whispers from the dark.

Malefic rises from his desk, turns, and puts his finger in the figure's face. "You listen to me, freak. I know you can't cause me any harm. So, why don't you get your mummified ass out of my face."

"You must rid yourself of all such things," the figure calmly responds.

"What things?" Malefic snaps back.

"Rid yourself of all such things as anger, rage,

malice, slander, and the filthy language that comes from your lips."

"Fuck you."

Flickers of light begin to glitter in the figure's face as if they were trying to escape from beneath the bandages. The figure's eyebrows are pulled down into a stare. "Rid yourself of such things," it says in a tone barbed with premonition.

"Fuck you," Malefic says again defiantly. As soon as the words leave his mouth, he experiences a sharp, excruciating pain in his midsection, forcing him to double over and fall to his knees.

"I do not want to cause you harm," the figure says solemnly.

Malefic attempts to catch his breath, but his efforts are subdued by the agonizing pain. He clutches his stomach and his face cringes in anguish, as he grovels before the figure. Malefic is minutes away from death. He gathers enough strength to yell, "Please stop!" between the tormenting waves of pain. The torturing affliction leaves him immediately, allowing his face to regain its customary shade. His wheezing pants are slowly succeeded by regular breathing. His muscles exhausted, he slowly lifts his head. Unable to lift it any further, he rolls his eyes upward to see the figure. He finds himself alone. Malefic remains in the middle of the dark room in a kneeling position.

Chapter 19

"I'm delighted you came over, James. I was afraid I wasn't going to see you again."

"I need to ask you something."

"I have a few things to tell you." Greg has an anxious expression on his face. "Last night I had a dream. It was about the one death and one birth fragment of the scrolls. In my vision a voice spoke to me saying that there will be a duration period. In this time span there will be one death and one birth, exactly the way I deciphered it. But the voice added that there will also be no death and no birth in the universe during this period."

"What does that mean?" James asks.

"Precisely what the voice proclaimed, I believe."

"That nothing in the universe will be born or will die?"

"Yes."

"When?" he asks skeptically.

"The beginning of the new year."

"January?"

"April."

"Of course, January makes too much sense," James says sarcastically.

"Ancient biblical calendars begin the new year in the month of April." Greg flips through a manual. "That leads me to believe that April is the month that the voice is referring to."

"How long will it last?" James asks skeptically.

"I could not locate that information in the scrolls, nor did the voice reveal any details about the length of the duration period."

"Well, I had a vision of my own that you might find interesting. One of my detectives was killed. I went to his house to inform his wife of the incident." James is speaking as if he shouldn't be talking about this out loud. "I saw him floating . . . . And glowing above me . . . And I think God was standing behind him."

"Was it a dream?" Greg asks.

"I thought it was until I went to the house again. Apparently, the wife saw it, too," he hesitates and leans back into the chair, "but I'm not sure."

"You're right, that is interesting . . . very interesting. If you didn't dream the vision, then you are being put into the next stage."

"Let me see if I understand this right. I have a vision that I don't remember. Then I dream about it, and I think it's just a dream. But later I discover it wasn't a dream, but it really happened, which puts me in the next stage."

"Yes," Greg says.

"So, I do something physically, and then my mind, in a delayed reaction, catches up in my dreams or in a vision."

"Correct."

"Do you know what an inconvenience that will be?" James says with a sarcastic grin.

Greg begins to shove papers about the desk, searching for something. "The visions are becoming aggressive. I'm afraid something sensational is about to occur and I will not be prepared."

"That wasn't sensational?" James asks.

"I'm anticipating something more dramatic than what has already transpired."

"Is there something you're not telling me?"

"There are a few sections I don't understand completely, but as soon as I decipher them I will inform you."

"You're beginning to worry me, Greg." James smiles. "More so than usual." He stands and puts his coat on. "I won't be around for a week. I'm going out of town."

"Where to?"

"California."

"Business or pleasure?"

"Both. I'll see you when I return."

*

"Professor Phault," Amsad whispers, poking his head in the door. "Professor?"

Professor Phault, engrossed in his work, is unaware of Amsad's presence. He has sections of a scroll spread across his desk, a single oil lamp burning beside him. He has been locked up in his room for days with his discovery.

Amsad appears worried. "Professor, you must eat," he says, holding a bowl of fruit. He walks over to the desk and sets it next to another bowl full of food. "Professor, please, you must eat."

Phault lifts his head in a weary manner, but his eyes are lit with excitement. "Amsad, do you have any idea what we have discovered?"

Amsad stares with a vacant expression. "No,

Professor, I do not."

"We have discovered a manuscript that dates back to the beginning of the first century. This scroll is an eyewitness journal of the crucifixion and resurrection of Jesus Christ. This individual was there." His voice is hoarse from lack of use over the last few days. "This part of the scroll contains the testimony of Pontius Pilate, viewing Christ after he crucified Him. And over in this section," Phault points to the upper part of his desk, "the documented testimonies of other prominent figures and leaders of the period who witnessed the incident. Herod Antipas is quoted right here." Phault runs his finger across the scroll as he reads it out loud. "'I, Herod Antipas, have witnessed the resurrected Jesus Christ, the Son of God. He stood before my eyes and allowed my hand to touch his wounds.' The writer of the scroll describes in complete detail his own encounter with Jesus before and after the crucifixion." Phault rests his elbows on the desk and places his head in his hands. He quietly asks, "But, who are you? Who is the author of this chronicle?"

"You must eat, Professor," Amsad says with concern.

"He was there," he says out loud to himself. "Who would have had access to all these prominent figures and leaders on a frequent basis, and daily encounters with the common people? Who would have been able to obtain so many witness accounts and government officials' testimonies?"

Amsad quietly closes the door behind him, leaving Phault alone in the room.

Chapter 20

It's warm for a winter day. The sun begins to descend toward the horizon. A sky colored every shade of orange imaginable begins to blanket the land. Arrays of purples and yellowish reds begin to consume the remaining blue above. The darkness isn't far behind.

A group of people are gathered in front of an abortion clinic. They are the anti-abortion activists, also known as the pro-lifers. They are holding their weekly rally, and it appears to be escalating to a level of intense friction. It's the usual routine, young women being escorted by police officers into the clinic as activists scream, "Murderer, baby killer, rot in hell!" Reverend John is leading the verbal assault with his wife beside him holding a sign that says 'SINNERS.' Most of the group, which ranges from the elderly to the young, are holding similar signs, and all are fueling the verbal attack. They judge and condemn the women entering the clinic. The mass media are getting their sound bites for the week. But this winter's day has enlightenment on its horizon.

A man appears wearing a gray suit and a tan trench coat. With the sun behind him, he casts a long shadow that reaches into the crowd. He stands on a brick wall beside the steps that lead to the entrance of the clinic, the same steps that held a sixteen-year-old girl splattered with animal blood a week earlier. The stains of last week's blood bath are still evident. The man standing beside those red-tarnished steps is Derrick Moore. He stands silently, staring with intensity in his eyes at the crowd. One at a time they notice him. The crowd slowly arrives at a silent stare. His large silhouette towers over them. The sound of his trench coat fluttering in the breeze covers the crowd. He begins to speak with a wrathful tone, "You dare pass judgement?" His words along with a sudden wind cut through their souls. "Who are you to judge another's servants?" He stares directly into Reverend John's eyes.

"They are murdering children in that house of sin you stand before." Reverend John points to the clinic with anger in his eyes.

"Judge not, that you be not judged. The measure you use will be used against you."

"Do you condone the murdering of children?" Reverend

John's voice rings with rage.

"I do not possess the power to condone, nor do I possess the power to condemn."

"You, sir, choose simply to close your eyes," Reverend John replies arrogantly.

"And why do you look at the speck in your brothers' and sisters' eyes, but do not consider the plank in your own."

"I've read your statements in the papers, candidate Moore. You don't believe in abortion. Why do you oppose us? Why do you defend them?"

"We are not here to judge. We are here to gather the lost sheep, the lambs that have strayed from the Shepherd. With love, compassion, and forgiveness we are to guide the lost, not by threats and intimidation."

A few of the signs in the crowd begin to lower. Derrick's words have penetrated the consciences of some, but others stand firm in their judgement.

"Therefore, let us not judge one another anymore, but instead resolve this. Let us not put stumbling blocks or a cause in the way of our brothers and sisters. Each of us shall account for ourselves to God." Derrick's words are laden with compassion.

"We must stop the killing now!" someone yells from the crowd.

"You say you are people of God. The Lord says,
This is my commandment, that you love one another as I
have loved you. You shall not take vengeance, nor
bear any grudge against the children of your people,
but you shall love your neighbor as yourself."

Slowly minds and hearts are turned. Enlightenment consumes most of the crowd, but there is still a feeling of negativity and anger in the air. Sensing it, Derrick continues, "It is God who justifies. Who among you shall bring a charge against God's children?"

Derrick's words begin to trigger thoughts and reminiscences among the activists. The presence of God begins to work through the crowd like a mystical mist. A college student is reminded of his blasphemy and his dishonesty. The blasphemous phrases continuously race through his mind uncontrollably. A thirteen-year-old girl's hands begin to itch and burn, reminding her that they have stolen. Mr. Walsh smells his mistress' perfume from fifty years ago. The scent becomes suffocating, and his body begins to ache and burn from the sinful deed. A man's mind flashes to his abusive past. The image of his wife lying on the floor, and him standing over her with his bloody hands balled into fists, devours his thoughts. The woman standing beside him is haunted by a neon light. It flashes over and over again, reminding her of a night that nearly destroyed her family. A man is reminded of his greed when his pockets feel as if they are on fire. The spirit begins to move toward Reverend John. The smell of alcohol seeps out of his pores, surrounding him in an aura of nauseating stench. An abominable feeling falls upon him as the memory of his bout with alcoholism is brought to the forefront of his mind. His wife is reminded of her lustfulness of the past as her heart burns. All are reminded of the stains on their souls, reminded that no one is without sin.

A young woman steps out of the crowd and walks toward Derrick. She stands in front of Derrick, looking up at him. She struggles to speak. The words eventually find their way out, "I'm sorry." Tears begin to form in her eyes. Derrick kneels down and reaches with his hand. The young woman takes hold of his hand and softly says again, "I'm sorry, please forgive me."

"Ask the Lord for forgiveness, and He will forgive," Derrick says with certainty in his voice.

One at a time, the crowd moves toward the young woman and Derrick, until there are twenty behind her.

"You will be damned to hell for condoning this abomination," Reverend John says with a small group behind him.

Derrick stands from his kneeling position to lock eyes with Reverend John and the remaining people behind him. "I say to you, man of the cloth, do you still dare to pass judgement on God's children?" He speaks with the Lord's voice rumbling through him. "Do any of you dare to condemn one of God's children?" Derrick scans the crowd for a response. Some hang their heads, while others stare with apprehension. "Pass your judgement and condemn yourselves. Break one of God's commandments and condemn yourselves. I witnessed your iniquities. I smelled and felt your sins, and I witnessed your pleas for forgiveness. The Lord has forgiven those with sincere hearts. Now you turn your backs on forgiveness. Where is the forgiveness in you? I say unto you, the Lord will not forgive the unforgiving heart." His words ring out like thunder, but he stops suddenly.

There is a calm between the two groups. The sound of a child's voice breaks the silence.

"Reverend John," says the young girl standing beside

him. "Reverend John, what are we to do?"

He looks down at the little girl and puts his hand upon her head. Then he lifts his head, and his eyes begin to tear as if he has been reminded of something comforting. He stares into the eyes of Derrick and softly says, "He who is without sin among you, let him cast the first stone."

One by one, the crowd leaves, convicted by their consciences.

Chapter 21

"Welcome to News Eleven. Our top story tonight, Congressman Derrick Moore. Earlier this evening, Congressman Moore prevented a potential riot at a downtown abortion clinic. Field reporter Jim Staff caught the congressman before he left the premises, and this is what he had to say."

The newscast flashes to a tape of the reporter and Derrick at the location. "I pass this clinic every day on my way to the support and counseling clinic down the street that I started a few years ago. Throughout the years, I have watched the activists demonstrate and express their beliefs. I, too, am pro-life. I have proclaimed that in the past and continue to support that statement. But I heard and saw things that do not reinforce my point of view. The activists have become aggressive and verbally violent, which I do not believe in, nor will I tolerate. This particular abortion clinic was generous to me. They allowed me to leave pamphlets and brochures at the front desk. They also advertise my free counseling program on their bulletin boards. The volunteers and I have counseled many young women to the correct decision with love and understanding, not with hate and intimidation. Seventy percent of the women we counsel come directly from this abortion clinic. The women that decide to have an abortion after speaking with us leave with the understanding that we will be there if they need to speak to someone. The volunteers at our clinic have been on both sides of the decision." The telecast flashes back to the news desk.

"We would like to apologize. We were unable to bring you video footage of the incident due to technical difficulties. We will have more on Congressman Moore later in the month in an exclusive interview about his thoughts on the country and his presidential campaign. Elsewhere in the city, a shooting . . . "

"I don't like that guy," Malefic says, staring at the television.

"Don't trouble yourself over Congressman Moore. You will be the next president of the United States," DeMynn reassures him.

"I don't know," he says, shaking his head in a questioning manner, "He's becoming strong with the people."

"You have to give a statement to the media. You must announce your position on the abortion issue." DeMynn says, fixing himself a drink. "That position will be pro-choice."

"Why?"

"This country is divided evenly on the issue. Congressman Moore is pro-life. By being pro-choice you immediately win half the country on that particular issue," DeMynn says, glancing over at the chessboard and noticing that the clear-glass bishop has been moved into an attacking position.

"You better be right."

DeMynn walks over and counters with a tinted pawn. A defensive move, but also a trap play. "Trust me," he says confidently, returning to the other side of the room. He hands Malefic a drink.

"Trust you? Like when you said that freak wasn't going to cause me any harm!"

"I said that I believed he wouldn't cause you any harm," DeMynn says defensively. "Anyway, you provoked him," he adds with a smile.

"All I know is, that hurt, and I don't want to experience it again."

"Next encounter with him, attempt to be agreeable."

"What?" Malefic's face is perplexed. "Be nice to that thing?"

"Upsetting him doesn't appear to be the proper way of handling the situation."

"What are we going to do about him? I'm sick of him popping in and out of my life," Malefic says in an aggravated tone.

"Be accommodating and pleasant. I'll come up with something. You focus on your campaign."

"Accommodating and pleasant. Maybe we can have tea," he says in a sharp, sarcastic tone. "You think he would like that?"

"That's the idea," DeMynn says, smiling.

*

A man enters the church and slowly walks down the aisle. He approaches Greg, who is seated in a pew in the front of the church. The man reaches Greg and sits next to him. The two men quietly stare at the golden glow of the candles that are beneath a life-size replica of Jesus Christ on the cross. The candles cast their warm light onto the replica, giving it the appearance of being alive. The setting sun's last rays filter through the stained-glass window that portrays the Apostle Paul's transformation on the road to Damascus.

"Are you all right, Martin?" Greg asks with concern.

"Remember the young boy that came before me last month for a drug charge?" Judge Russell asks. "The one I told I wouldn't send to jail if he were to go to the drug program and the Bible study."

"Samuel?"

"Yes," Judge Russell says as his eyes begin to water. "He was shot and killed yesterday leaving the Bible study."

"Why? What happened?"

"They said it was drug related," Judge Russell says painfully.

"I'm so sorry, Martin," Greg says, putting his hand on the judge's shoulder. "I know you think you should have dealt with the situation differently, but you must understand, you tried to do what you thought was best for him," he says consolingly.

"I should have sent him to the Juvenile Correctional Department," Judge Russell says, looking down at his hands.

"You cannot blame yourself for having good intentions," Greg says.

"Good intentions," Judge Russell says in a raspy tone. "We know where that road leads to."

"Think of the other offenders and young people you have helped and put on the right path using the same manner you employed with Samuel," Greg says. "And there are many."

Judge Russell stares tearfully for a moment. "Thank you, Greg," he says quietly.

Chapter 22

"Excuse me. Where can I find the owner?" James asks a man of Mexican descent.

He says he doesn't speak English. So James begins to speak Spanish, but a white man in a suit comes out of an office and approaches them. The dock worker departs immediately.

"Can I help you?" the man asks.

"Are you the owner of this business?"

"No. Why?"

"I'm doing research for my book," James tells him.

"Oh really, about what?"

"The American fisheries and their importance to the economy of the country."

"I'm sorry, but the owner isn't here and you are trespassing."

"Can I ask you some questions?" James asks.

"Like what?"

"How many restaurants does this fishery distribute to?"

The man thinks for a moment, determining if there would be any harm in answering the question. "Around six thousand," he says.

"West Coast?"

"Eleven states on the West Coast and Midwest."

"That's a lot of fish," James says, smiling.

"The place runs twenty-four hours a day."

"Can you describe a routine workday?"

The man again appears to be contemplating his answer and the possible consequences. "The first shift comes on at six a.m. They spend twelve hours unloading the boats, separating and cleaning the catch. The night shift comes on at six p.m. They're responsible for crating the product in ice and loading it onto delivery trucks. The night shift works for ten hours. The two-hour downtime is when the cleaning crew comes in. Then, it starts over again. This goes on seven days a week."

"Would this be considered a large operation?" James asks.

"One of the largest in the country."

"I'm going to be in town for a week. If the owner shows up, tell him that I'll be back in two days. I would like to take some pictures of the site and ask a few more questions."

"I doubt he'll be here," the man tells James.

"That's all right, I may have enough information. What's your name?"

"Anthony Fitsdrew."

James writes it in his pad along with the other information he has been writing down.

"Am I going to be in your book?"

"Looks like it," James tells him. "Would you mind if I take some pictures of you?" he asks.

"No, go right ahead," the man says with a smile.

James points the camera at the man, but he focuses on the building and the license plates of the trucks that are parked behind the man. He takes a few quick photographs and thanks the man before he leaves.

Chapter 23

Down in the cellar of the church, Greg labors rigorously on the scrolls. The candle wax grows higher on the shelves behind Greg. There are many scrolls to decipher and interpret. He searches frantically through them, hoping to discover the answers to the numerous questions plaguing his mind. He lights more candles, anticipating another long night.

"Beneath the scrolls, in the folder," a voice says from the corner of the cellar.

"What?" Greg blurts out in a startled voice.

"In the plastic," the voice says.

"Who are you?" Greg asks quietly but sternly. He lifts a candle in the direction of the voice.

"You have no reason to fear me. I, as yourself, have been created to serve."

"To serve?" Greg asks, extending his arm in an attempt to direct the candlelight into the dark corner.

"To balance the scales," the voice says.

"Who are you?" The flickering light reveals a pair of eyes, piercing out from the dark.

"One of the brethren."

"What am I to do?" Greg asks.

"Continue on your path."

A look of amazement appears on Greg's face. The shimmer of candlelight outlines a figure. Greg thinks he sees wings on the figure. "Are you here to help?" he asks.

The voice doesn't answer. He is gone. Greg moves aside the pile of scrolls and locates a folder. It's a folder with plastic sleeves for the fragile fragments of scrolls. In it are fragments that he either hasn't had time to translate or has neglected in the past. The first things he observes are four Hebrew words, which cause him to hesitate. "Wars of the Lord," he reads out loud to himself. "Oh my God, it's one of the lost books," he says, his voice vibrating with excitement. There are only six readable lines on the fragment. He begins to decipher them out loud.

" . . . Wars of the Lord . . . prepare my children, for the battleground is of a flesh realm . . . but fought in the spiritual sphere. I, the Lord, will gather the righteous, before the beasts come from the sea and the earth, joining the great dragon, the prince of the air, that will make war with my children. The era of the Great Deliverance goes forth in the beginning of the last millennium. Prepare my children, . . . the blind will see and the deaf will hear, . . . the trumpets from heaven, and the battle for souls . . . "

Greg stares at the portion of the scroll in wonderment. The battle for souls appears to have begun on a new level, and for the last time . . . . And he is one of the principal commanders on the battlefield.

Chapter 24

"Congratulations, Mr. Malefic. The shark oceanarium is a success," the oceanologist says with excitement.

"The great whites survived," the marine biologist adds.

"That's good to hear, after all the money I dumped into it," Malefic tells them.

Malefic has financed the construction of the largest aquarium in the world. The oceanarium was built to house the great white shark. Until now, keeping great whites alive in captivity had never been accomplished. The oceanarium is larger than three football fields laid side by side and taller than a ten-story building. It has three transparent tunnels that run beneath the water from one end to the other. All three begin and end at different points of the oceanarium. The three transparent tunnels run at three separate levels, intersecting at the midpoint of the aquarium. The oceanarium has been hailed as one of the new man-made wonders of the world.

"We are on our way to a press conference to announce the grand opening of the Great White Oceanarium. It would be our pleasure if you would attend the opening."

"Sure."

"Thank you, Mr. Malefic. Thank you for everything you have done."

The two men begin to leave the office.

"Did you see the paper?" a man says, walking into Malefic's office waving a newspaper, nearly running over the oceanologist and the biologists that are on their way out.

"Yes I did, Mr. Sims, and I saw the news last night."

"We have to counter."

"I made a statement this morning. I told the media that I support the rights of the individual. Americans should and will have the right to choose if I'm elected president of this country," Malefic says.

"Very good."

"I figured you, as my political adviser, would like that."

"We have to plan our next move before Moore makes another unexpected bleeding heart speech."

"What about the gay rights issue? I was asked again this morning."

"We have been eluding the issue too long." He begins to walk about the room, thinking. "What do you think about the issue?" he asks.

"I could care less. I'm concerned about the numbers. How many of them are out there? How do I get their votes?"

"Well, Moore has stated that he doesn't condemn the individual, but the lifestyle. We've received no public feedback on that statement. So we don't know if it helped or hurt him."

"So we're looking for something neutral," Malefic says.

"I suggest you make a statement like, an American is an American, and every American has rights," Mr. Sims offers.

"That's good for now."

Chapter 25

In a small motel room on the oceanside of Imperial Beach, California, James has fallen into a deep sleep. The cool night air blows through the room, and the rhythmic sound of the surf provides a soothing backdrop. The drapes sway from the breeze coming through the open windows. A figure emerges, standing within the drapery. The drapes appear to pass through the figure. The drawer of the lamp table slides open; there is a Bible in it.

The morning has come, and James is greeted by a beautiful day and a Bible resting on the pillow beside his head. He isn't surprised, nor is he befuddled by the discovery. Nothing surprises him anymore. There's a piece of paper hanging out of the Book. He opens the book and finds a fishing license. His first order of business for the day was to purchase a fishing license. He doesn't dwell on when or how it got there, but simply accepts that his life has taken a turn for the bizarre. He also discovers a black piece of fabric in the section of the Book where he found the license. The name 'Matthew' and the numbers '4:19' are written on the fabric. The name and numerals glitter and appear to be three dimensional, as if they were levitating from the surface of the cloth. James begins to read the passage to himself, "'Then He said to them, "Follow Me, and I will make you fishers of men."'" Immediately after he reads the last word in the passage, the markings on the cloth float upward, sparkling, and slowly diminish into the air. The cloth dissolves into his hand. He shakes his head and closes the book. He heads for the shower.

James, dressed like a tourist, spends the day observing the charter business from a small cafe on the dock. He notices that there are three boats that operate on four-hour cycles, starting at seven a.m. and ending at seven p.m. He signs on for the three o'clock charter. He boards with two other paying clients. They join the captain and two crewmen.

"All right, land lovers, let's see if we can make it a Kodak moment!" the captain yells out. He's wearing a grimy white captain's cap and a shabby beard. He's slightly overweight and has a half dozen tattoos running up both arms. The two crewmen are of Mexican descent and keep to themselves.

The crewmen begin preparing the rods. That's when James notices that there's no land in sight. He begins to realize that he doesn't like the ocean.

"You look a little green," the captain says grinning.

"I don't think I was built for the ocean," James says.

"Why are you here? Does it have something to do with that little pad you keep jotting in?" The captain points with his toothpick.

"I'm writing a book on activities on the West Coast, something like a tourist's guide, a traveler's advisor of sorts," James tells him.

"I hope you advise your readers to stay away from that store you bought those clothes from." He grins with the toothpick hanging out of his mouth.

Suddenly, there's a tug on James' line. The captain quickly lunges toward James, pulling James' belt tight in the chair he's sitting in. "Are you ready?" he asks, smiling.

"Ready for . . . " James is abruptly jerked forward. He feels as if his shoulders have been pulled out of their sockets. "Oh shit! What am I supposed to do now?" he screams.

"Lean forward, reeling at the same time. Then pull back and do the same thing over again," the captain says in a manner that suggests he's enjoying James' lack of experience.

"By myself?"

"It's gonna make one hell of a chapter in your book," the captain laughs.

James grunts and moans as the veins in his arms bulge from the relentless struggle with the marlin. He watches the marlin propel itself above the dark turquoise surface of the water into the perfect, clear blue sky. The marlin crashes back into the ocean. Then once again breaking the surface and dancing across the shimmering water. An hour and a half has passed. James is thinking of surrendering.

"Don't give up. A couple more minutes and he's done!" the captain yells from the bridge.

"Who are you talking to, me or the fish?" James yells back.

The two crewmen run to the side of the boat, and begin to scream up at the captain in Spanish.

"They say it's a big one."

James glances over with an expression that states, "No shit!"

They bring the marlin up the side of the boat onto the deck. It's seven feet long and beautiful. James stares at its multishaded blue scales that fade into a pure white belly. The sun beats down on the creature, leaving James in astonishment of its beauty. James' hands feel as if they will remain permanently in a grip position, and his back feels like it will never recover. The captain takes a photograph of James and the blue marlin. James smiles with pride and, for a moment, the pain isn't there. Then the two crewmen cast the creature overboard. They watch it swim away into the depths of the ocean.

"Well done, land lover," the captain says as he hands James a beer. "Let's head on back. We got some lies to tell."

Chapter 26

"Derrick."

"Thomas, how are you?"

"Fine."

"Please join us." Derrick turns to his lunch companion, Senator Margaret Long. "Margaret, I'd like you to meet a very old and dear friend of mine."

"Nice to meet you, Thomas."

"Likewise, Margaret."

"I heard a rumor, Thomas, that you were seen hanging out at political dinner parties. You were overheard giving out political advice," Derrick says, grinning.

"I gave up politics for Lent."

"Really?"

"On occasion I have to get my feet dirty. When you're head of the Environmental Protection Services, you must kiss up a little. If a bit of free advice helps them pucker up, so be it."

"You have experience in the political arena?" Margaret asks.

"Thomas was once the most sought after political adviser in the field," Derrick explains.

"What happened, if you don't mind me asking?" Margaret inquires.

"No, I don't mind, Senator. It became all bullshit. Excuse my language."

"I believe he means too commercial," Derrick says.

"I think I understand, but I do believe it's improving," Margaret says, slightly on the defense.

"I don't see it that way," Thomas says as he takes a sip of water.

"It is improving." Derrick attempts to be reassuring.

"In my political era, the standard quote was, 'Did I say that?'" Thomas says mockingly.

"Was it that bad?" Margaret asks.

"Faulty product, and no guarantee."

Derrick glances over at Margaret. "Can you feel the love in the air?"

"I'm getting the impression that you don't like politics," Margaret says smiling.

"Politics don't bother me, it's the politicians that annoy me."

"Thanks," Margaret and Derrick say simultaneously.

"I trust you, Derrick." He looks across the table.

"I don't know you, Margaret. So it wouldn't be fair to say either way, but I do trust you, Derrick." He pours water into his glass. "That's the sad part."

"What?" Derrick asks.

"Someone like yourself won't get elected. You're too honest."

"Thanks . . . I think."

"I understand what Thomas is saying," Margaret says with a discouraged expression on her face.

"There's no place for honesty in politics," Thomas says mordantly.

"That's very true concerning the last couple of presidential terms," Margaret says.

"I plan on changing that," Derrick says with a wink.

"I hope so," Thomas says lifting his glass in a toasting manner. "We need someone to get things back on track because our country is still hurting from the last scandal that came out of the White House."

"That one was pretty ugly," Margaret says shaking her head.

"I'll never look at a cigar the same way again," Thomas mumbles. "Well, since I have your undivided attention, what's your position on the environmental issue, Derrick?"

"What's on your mind, Thomas?"

"I'm looking for a reason to support you."

"You need a reason?"

"I'm responsible for a large committee. Before we support a candidate, I have to be assured that my organization's interests are catered to," Thomas says earnestly.

"Even if you disagree with the rest of the platform?"

"The environment is my platform . . . My number one priority."

"I'm sorry, Thomas, but the environment issue doesn't take precedence over the other issues."

"I understand, Derrick. I wanted to hear you say it. Now that the political crap is out of the way, let's have a couple of beers later, for old time's sake."

"That sounds great. I'll meet you at Capital's in a couple of hours."

Thomas says his good-byes to Margaret and leaves.

"Politics left a bad taste in his mouth," Margaret says quietly.

"Well, Margaret, without getting into a long story, I can tell you this much. He took the fall for another man's mistake. He basically got screwed. Excuse my language."

Chapter 27

"Mr. Malefic, may we have a word with you?"

"What can I do for you officers?"

"It's about the burglary. We need some more information."

"I told a Sergeant Wills everything that night."

"Yes sir, I know, but there was a problem with the weapons check. Can you tell us again why you have machine guns on the premises?"

Malefic takes a deep, frustrated breath. "We are an International Telecommunication Service. We handle classified communications for our Federal government and other governments all over the globe," Malefic speaks as if he were addressing a child. "We maintain one of the primary databases for our military's satellite information retrieval program. All the data is stored in this building. So, as you can see, it's imperative that we have a well-developed security system in place. One part of that security system is heavily armed men. I gave the police department a copy of the license for the weapons and a telephone number for my lawyer at the Pentagon."

"Thank you, Mr. Malefic, for your cooperation and patience. I'll take care of it personally," the officer says.

DeMynn enters Malefic's office as the two police officers are leaving. "How many policemen's ball tickets did you buy?"

"Where have you been?" Malefic asks sharply.

"Here and there. What did they want?"

"There was a mix-up with the weapons license."

"Did you politely explain to them that we need automatic weapons for our rodent problem?" DeMynn says with a grin.

"The only rodent problem we have is a seven-foot, three-hundred-pound rodent."

"Has he returned?"

"No, and I hope I never see that son of a bitch again." Malefic's face cringes in pain as the words depart his mouth.

"Are you all right? What's wrong, Charles?"

"Give me a second," he says as he attempts to catch his breath.

"You should really deny yourself those hot peppers that you fancy so frequently," DeMynn says, glancing at the chessboard across the room.

"It isn't hot peppers."

"What is it?" DeMynn asks as he walks over to the chessboard. He stares at the board for a moment. Then he moves his tinted knight, removing a clear pawn from the chessboard.

"That thing put a hex on me." Malefic's expression displays irritation and his voice is imbued with animosity.

"Pardon me?"

"Every time I cuss, I get a sharp pain in my midsection."

DeMynn begins to laugh. "What happened to the bar of soap days?"

"You think this shit is funny?" Malefic doubles over from the pain in his abdomen.

"How bad does it get?" DeMynn asks, attempting to hold back his smile.

"Bad enough." He sits down, holding his stomach. "That isn't the half of it."

"What do you mean?"

"When I swear, it's worse."

"Do you mean blasphemy?"

Malefic nods his head.

DeMynn smiles. "He's attempting to change you."

"It's definitely going to change my vocabulary."

"I believe it will be for the best," DeMynn says, amused by the entire situation.

"Can you stop it from happening?"

"Don't curse."

Malefic stares out into space with a blank expression. "What's going on?" he asks; his voice is weak and tired.

"You wouldn't believe me if I told you."

"What choice do I have?"

"It has to do with that subject you hate," DeMynn tells him.

Malefic rubs his eyes in frustration. "This thing pops in and out of my life when he pleases. I experience excrutiating pain because I use particular words. What choice do I have, but . . . ." He stops speaking and sinks down into his chair with a weary look on his face.

"He's from the spiritual realm and has elected to enter your life for a specific reason."

"Great," Malefic mumbles under his breath.

"I have a theory on why you were chosen, and I believe I know what he has planned . . . and I do have a solution."

"How do you know this stuff?"

"I read a lot."

"Well, read faster. I may be dead soon."

"Perhaps."

"What?" Malefic asks fretfully.

"That was humor, Charles."

"My suffering is your humor," he says in a resentful tone.

"Please accept my apology. It was in bad taste." DeMynn attempts again to hide his smile.

"Thank you." Malefic straightens up; the pain has diminished.

DeMynn begins to walk out of the office, but stops and pokes his head back around the door. "Oh Charles, don't forget."

"What?"

"Thou shall not take the Lord's name in vain." His laughter can be heard down the hall.

Chapter 28

The sun begins to sink into the ocean, and the cool evening air blows through the windows. James sits at a small desk in his motel room. The desk is covered with papers and folders. They appear to be randomly spread across the table, but to him they are precisely positioned. He's one phone call away from piecing the puzzle together. One phone call and he'll be able to place a name with the letter . . . the name of his wife's murderer. That call will have to wait until morning when the bank opens. He begins to doze off, thinking about the serene sound of the surf and the peaceful feeling the breeze on his skin gives him. The idea of starting over here crosses his mind.

"Have the brakes felt strange to you?"

"I haven't noticed," Faith says, looking through a book of children's names.

"The cruise control has been acting up, too."

"The car is still under warranty, isn't it?"

"Yeah, but it's such a pain taking it in," James says in a whining voice.

"I'll take it. You should slow down, honey. It's beginning to rain harder."

"Man, why in the hell would they put all these sharp curves on a mountain road?"

"To make people like you drive slower," she says smiling.

James takes a curve riding the brakes. There's a hissing sound, then a pop. The brakes are gone. "Oh shit!"

"What?"

"No brakes."

"What are we going to do?"

"Hold on." James begins to scrape the car against the mountain.

"Why are you speeding up?!"

"I'm not. It's the cruise control. It came on and I can't turn it off.

The car continues to scrape against the mountain, gaining momentum and heading toward a sharp curve. Sparks fly into the misty air. James tries to hold the car against the rocks with all his might, but the vehicle doesn't slow down. The steering wheel locks into a straight position. James reaches over to Faith's seatbelt and attempts to unfasten her and himself. Jumping out could save them. But the seatbelts are stuck and the door locks are jammed. The front tire bursts and the hood peels off, flying over the car. The vehicle runs off the road and proceeds toward the guardrail. It strikes the guardrail at an angle, causing the car to flip over and tumble down the fifty-foot cliff into the trees.

James wakes from the dream, realizing he has obtained the answer to a question that has been tormenting him since that fatal night. The doctors said he had a mild case of amnesia due to a severe concussion. He wasn't able to remember the chain of events leading up to the accident. They also said he was suffering from denial and depression. He started to believe them. But the letter, the memory, and some investigating will prove them wrong. James finds no comfort in proving them wrong. The satisfaction will come in the form of revenge.

Chapter 29

"Thomas, what happened last night?"
"Is that you, Derrick?"
"Yeah. What happened last night?"
"What do you mean? We had a couple of drinks and some shooters."
"I woke up in a motel room," Derrick tells him.
"What?"
"Tell me what happened last night. All I can remember is the first half of the Skins game."
"We drank until about midnight, and you said it was time for you to go. I stayed with the girl I was talking to."
"So I left around midnight without you?"
"Right. Are you all right, Derrick?"
"No, Thomas, I'm not. I don't remember leaving or how I got in that motel room," Derrick says with a sharp tone.
"Relax, buddy, I'm sure there's nothing to get upset about."
"There's seven hours of my life I have no recollection of. That sort of thing upsets me."
"Listen to me. You probably thought you were too drunk to drive home and decided to get a room. You got into the room and passed out before you could call your wife."
"Are you forgetting anything?"
"No, that's it," Thomas says, sure of himself.
"I'll talk to you later, Thomas." He hangs the telephone up and looks at his wife.
"What did he say?" she asks with concern.
"He said I left around midnight without him, that I must have gotten a room because I was too drunk to drive home."
"Do you remember anything like that?"
"No." He rubs his eyes in frustration. "Something is wrong here. I would not have gotten a room and not called you."
"I know," she affirms.
"I have never had a blackout in my life. And I know I didn't drink enough last night to do so."
"What's going on, Derrick?"
"I don't know," he says wearily.
Derrick and his wife stare at one another with fear in their eyes. The telephone rings, breaking the silence.
"Hello, Moore residence."

"Derrick, did you page me?" James asks in a tired voice while he unpacks his suitcase.

"James, I need to talk to you."

"Are you all right? You sound funny."

"Listen to me. I woke up this morning in a motel room in the city. I don't remember how I got there."

"Meet me at the station, and don't take a piss."

"What?"

"Meet me at my office, leave now!"

Derrick stands holding the telephone.

"What did he say?" his wife asks.

"He said to meet him at the station and not to use the bathroom."

Chapter 30

A man casually walks into the garden. "Strange weather we're having, isn't it?"

Greg glances up from his reading. "Yes, it is . . . a pleasant surprise."

"May I?" The man waves his hand toward the bench Greg is sitting on.

"Yes, of course." Greg slides over to make room.

The man takes a deep breath and looks around the garden. "I can't believe it's this warm at this time of year."

Greg smiles. "Do I know you?" he asks politely.

"I'm sorry. My name is Luke DeMynn," he says, extending his hand.

"Professor Greg Orfordis," Greg says, shaking DeMynn's hand.

"Yes, I know." He smiles slightly.

"Your name sounds familiar. Have I met you before?" Greg draws his hand back and glances down at it, feeling as if there were something on it.

"It's possible," DeMynn says, staring out into the garden. "My activities occasionally have me working closely with the church." He turns and smiles at Greg. "That is why I'm here. I believe you can assist me."

"What can I do for you, Mr. DeMynn?" Greg asks.

"I have two friends that are interested in the same woman. My best friend, Chuck, would suit her perfectly, I believe. My other friend, Rick, on the other hand, isn't right for her at all, considering her grandeur. But Rick is being encouraged by his best friend to pursue this woman. I believe it would be unhealthy for Rick to continue this fantasy, fearing his heart may be broken. If I could in some way speak to the fellow that is encouraging Rick, I may be able to save him a great deal of pain in the future."

"That is very considerate of you." A gust of wind suddenly blows furiously through the garden, causing the pages in Greg's Bible to flip. The pages rest with the withdrawal of the wind. Greg stares down at the first passage that catches his eye. He quickly reads it to himself. 'Put on the whole armor of God that you may be able to stand against the wiles of the devil.' The gust of wind suddenly returns, causing the pages to flip again. Greg looks up into the sky, checking to see if there is a storm coming, but the sky is perfectly clear. The wind subsides and the garden becomes calm. Greg glances down. The book is now opened to the section called '1 Peter.' Chapter 5, passage eight draws his eyes. 'Be sober, be vigilant, because your adversary the devil walks about like a roaring lion, seeking whom he may devour.' Greg looks up to discover DeMynn staring at him.

"Strange weather we're having." DeMynn says, smiling, but his eyes stare coldly at Greg.

"Let me see if I understand you correctly," Greg says in a defensive but confident tone. "You have a friend named Chuck that is appealing, charming, and financially secure, which in your opinion would be preferable to the woman."

"Correct."

"Now, the other friend, Rick, is modest, ordinary, and has a nice personality, which causes you to believe that the woman in question would merely break his heart, because he doesn't possess the material success and the appealing image of Chuck. He wouldn't be able to keep her happy."

"Precisely."

Greg continues. "The fellow that is encouraging Rick is leading him toward guaranteed heartbreak and pain. You would like to speak to the gentleman that is encouraging Rick in hopes of deterring him from making a mistake."

"I believe you understand precisely the dilemma I am experiencing."

"I'm sorry, Mr. DeMynn, I can't help you. I tend to side with the individual with character."

"Is there anything I can do to sway your decision?"

"You look quite capable of resolving your own problems."

"Thank you, Professor, that is very kind, but I'm considerably lazy. I always attempt to recruit others to make my life simpler."

"Really?"

"I remember a few years back. I believe it was in this very city that an inspiring actor lent me a hand. There was a gentleman that had a genuine chance of beginning a great era. He spoke about a nation conceived in liberty and the equality of all men. But the inspiring actor put an end to it all, ironically in a theater. Personally, I believe it was his greatest performance." DeMynn grins with satisfaction. "I also remember one sunny day, I believe it was November, in a charming little town in Texas. That's where I met a young, skinny lad who aided me with a chore. Except he wasn't as reliable as I believed. Fortunately, I was there to assist. Then there was the man that assisted me in Memphis." His voice and demeanor reach a climactic level. "That day was very special for me, because there was a man of God at that time who worried me quite a bit. He was a serious threat to my plans. But it had a happy ending . . . for me, of course." He stops speaking and stares out into the garden. He appears to be reminiscing about a fond memory. The memory fades and he glances at Greg. "Professor, are you all right?" he asks in a caring tone. "Are those tears forming in your eyes?"

"I think you should leave," Greg says solemnly.

"I assume you are not going to help me."

"I'll help you the day your place of residence hosts the Winter Olympics."

"I assumed correctly," he smirks.

"Good-bye, Mr. DeMynn," Greg says coldly.

DeMynn stands and begins to leave. "We will see one another again, Professor."

*

The sun begins to ascend into the sky and the morning chill begins to leave the air. All the drops of dew in the garden sparkle like little chips of diamonds, before they eventually evaporate into the air or are absorbed by the ground.

James' late night has brought him to the church. He stands at the entrance of the corridor. He feels a peace within himself as he stares down the passageway. He focuses on the light at the end of the corridor as he walks toward the garden. A figure appears and is approaching James. His first thought is that it is Greg, but the shape of the figure reminds James of what Greg had said, that Judge Russell occasionally visits the garden. They near one another; the man passes James with his eyes staring downward at the cobblestone walkway.

"Judge Russell?" James asks, unsure of himself.

The man stops and turns around.

The Biblical events portrayed on the stained glass windows have now begun to glow from the sunlight.

"Detective Rood?" Judge Russell asks, putting his hands into his pockets.

James steps closer to Judge Russell.

"What are you doing here?" Judge Russell asks softly.

"Sometimes I come here after work to talk to Professor Orfordis."

Judge Russell stares at James as if his mind were

elsewhere. "Men in our position, there is no after work," he says in a tired tone.

James stares into Judge Russell's weary eyes for a moment. "Is the professor in the garden?" he asks, glancing at the end of the corridor.

"No," Judge Russell answers. "Do you need to speak to him?"

"I need to ask him something."

Judge Russell glances up at the stained glass window that has the Archangel Michael spearing the serpent. "Sometimes the answers are right in front of you," he says in a soothing voice.

James looks upward at the stained glass windows. "Sometimes there are no answers," he says, looking back at Judge Russell.

Judge Russell cordially says good-bye and walks out into the city. James enters the garden and sits on a bench under an oak tree.

Chapter 31

"Beer?" Anna asks.

"Ice water, thanks," James says, pulling a stool next to Derrick.

"What's going on, James?" Derrick asks with concern.

"They found traces of Zendan in your blood and urine, along with alcohol."

"Zendan?"

"It's a type of sedative, primarily used in mental institutions," James explains.

"I was drugged?"

"Who were you with last night?"

"An old friend," Derrick says, putting his elbows on the bar and his head in his hands.

"Do you trust this friend?"

"I guess," Derrick mumbles.

"I went to the bar and talked to a bartender named Sam. A long-haired guy, do you remember him?"

"Yes."

"He said he was working last night and he remembered you. He said you and your friend, and a woman with red hair, left together around eleven o'clock after the Skins game."

"Thomas said I left around midnight and alone," Derrick says glancing up.

"The bartender said the only reason he remembered you was because he recognized you. He remembered you needing help walking. He also said your friend and that woman helped you out the door, and he didn't see them come back." James takes a drink of his water. "He and I agreed that a couple of shots and a beer wouldn't have put you in that state."

"What's going on, James?"

"Someone is trying to take you down."

"What am I going to do?"

"I want you to talk to a friend of mine." James glances at the door. "She's coming in the door now."

"She's a reporter!" Derrick exclaims.

"I know."

"Someone in the media is a friend of yours?"

"Well, Detective, I must say I was shocked to hear from you," Hope says as she approaches.

"Hope Naples, Derrick Moore."

"Senator Moore, it is a pleasure to meet you. I'm a big supporter of your platform."

"Thank you."

"How big of a supporter are you, Ms. Naples?" James asks.

"What does that mean, Detective Rood?"

"Do you want a big story?"

She stares at him suspiciously.

"You are the first and only person we are going to talk to from the media," James says.

"You have my undivided attention."

"James, are you sure about this?" Derrick quietly interrupts.

"The senator was drugged and abducted last night. He woke up this morning in a motel room in the city, unable to remember a large part of last night."

"Alone?"

"He woke up alone, but I have a suspicion he wasn't."

"How do you know he was drugged?" she asks, pulling out a small pad.

"Blood and urine tests," James replies.

"Did you have the results officially documented?"

"Yes."

"What is going on?" Derrick asks nervously.

"Beginning right now, this is an official extortion investigation," James announces.

*

The day gives way to the darkness, and loyalty closely ensues. The city streets are active with dark intentions, but what occurs in the uppermost office of the Malefic Building makes the city streets pale in comparison.

"Mr. Malefic?"

"Yes, Mr. Sims, what can I do for you?"

"I have some information that you may find interesting."

"I'm listening."

"I've come across some photographs of one Senator Moore. Unflattering, I must say." Mr. Sims grins a corrupt smile.

"Photographs of such compromising proportions must be quite valuable," Malefic says, grinning slightly.

"I was hoping you would perceive it that way."

"Of course you were. What is the going price for scandalous photographs these days?"

"A half million dollars . . . and keep DeMynn off Moore."

"The price I find reasonable, but as for DeMynn, I have no control over his extra activities."

"When can you pay?"

"I can provide the money now. Will cash be suitable?"

"That will suit me just fine," Mr. Sims says with a grin.

Mr. Sims leaves the office with a leather briefcase. He steps into the elevator. Slowly the doors come together. The elevator begins going down to the garage.

Malefic spins his chair around to stare out over the city through the large office window. He crosses his legs, knee over knee, with a satisfied expression on his face.

One of Malefic's associates enters the office. "I just saw Thomas Sims leaving the building," the associate says, throwing a pile of paperwork on the desk. "Is he still working for us?"

"Yes," Malefic says quietly, continuing to stare out the window.

Chapter 32

"I got your message."

"James, nice to see you."

"Nice to see you, too, Greg."

"The time has arrived," Greg says, looking through his papers.

"What are you talking about?"

"Remember the part of the scroll that speaks about an Agent of God, also referred to as the Guide?"

"Yeah, the person I'm supposed to be," James says with a half smile.

"I believe it will be known to the other side that you are the Agent. In turn, that will put your life in grave danger."

"The other side?"

"The side against God's plan."

"That's right, the goblins and devils."

"I suggest you don't take this lightly," Greg says sternly.

"Sorry Greg, it's difficult for me."

"In your line of work, it's your job to enforce the law. That's the right side, the good side. The people who make a living at breaking the law are the other side."

"I understand, at least most of the time, the things I see every day, but the things you talk about are very difficult for me to comprehend. I'm having a hard time believing that any of this has really happened."

"You have to go beyond the secular mind. In the big picture, there is God and the forces working against God's plan."

"Every day I try to convince myself that this is really happening." He rubs the side of his head. "Then I try to convince myself that it isn't," he says, now rubbing the bridge of his nose.

"It is happening, and in the middle of it all are a great deal of people, and if the wrong circumstances occur, they will be led to a path of self-destruction."

James stares at Greg, sensing the importance of what he's saying.

"You must understand that the time has come. The days of fence straddling are over. Sides must be chosen." Greg stands and walks to the front of the desk. "I know how you would like to believe you are delusional or insane. It would be easier to accept, but you are far from insane."

There's a lingering silence between them. James stares down at the floor and asks quietly, "What kind of danger are we talking about?"

"They will attempt to turn your soul. If they can't get your soul, they will destroy you."

"Why me? What will that accomplish?" he asks with his head still down, now staring at his wedding band.

"You are the Guide, the one to deliver the man of God to the people. If they can redirect your soul or destroy you, the prophecy will not be fulfilled. The chain will be broken."

He glances up at Greg. "Why not the man of God? If they got rid of him, wouldn't that stop the fulfillment of the prophecy?"

"I'm sure that would break the chain, but the scrolls suggest that the 'Fist of God' was sent to protect him, making you the easier target."

"What about me? What's going to protect me? I'm the one delivering the man of God. He's almighty, He can send another one. He has two fists."

"The scrolls say that the Agent of God's greatest weapon is his faith."

"I'm in serious trouble then," he says, smiling slightly. "What should I expect?"

"I don't know. I don't know when or how, or in what form they will appear."

"Form? What does that mean?"

"Flesh or spirit."

"Great," James says, shaking his head and rolling his eyes.

"I will continue to search the scrolls. They may be able to alert us to future dangers."

"That would be helpful," James says looking down at his hands. "Why is this happening, Greg?" he asks quietly.

"From what I gathered so far, it appears that God is attempting to save as many people as He can through Derrick, by positioning him in the presidency. I believe He's intervening once more in human history, because the end is near." Greg picks up a scroll and stares at it for a moment. "The scrolls say that there will be a battle for souls. They seem to be speaking about our current situation. They also say shortly after the battle, the demonic trinity will surface."

James looks up. "What's that mean?"

"The scrolls say that the beast of the earth and the beast of the sea will join the great dragon after the battle for souls has ended," Greg explains. "Becoming the demonic trinity."

"What beasts? What great dragon?" James asks.

"The Antichrist, the false prophet, and Satan," Greg says in a low voice.

James shakes his head and leans back into the chair. He stares at Greg with a bewildered expression. "That's pretty wild stuff, Greg."

"I know. And there's a great deal more," Greg says, smiling.

"I don't think I can handle anymore. You're going to give me nightmares."

"By the way, how was California?" Greg asks, returning to his chair behind the desk.

"The weather was beautiful."

"The business?"

"Insightful."

"Do you want to talk about it?"

James stares down at the floor again. "What do you know about the accident?"

"Everything that you told Dr. Leanman. I also remember reading about it in the papers."

"The papers?" A quick expression of anger crosses James' face.

"Yes, they said you were intoxicated and driving too fast, and you lost control of the vehicle. They also said that no blood tests were done, so no charges were filed. You lost your memory, and you were unable to remember what caused the accident. You were in the hospital for six weeks, and the department suspended you for four weeks."

"Six weeks . . . I was suspended for six weeks."

"It ran in the papers for four weeks."

James leans over and puts his elbows on his knees, staring downward. He begins to repeatedly turn his wedding band around on his finger. "It makes me wonder why God would choose a man like me for His plan."

"I don't believe the papers, and God knows the truth."

"Do you know the truth?" James asks, glancing up at Greg.

"It has something to do with why you went to California."

He lowers his head again. "My wife was murdered."

"Why?"

"She was a political journalist for the Washington Post. She was working on a story about a man that had underground connections. This man was and continues to bring drugs into the country. She was close to exposing him, but he had her killed before she linked him to the drug trafficking. A box of her personal belongings ended up at her brother's house. He's the one who delivered the box to me. I believe she somehow had her belongings sent there, knowing they would search our house and her office."

"Smart lady."

James rubs his eyes. "Yes, she was."

"Who murdered her, James?"

"Charles Malefic," he says vengefully.

"Are you sure?"

"When I was in California, I investigated the information that Faith had gathered. I had bank slips and receipts, along with other documents from Faith's folder. They were primarily related to three businesses. A fishery and a charter company in southern California, and a yacht club in Tijuana, Mexico. All three had a common account number. While I was at the yacht club, I had a conversation with one of the employees. That's when I discovered that Malefic owned the club. I called and verified the account number. He owns all three businesses and a half dozen restaurants on the West Coast. I believe it all begins in a rain forest project of his in South America and ends at the restaurants that are distributing points for the fishery. I also believe he has a similar operation set up on the east coast of Texas. He owns two flight schools. One is located about two miles outside of Port Issuable, Texas, the other in a small town in Virginia. I'm flying the yacht club employee in tomorrow. He's going to tell me precisely how the operation runs. I gave him the address of the church. I was hoping he could hide out here."

"Yes, he can."

"Thank you, Greg."

"In return, I want a favor from you."

"Sure."

"Promise me you're not going to do anything irrational."

James smiles and walks away.

Chapter 33

"Did you see the paper this morning?" DeMynn asks, holding up the newspaper in his hand.

"No," Malefic responds as if he were already irritated.

"It appears Senator Moore was drugged and abducted."

"What?" Malefic asks, acting surprised.

"It seems to me someone has made a feeble attempt to tarnish his reputation and destroy his candidacy for president," DeMynn says, staring down at the chessboard.

"Thank you for your opinion, but what do the papers say?"

"That someone has made a feeble attempt to tarnish his reputation and destroy his candidacy for president," DeMynn says again, glancing over his shoulder with a grin.

"Anything else?"

"The senator woke up in a motel room, and he had no recollection of the night before, nor could he remember how he got there," DeMynn explains as he contemplates a move.

"Alone?" Malefic asks, walking over to the bar.

"There's a photograph with an unidentified woman in it, but no one seems to believe the senator was there by choice," DeMynn says, moving his tinted queen out of trouble.

"What else?" Malefic asks, fixing himself a drink.

"He went immediately to the police and filed a report. They conducted blood and urine tests and discovered a very potent sedative in his system," DeMynn tells him. "Oh, did I mention the witnesses?" he asks, walking over to Malefic.

"What witnesses?" Malefic asks, quickly shooting his drink down.

"A few good citizens and a bartender witnessed the senator being carried out of the bar by a man and the unidentified woman in the photograph. They escorted the senator out the door to a waiting limousine."

"What are the police doing?"

"Investigating."

Malefic walks over to the window and stares out over the city.

"Whoever did this," DeMynn says staring into Malefic's eyes in the window's reflection, "may find it backfiring on him."

"I don't want to talk about it."

"Stay out of the gutter, Charles, muddy feet leave

trails."

Chapter 34

The snow drifts peacefully down to earth, covering the church grounds with a white blanket. The neighboring houses are decorated with Christmas lights and other festive decor. Snowflakes float quietly into the bell tower of the church. There in the tower, a creature dreams of an ancient entombed memory.

The road is narrow and dusty. The buildings along the cobblestone road appear whitewashed. The streets are crowded with people, and they seem to be anticipating an event. The sight of a group approaching around the bend prompts the crowd's murmur to become louder. The group approaching consists mainly of men wearing uniforms, but in the middle of the group are three other men carrying large wooden objects. The group presses through the crowd toward a hill. The soldiers and the three men dragging the heavy objects reach the summit of the hill. They are met by additional crowds. Then the dream is consumed by the echoes of metal striking metal. The dream has turned into a nightmare, bringing the figure abruptly out of his dream. He begins to radiate, melting the snow around his body. He begins fading into the darkness . . . reappearing across town.

"Malefic," a voice says from the darkened corner of Malefic's office.

"I was beginning to wonder if you forgot about me."

"I must talk to you."

"Sure, can I get you a drink? Tea maybe?" Malefic asks in a polite manner.

"You cannot be president of this country."

"Why?"

"Through you, many souls will be lost."

"What?"

"You are being used."

"What are you talking about? No one uses me!" Malefic has become angry and defensive.

"You are beginning to worry me, Charles. Talking to yourself in the dark?" DeMynn asks, entering the office.

"I'm not talking to myself. I have company," Malefic says, looking toward the dark corner.

DeMynn notices a pair of eyes in the corner. "Why was I not invited to the tea party?" he says, as if his feelings were hurt. "Introduce me to your friend."

"Excuse my lack of manners. Luke DeMynn, meet . . . "

Malefic's face strikes a muddled expression. "How embarrassing, I don't know your name."

The figure quietly says his name, but he says it in Hebrew.

"I'm sorry I didn't get that," Malefic says.

DeMynn repeats the figure's name, but in ancient Greek.

"Excuse me, is there an interpreter in the house?" Malefic blurts out.

"He said his name is . . . " DeMynn hesitates, "the Fist of God."

Malefic and DeMynn stare speechlessly at one another for a moment.

"Should I be worried?" Malefic asks.

"I don't know," DeMynn says glancing back at the figure. "Should he be worried?"

The figure begins to speak in the Hebrew language, combined with ancient Greek, and DeMynn responds in the same manner.

"That is really rude," Malefic interrupts. "Did the two of you forget how to speak English?"

"It appears that our friend here believes that I am a bad influence on you," DeMynn says grinning.

"He will use you for his personal agenda," the figure says as he begins to glitter and slowly fade into the darkness.

"Hey, what does that mean? What is he talking about?" Malefic asks with a confounded expression.

"He is trying to play us against one another," DeMynn says to reassure Malefic. "It's an old trick, Charles."

"An old and effective trick."

Chapter 35

"Senator Moore, have the scandalous photographs damaged your campaign and the way the country perceives your character?" a news reporter seated with Derrick asks.

"I do believe some have speculated about my guilt, but I do believe they are the same people who had illegitimate speculations about me for one reason or another from the beginning. The same people have me connected to foul play."

"Would those people be incorrect?"

"Yes. I was a victim of a clumsy attempt to destroy my candidacy for president."

"Is it true that the photographs have been investigated by a specialist? And, if so, have the results been concluded?"

"The examination of the photographs determined that I was unconscious at the time they were taken. Adding these results to the tests taken the morning after affirms that there was no sexual interaction that night, making it clear that I am innocent of any sex scandal or infidelity."

"Is there any evidence pointing toward the party responsible for the abduction and photographs?"

"I'm not permitted to comment on that."

"Do you have a personal opinion on who it may be?"

"No, I don't."

"Do you believe you still have a chance in the election?"

"Ask me ten months from now."

"One more question, Senator. What can the country expect if you are elected?"

"My four years will be dedicated to rebuilding the moral foundation of this country."

"Precisely what does that mean?"

"If we can teach the young generation a moral and ethical way of life, that would lead to our future parents, business owners, and congressmen making moral and ethical decisions. Every young generation is a new foundation, and it is the responsibility of the elder generation to build, and repair if needed, the new foundation. Moral and ethical decisionmaking is what shapes a country. This country has made many immoral and unethical decisions in the past. It is time for a new foundation."

"Thank you, Senator Moore."

*

A taxicab arrives and a man of Mexican descent steps out onto the freshly fallen snow. He carefully walks with his small suitcase in one hand and a piece of paper in the other. He approaches a man who is shoveling snow off the sidewalk leading to the church.

"Could you tell me where can I find a Professor Orfordis?"

The groundskeeper gives the man directions to where the professor can be found. The man begins to enter the two large wooden doors of the church, but he's met by a tall, lanky man before he is able to enter.

"Are you Pablo Sanavas?"

"Why?"

"Jim sent me to pick you up and take you to a rendezvous spot."

"He told me to come here," the man says, glancing at the little piece of paper in his hand.

"He thinks someone was tipped off, and they know you're coming here."

"Who are you?"

"I work with Jim." The tall man shows him his identification.

"Where am I supposed to meet him?"

"The aquarium."

They enter a black BMW and pull away from the church. Pablo and the man driving the car drive in silence for forty-five minutes. They reach the parking lot behind the Baltimore Aquarium. The man stops the car at the sidewalk in front of the entrance.

"Go through the back doors, and follow the signs to the oceanarium. It's the great white exhibit. He'll meet you there."

"The aquarium looks closed," Pablo says nervously.

"It is, but we know the security guards."

"Are you coming?" Pablo asks.

"I have to run another errand for Jim."

Pablo gets out of the car and closes the door. The car quickly pulls away. He stands for a moment, contemplating of leaving. He slowly opens the metal door and follows the signs to the oceanarium. The exhibit tanks provide the only source of light, giving the inside of the building a cold, blue ambiance. He locates the shark exhibit, but no one is there. He backs into a dark corner and waits.

An outline of a figure begins to slowly appear behind Pablo.

"Good evening, Pablo," someone says from behind him.

"DeMynn," he says, turning and stumbling backward with a surprised expression.

"Are you lost? You're a long way from the West Coast."

"I'm . . . I'm visiting a friend."

"Here?" DeMynn asks smiling and glancing around. "At the aquarium?"

"I . . . I got a phone call to . . . to meet him here."

"The aquarium is closed, Pablo. Are you certain he said to meet him here?"

"I think he works here."

"Is one of these two guards your friend?" DeMynn asks, as two men step out of the shadows.

"No."

"Well then, while we wait for your friend to arrive, why don't we seize the opportunity." DeMynn smiles. "Let's take a tour."

DeMynn, followed by Pablo and the two men, walks over to a platform.

"Would you like to see a thing of beauty?" DeMynn asks, staring with a grin. "Look there." He points down.

Pablo looks down and observes two fifteen-foot great whites cutting the water ten feet below him. At the moment, he does not perceive them as beautiful.

"Their names are Adam and Eve." DeMynn smiles. "But I like to call them: The judge and jury."

"I didn't do anything wrong," Pablo says defensively and obviously frightened.

"I don't remember saying you did. But I do have a few questions. For instance, who were you having a conversation with at the yacht club? And is he the friend you were supposed to meet tonight?"

"I don't remember anyone at the yacht club."

"Really?" DeMynn steps to the edge of the platform. "Have you ever witnessed a great white feed, Pablo?"

"DeMynn, I didn't . . . "

"Maybe I can rejuvenate your memory." DeMynn stares out over the water. "He was approximately a hundred and eighty pounds, perhaps a little over six feet tall and . . . oh yeah," DeMynn turns around, "he was the only black man in the yacht club."

"I don't remember, DeMynn." The sweat begins to gather on Pablo's forehead.

"Here's the deal, Pablo. You tell me the name of your

friend, and I will simply forget I saw you tonight. And please don't tell me you don't know his name. That will truly upset me."

Pablo stares at the wake on the surface of the water, made by the dorsal fin of one of the great whites.

*

"Daddy, Daddy!" a little girl yells, running to the door to catch her father before he leaves for work. "Did you tell Santa about the doll I want?" Her face shines with excitement.

"Yes, I did, honey." Anthony kneels down. "Did you send your letter?"

"Yes, I did," she says proudly.

"Then, Santa knows, and he will get it for you," he says with a reassuring smile.

She hurries up the stairs and turns around at the top. "I love you, Daddy." She quickly disappears down the hallway.

Anthony's wife, Beth, walks up to him and whispers, "Did you find it yet?"

"Not yet. I'll look again after work, before I go to my meeting."

He works for UPS and attends drug abuse meetings at the clinic three nights a week.

"She's so excited. I hope we can find it," Beth says, glancing up the stairs.

"We will, honey," he says optimistically.

Chapter 36

    The sun sets on the Caribbean Islands, and the winds carry an ancient message to their shores from the Field of Blood.
    In a small bungalow on the beach, a man relaxes. He lies on the cool white sheets of his bed, enjoying one of the most beautiful tropical settings in the world. He sips a colorful island concoction and attempts to fill his mind with fantasies about his newfound wealth. The swaying palm trees mesmerize and the shimmering ocean captivates his mind. The surf glitters with the moon's alluring light as it quietly crawls onto the sand. But something is troubling him. The man falls into a surreal dream state. An unusual cool breeze enters the room, but the man continues to sleep. The breeze takes form, becoming a cosmic mass. The blackness hovers above the man like a dark cloud. It pours itself into the man's body, seeping into every pore, flowing into his bloodstream. It spreads throughout the body like a cancerous disease, oozing throughout the organs and saturating the brain. It desires to recover and awaken the subconscience of accountability, but it is hidden deep in a suffocating world, a world where everything dies a slow, agonizing death. The mass steadily travels throughout the body. The lungs collapse as it departs from them. It shreds the liver like paper as it moves through it. It climbs the spinal cord with the corkscrew motion of a snake, slicing the nerve endings with razor-like moves. It reaches the heart and coils around it, constricting its last beat. It then follows the throat up to the roof of the mouth, entering the brain. It searches for the final thought. It searches for a confession, a plea, a reason to save his soul. The mass begins to radiate, becoming a source of burning heat in the brain. It will be the destroying blow, but the mass hesitates. It hears a distant voice, a voice repressed and screaming for forgiveness. The mass becomes a brilliant light and a harbor for the crying voice. One claw at a time is detached from the voice, releasing it from the bondage of pain and bitterness. The strangling tentacles of the murky world are severed. The light consumes the voice like the warm embrace of a mother. The voice of the soul has been heard. The mass departs from the flesh and leaves on the tropical winds.

*

Washington, D.C.

"Where's Pablo?"

"I don't know. He hasn't arrived."

James places a call to the airport and discovers that the flight did arrive on time.

"Where are you going?" Greg asks.

"To talk to the groundskeeper. He's been out there all day. Maybe he saw him."

They locate the groundskeeper near the side entrance of the church.

"Did you see or talk to anyone looking for the professor?" James asks.

"A man did ask me where he could find the professor," the groundskeeper says.

"And?"

"I told him, but another man met him at the doors. They never went in. They left together."

"Do you know where to?"

"I did hear one of them say something about an aquarium."

James begins to run down the sidewalk.

"They got into a black BMW!" the groundskeeper yells.

*

James quietly slips through the back doors of the Baltimore Aquarium building. He moves through the dark corridor with his gun drawn. He comes to a blue tinted room where the dolphins are displayed. The motion of the water casts a rippling reflection on the walls. He slowly works his way along the curved glass aquarium as a sea turtle drifts past him. He enters a different part of the building. It's the shark oceanarium. James climbs a platform to view the entire floor area. There's no sign of Pablo or anyone else. He enters one of the transparent tunnels that extend through the shark oceanarium. In an effort to quickly reach the other side of the building, he walks along the clear tunnel, routinely checking behind him. A feeling of claustrophobia begins to set in as he realizes that he's under a hundred feet of water and three hundred feet away from the nearest exit. Motion from above draws his attention. He encounters one of the occupants of the oceanarium, a fifteen-foot great white swimming gracefully above his head. He stands staring in astonishment at the beauty of the large beast. The shark slowly glides out of sight. Something below the clear walkway that he's standing on catches his eye. He bends down on one knee to get a closer look, but the bottom is ten feet below. There's something entangled in the swaying seaweed. He waits for the seaweed to move for an unobstructed view. The seaweed sways, and James gets a clear view. The sight causes him to turn away in disgust. A man, or what is left of a man, is floating in the midst of the seaweed. Half of the chest and head, and part of the right arm remain of what once was Pablo. By morning, the bottom feeders and scavengers will have done away with what is left.

*

Washington, D.C.

"Hello, Ms. Naples. May I join you?"
"It's still a free country."
"I'm a fan of your column."
"Really?" Hope asks sarcastically.
"Yes, I truly enjoy it."
"What do you want, Mr. DeMynn?"
"Well, I'm flattered that a celebrity such as yourself knows my name."
"I know you're Malefic's righthand man, or business partner, or political advisor, or something like that."
"Something like that," he says staring at her, grinning.
"What do you want?"
"So much for the pleasantries. The truth of the matter is, I have a suggestion."
"What are you talking about?"
"A suggestion on how you could improve your column."
"This should be good."
"I believe it would be a great improvement if you didn't write a negative piece on Charles."
"Who said I was going to?" she says, swirling the straw in her drink.
"You wrote a pleasant article on Moore, and I heard you support his platform. That leaves me with the impression that the article on Charles will not portray him in a positive light."
"Very insightful, Mr. DeMynn."
"Thank you, Ms. Naples."
"But I'm sorry, Mr. DeMynn, I have to do what I have to do."

"I presume bribery is out of the question?" he asks smiling.

"Not for sale."

"OK then," he says, as his expression becomes serious, "you leave me no choice." He stares solemnly at her. "Bartender, a pretty drink, and please put one of those cute little umbrellas in it." His smile returns. "Would you like to join me, Ms. Naples?"

"Sure, why not?"

*

"You know, Hope, I'm beginning to understand your point of view. Of course, it may have something to do with the seven drinks I've had. But after talking to you, I believe Moore will make a good president."

"Great," she smiles, "but I know you still prefer Malefic."

"Charles would make a good president, Hope."

"No, he'd make an OK president, but he'd make a great dictator."

DeMynn stares at her for a moment with a blank expression. Then he begins to laugh out loud. DeMynn extends his arm outward and says, "Heil Hitler."

Hope begins to laugh with him. Their laughter becomes loud enough that people begin to stare.

"I must be going, Hope," DeMynn says as he stands and steadies himself.

"Thanks for the drinks," she says.

He pays the bartender and chuckles to himself. "I haven't had this good a time in a long time. Thank you."

"I'll see you around, DeMynn."

"Hope, take care of yourself."

"Hey, DeMynn."

He turns around before he walks out the door.

"Tell Adolf I said heil."

DeMynn smiles and walks out the door. She sees him laughing and shaking his head as he walks down the sidewalk.

*

It's another perfect day in the Caribbean Islands. The morning breeze is warm, and the sky is a beautiful shade of royal blue.

A young man approaches a bungalow carrying a tray with

a complimentary breakfast. He knocks and waits. There is no answer.

"Room service," he says and knocks again.

The room remains silent. The young man knocks and pushes the door slightly open.

"Room service, Mr. Sims," he says a little louder.

The young man pokes his head into the room and sees Mr. Sims lying on the bed. "Are you all right, Mr. Sims?"

He nears the bed and discovers that Mr. Sims is pale white. He quickly checks for a pulse but doesn't find one. He begins CPR, but realizes that Mr. Sims has been dead too long. He quickly calls the front desk. He hangs the telephone up and begins to leave the room, but a reflection of light on the other side of the bed catches his eye and he stares at it with a dumbfounded expression. Thirty ancient silver coins lay in the bed with Mr. Sims.

Chapter 37

The prevailing winds blow steady from hell and the beast's breath lays heavy on the world.

Spray painted on an abandoned building are words of warning. They read, 'He is amongst us . . . gathering souls to burn in hell.'

The steam rises from the sewers and crawls onto the streets. The snow's beauty has disappeared beneath the feet of the 9-to-5'ers, but there are worse sights hidden in the alleys. The night grows cold, and the traffic dies down. The city appears abandoned, but in the shadows in the alleys, it's business as usual.

"Bitch, you better stop stealing from me," the pimp says with his finger in her face.

"Shit, Butch, that's all I got," she says with her back against the alley wall.

"Bullshit! Where the fuck is the rest?"

"I told you . . ."

The pimp slaps her across the face. A drop of blood trickles from her lip. The blood droplet falls onto the only piece of white snow in the city.

"You're two hundred short, bitch," he says, counting the money.

"I gotta feed my kids," she cries.

"No, you gotta feed me!"

The little red droplets continue to fall.

"Please Butch, I'll make it up."

"You're goddamn right you will."

The little white patch of snow has become a little red patch.

"I'm gonna take it out of your ass," he says, drawing his fist back, ready to unleash a punishing blow.

"I have three hundred dollars," a low, soothing voice says from a dark place in the alley.

"Who the fuck is that?" Butch says, snapping around.

"I . . . I don't know," she says nervously.

"Step out motherfucker," Butch says, sliding a pistol out of his coat.

"I have three hundred dollars . . . two for you and one for her. All three of us can be happy," the voice says calmingly.

"I'll tell you what, Joe. How about three for me and none for you and the bitch, and we can all still be happy," Butch grins. "You know why? Because I'll have the money, and the two of you won't have bullets up your asses."

"You want it all?" the voice says quietly.

"We got ourselves a brain surgeon," Butch laughs.

"Greed is an ugly thing." The voice has become darker.

"Shut the fuck up and give me the money."

"Butch, Butch," the woman whispers, "that might be the Garbage Man."

"Well then, the garbage is gettin' taken out tonight."

Butch fires five shots into the shadows in the direction of the voice. The sparks from the bullets dot the wall, followed by the rustling stir of trash. The last echo from the blast rings through the alley, as the gun smoke floats slowly upward.

"Maybe I'll get a reward," Butch says, pleased with himself.

The silence lingers for a moment before the pimp carefully walks over to the dark side of the alley. The trash beneath his feet is thick and rustles loudly. He stands quietly, listening for some motion or sound. Then, a sudden and unexpected thrust from behind lifts him up to his toes. He groans in agonizing pain, as the soft sound of clothes and flesh separating fills the air. A nine-inch stainless steel dagger penetrates his back, ripping through muscle tissue and slicing past the rib cage. The dagger pierces the cardiac muscle and right atrium of his heart.

"Consider that your reward," the voice says in a raspy tone.

The woman stands staring, paralyzed by fear. Unable to see clearly, but without doubt, knowing what she has witnessed. The numbness in her legs wears off. She slowly begins to back out of the alley.

"Woman," the raspy voice says, numbing her legs once more. He stares at her from the dark and says, "Sin no more."

She stares, unable to move, at the large silhouette standing in the alley as steam hovers around him.

"Go home to your children," the voice says in a warm and soothing tone.

He turns and begins to walk into the shadows. She watches and listens as the sound of his footsteps fades into the darkness.

*

Anthony clocks out from work and cashes his check at a

liquor store. He was informed that his hours will be cut back after the holidays and that he would eventually be laid off. He stands in front of the liquor store, thinking about his bills. He ponders the thought of being out of work. He tells himself he can find another job. He begins to think of his daughter and the gift she wants. He walks along the sidewalk, glancing into the store windows as the snow begins to slowly float down from the sky. He looks at his watch to see how much time he has before his meeting at the clinic. Anthony goes to one store after another, searching for his daughter's gift. But the thought of losing his job continuously enters his mind, bringing the pressures of his past back, a past he has fought off one day at a time for two years. He continues from one store to the next. He stands on the sidewalk staring, at a window display full of toys, but none of them is the gift he has been searching for.

"Do you want some?" a voice asks from a nearby alley.

Anthony looks over and sees a silhouette of a figure standing in the shadows of the alley. "What did you say?" he asks.

"I got the best," the dealer says.

Anthony's head slumps down. He stares at the freshly fallen snow on the sidewalk. The thought of his circumstances has left him vulnerable. The idea of succumbing to the enemy gives him a serene sensation. The feelings of calmness and relief wait patiently for him in the alley. The battle within him has reached its peak. The snow has turned into icy sleet. He slowly walks into the alley and disappears into the darkness.

*

"Greg, over here," James says, extending his arm above the crowd.

"I'm not accustomed to establishments of this nature," Greg says, glancing around the bar.

"On occasion, Jesus hung out with sinners," James says smiling. "Don't worry, Greg, I don't think any of their vices will rub onto you."

An attractive woman rubs up against Greg as she attempts to squeeze past him in the crowd.

"But I have been wrong before," James says, as she smiles at them while she makes her way by.

"What did you want to talk to me about?" Greg asks.

"Do you want something to drink?"

"A glass of wine, please. Did you find Pablo?"

"Yes, I did. I need to ask you something. This Fist of God that you were telling me about." James leans in toward Greg and lowers his voice. "Would he kill a man?"

"I don't know. Why?"

"A man attempted to destroy Derrick's political career. That man is dead."

"What makes you think the Fist of God killed this man?"

"They found the man lying in bed. He didn't have a mark on him. Not a single cut, not a bruise, not a puncture was found on the entire exterior of the body. They performed an autopsy. They discovered his organs in complete disarray. His lungs were turned inside out. The heart was pulverized, as if someone held it in their hand and crushed it in their grip. The liver was shredded, along with the nerve endings of the spinal cord. His intestines, appendix, kidneys, and stomach looked as if they had exploded," James says, shaking his head. "Another strange thing was the brain. It was fried. It looked like someone had taken a torch to it." James shoots his drink down. "Not a single bone was fractured. They searched for poisons or any other chemical affliction, but found none. What they did find just added to the mystery. He had three different fatal cancers and a variety of other terminal diseases, but to be in the stages that these diseases were in, he would have had to be at least eighty years old." James stares for a moment. "He was thirty-eight," he says, looking down at his empty glass.

"I have never heard of such things in my life!" Greg exclaims.

"No one has," James says. He gets an odd expression on his face as he reaches for his fresh drink. "There was something else," he says, glancing down and stirring his drink. "They found thirty ancient silver coins in the bed with him."

They stare at one another, searching for words to express what they are thinking.

"What are you thinking, Greg?"

"Judas was paid thirty pieces of silver to betray Jesus."

"The guys in forensics dated the coins to be around two thousand years old," James mumbles. He shakes his head and sits on a barstool. "Do you know how hard it is for me to think this way? That some guardian angel killed this man?"

"I know it is, James."

A man standing nearby stares strangely at James because he overheard James' comment.

"Can I help you?" James asks sarcastically.

"No, man," the man says, backing up and throwing money on the bar. "You have a good night," he says as if he were speaking to a crazy person.

"Did you tell anyone what you know?" Greg asks.

"Are you kidding? They would lock me up. Our future conversations would be held in a padded cell."

"Good, I need you out here."

Greg notices that James is periodically glancing at the front door. "Are you expecting someone?" he asks.

"Derrick is meeting me here. I have to tell him about Thomas Sims, the man I was telling you about earlier."

"Good, I also have to speak to your brother-in-law."

"Why?"

"I have a message for him."

"From who?"

Greg smiles and says, "From a voice."

"Oh no, Greg. I don't think so."

Derrick makes his way through the crowd, closely surrounded by Secret Service agents. After a dozen handshakes and a little campaigning, he reaches the bar. James introduces Derrick to Greg. The three of them engage in general conversation for a few minutes. During the conversation James secretly insists by expressions and shaking his head that Greg not bring up the voice.

"What's wrong with you?" Derrick asks, noticing that James is acting strange.

"Nothing. Why?" James throws his hands out defensively.

"Professor, what's going on?"

Greg stares at James, smiling and waiting for permission.

"Go ahead, Greg," James says reluctantly.

"I have a message for you."

"From who?" Derrick asks.

"Without going into a great deal of detail, I heard a voice in my study. The voice told me that God has chosen you to lead this country."

James looks over at Derrick and shrugs his shoulders, signifying that he knows it sounds crazy. "You couldn't get a better endorsement than that," he says with a half-smile.

"I also heard a voice a few nights ago," Derrick says.

"What?" James says with his eyebrows raised.

"I also heard a voice," Derrick repeats quietly.

"Oh man, not you, too," James says, getting the bartender's attention for another drink.

"What did the voice say to you, Derrick?" Greg asks.

"Through me, the church will be reformed."

James shakes his head and says, "Between the three of us, we are going to make one psychiatrist a very rich person."

"I thought I dreamed the incident."

"There is more, Derrick," Greg says, "The voice said you must make it a public prophecy."

"What does that mean?" James asks.

"I believe through the media," Greg explains.

"The media?! They will eat him alive."

"What do I have to say?" Derrick asks.

"Hey, wait a minute," James interrupts, "you can't do this. You'll look like some religious nut."

Greg and Derrick stare at James as if he were the insane one.

"Fine, destroy your career," James says.

"What do I have to say?" Derrick asks again.

"Good-bye political career, is what you say," James mumbles into his drink.

"You must state that you were chosen by God to lead this country." Greg explains.

"So much for being president," James says quietly staring down at his drink.

"God will provide a sign to the world, demonstrating that you speak the truth."

"And if the sign doesn't appear?" James asks.

"Derrick will have to terminate his candidacy for president," Greg explains.

"What is the sign?" Derrick asks.

"There will be a period of time in which there will be no death and no birth in the universe, with the exception of one death and one birth that all will witness."

"When?"

"April."

"Derrick, you should think about this," James contends.

"I don't need to, James. It's already been thought out. But I do have a question."

"Only one?" James asks, half smiling.

"I felt an incredible surge of energy pass through me the day I spoke to the activists at the abortion clinic. Something compelled me to stand up there. I didn't have to think about what to say. The words simply came out."

"Welcome to the plan," James says under his breath.

"God is working through you," Greg says.

"Like it or not," James adds.

"I spoke to one of my advisors a few hours after the incident. She was at the clinic, and she said she heard my voice and another in harmony while I spoke. I don't remember hearing it myself, but I do recall a presence working throughout the crowd. I also remember seeing visions."

"Sounds familiar," James says, glancing at Greg.

"I could see the crowd's inner conflicts with their hidden sins."

"It's just the beginning," James tells him.

"James is correct. It is beginning, and you are the cornerstone of His plan."

"Am I to do anything?" Derrick asks.

"Continue doing what you have been," Greg tells him.

"And hold on," James adds, "cause it's gonna be a bumpy ride."

"I must be going. Derrick, it was nice meeting you. James, I'll speak to you later."

"Sure, Greg."

"Good-bye, Professor, and thank you," Derrick shakes his hand.

"Yeah, thank you," James mumbles.

"How do you know Professor Orfordis?" Derrick asks James after Greg has left.

"I met him through my psychiatrist. Do you know that going public with this prophecy will be committing political suicide?"

"Or . . . it may be the beginning of salvation."

*

A long, black limousine pulls up near the curb. The limousine's tinted back window glides halfway down.

"Professor," a voice calls out from the backseat.

Greg stops and glances over at the limousine.

"May I have a word with you?" the voice asks.

"What can I do for you, Mr. DeMynn?" Greg asks bluntly.

"Please, join me."

The back door of the limousine opens. Greg slowly enters the dark backseat.

"Thank you, Professor."

The door shuts behind Greg. The limousine begins to drive off into the city.

"What do you want, Mr. DeMynn?"

"I have a proposal," DeMynn says, smirking.

Greg stares at him and waits.

"You and I understand one another's obligation." DeMynn pours Greg a glass of wine and hands it to him. "We both have a goal to accomplish. The responsibilities are heavy burdens, but the reward of success is great."

"Yes, it is," Greg says, setting the glass of wine down. "And very costly."

"I must succeed. My reputation is at stake," DeMynn says, slightly smiling.

"And your existence," Greg says with a hidden grin.

"Correct me if I am wrong. It appears I'm up against a three-headed antagonist, which in turn puts me in an interesting predicament." DeMynn sips his wine. "But I do have a solution."

"I knew you would," Greg says with a sarcastic expression.

"Sever one of the heads, and the entire adversary dies," DeMynn says as if he has given it a great deal of thought. He stares at Greg, waiting for a reaction, but Greg appears unaffected by the statement. "One of the heads I prefer not to engage, and the second keeps itself hidden. The third, and most admirable, confronts me with confidence, and out of respect, I offer an alternative."

Greg's eyebrows lift in anticipation.

DeMynn's expression instantly becomes solemn. "Reveal the hidden head and live," he says in a sinister whisper.

Greg stares at him for a moment. "I shall live regardless," he says with certainty.

"Your faith is honorable, but will you die in the same manner?" DeMynn asks.

"I embrace death," Greg says, staring at DeMynn fearlessly. "Mind you, I will only die once."

"Professor, I have given you an alternative. You can avoid death."

"Either way, I will die."

"The conscience is quite a nuisance," DeMynn says in a disappointed tone.

"To me, it is a warm companion."

"You are a remarkable man, Professor. I will miss our conversations."

The limousine stops in a dark parking lot. DeMynn and Greg, followed by two other men from the front seat, walk to the back door of a building. They walk along a dark corridor that brings them to the glass-walled oceanarium . . . the shark exhibit.

"Last chance, Professor," DeMynn says, as one of the men chums the water.

"I'm prepared to die in the name of the Lord," Greg says confidently, standing on the edge of the platform.

"So be it."

The great whites become active in the cloud of fish parts and blood below.

"DeMynn, maybe we should think about this," one of the men says.

"Do you think so?" DeMynn stands on the platform, contemplating the suggestion.

"Well, yeah . . . you know, he's like a priest or something," the man says.

DeMynn appears to be pondering the suggestion some more. "Perhaps you are correct," he says. "Good news, Professor." DeMynn walks over to put his arm around Greg, but the force of his arm knocks Greg off the platform. "Oops," DeMynn says, pretending he didn't mean to do it.

Greg falls fifteen feet and splashes into the oceanarium with the two sharks.

DeMynn begins to walk away, but he stops beside the man who questioned him. "Be thankful it isn't you," he says in a sinister whisper.

Chapter 38

"Where have you been? Your friend added another one last night," Captain Ross exclaims.

"East side?" James asks knowingly.

"Right on schedule."

"Where?"

"Independence and Massachusetts, in an alley."

*

James stands in the alley watching the litter revolve in little whirlwinds. The cold breeze whistles through the alley as James begins to think out loud. "The victim has a puncture wound from a daggerlike instrument, which entered the back and pierced the heart. But there's no message or clue, just the victim lying in a pool of frozen blood. The body was left in the same position it fell in, unprepared for our viewing . . . a sloppy kill by his standards . . . different from the rest, but why? The gun found near the victim was fired five times. All five bullets found their destination, but none their intent. There is a small puddle of blood near the wall on the other side of the alley. A second victim? The blood on the victim's hand will undoubtedly match the small pool of blood. A pimp and his whore arguing, and it became physical. Unknown to both, death lurked in the shadows, but they became aware. Five shots and a dagger through the heart later, we have a witness, standing over a small puddle of blood. Was this an act of mercy? Yes, but why?"

"How does he do that?" a young police officer asks.

"Too much experience," a detective quietly answers.

James has walked to the far end of the alley. He stands there, staring back at the murder scene, watching the flashes of light from the department's photographer. He slowly turns away and begins walking down the sidewalk, disappearing around the corner.

*

"Did you see the game last night?" a janitor working at the aquarium asks his young assistant.

"Yeah, I lost twenty bucks," the young man says disappointedly.

"If you had listened to me, you could have made some

money."

"Yeah, yeah, sure."

"Never bet against the Skins at home," the older man says. "They're tough at the Jack," he adds, smiling.

"Yeah, yeah, I know."

"Sweet mother of God."

"What?" the young man asks. "Oh, shit!"

"Get the lifeline!" the older man yells.

The young man runs off to get the lifeline. The other man stands at the edge of the platform, staring down at Greg, who's floating face up in the water. The two great whites gracefully circle Greg, but never approach him in a threatening charge.

"Mister, mister, are you alive?" the older man asks, not expecting an answer.

Greg's eyes open. He smiles for a second and closes them again. The two men pull Greg out of the oceanarium and wrap a blanket around him.

"How in the hell did you get in there?" the old man asks.

"I don't know," Greg answers quietly.

"I can't believe you're alive," the young man says, astounded.

"You're a lucky man, mister," the older man says, glancing down at the water.

"No one must know of this," Greg says.

"What?" both men say simultaneously.

"No one must know of this incident," Greg says again.

"We have to report this," the older man says.

"Why?" Greg asks.

The two men stare at one another.

"Why don't you want us to report it?" the young man asks, suspiciously.

"I wouldn't be able to explain how I got here," Greg says. "I would have to fabricate a story . . . I guess I could say that I got lost and slipped on an unmarked platform into a shark tank . . . and the security is so inferior that I wasn't noticed for nine hours," Greg explains. "I may be forced to sue. The publicity wouldn't be good for the oceanarium. The authorities may even have to close the oceanarium."

Once again the two men stare at one another.

"He has a point," the older man says, thinking about his job and family.

"I believe it would be for the best," Greg says, glancing down at the sharks.

Washington, D.C.

"Thanks for coming."

"No problem," Hope says, pulling a stool up next to James.

"I just wanted to thank you," he says.

"For what?"

"For helping Derrick and me."

"I like Derrick. I'm glad I could help," Hope tells him.

"There's something different about you, James," Anna says, as she hands Hope a drink. "I know what it is . . . you're having a civil conversation with a media type," she says, smiling.

"I'm a changed man," James says with an unconvincing grin.

Anna walks away smiling and shaking her head, indicating her disbelief.

"It seems that she doesn't believe you," Hope says, smiling as she takes a drink.

"I'm just misunderstood," he says with a half smile.

Hope smiles as she fishes with her straw for the cherry at the bottom of her drink.

James watches her struggle for a few moments, unable to retrieve the cherry from the bottom of the drink. He leans over the bar and reaches down for a bowl of cherries. He slides them over to her.

Hope pops a cherry into her mouth. "Thanks," she says, as she returns to fishing for the one in her drink. "Derrick is fortunate to have a friend like you," she says.

James stares down at his drink. "You think so?" he quietly asks.

"Yes, I do. If it wasn't for you, things could have been very different," she says, looking over at him.

"Maybe," he says, glancing up at her.

"Well, I know he wouldn't have a political career to speak of, if it wasn't for you. And I know it must ease his mind knowing that you're seeing to the personal distractions that go hand in hand with Derrick's position," she says earnestly. "You're good at what you do and, personally, it's comforting knowing that you are there for him."

James is staring down at his drink again. "Thank you," he mumbles, clearly uncomfortable with the compliment.

"You're welcome," she says, mocking him.

James glances up with a shy smile. "Are you making fun of me?"

"Yeah."

"I thought so." James stands and throws money on the bar for the tab.

"Was it something I said?" Hope asks, smiling.

"I have to go and see someone."

"I'll give you a ride."

James stares at her for a moment, unsure if he wants to accept the offer. "Thanks," he says with some hesitation.

*

"I hate this time of year. It's so cold and the days are too short," Hope says, waiting at the stoplight.

"At least it snowed," James says, staring out of the window on his side of the car.

"Where are we going?" she asks.

"Make a left here."

"In the cemetery?" she asks, glancing over at him.

"Yeah," he says quietly, still staring out the window.

Hope pulls beside a curb, and James gets out alone. He walks through the snow along a worn, muddy path leading to Faith's gravesite. Hope watches him from inside the car while the radio plays "I Wish It Would Rain" by the Temptations. The sun seems to be hovering above the horizon, refusing to set. James' trench coat flutters in the cold breeze as he stands in front of Faith's headstone. Hope curiously watches him, as a sorrowful feeling comes over her. "God help him," she says to herself.

James falls to his knees. "I'm struggling without you," he says, slumped over. "I'm not going to make it," he says with a hopelessness in his voice. "I can't live here without you." He remains in a kneeling position for several more minutes before he eventually makes his way back to the car. The sun begins its decline into the horizon. He glances over at Hope, discovering that she has been crying.

"Are you all right?" he asks, handing her a napkin.

"I will be," she says, wiping her tears. She sees that his eyes are red and glassed over. "Are you all right?" she asks.

"Yeah," he says, looking away. "What's wrong with you?" he asks, staring out the window on his side of the car.

"My husband left me a couple of years ago," she whispers.

"Sorry," James whispers back.

"I guess I really never got over it. He said he fell out of love with me."

"I don't believe you can fall out of love," he says, turning to look at her, "if you're really in love. My mother used to say, 'You can't fall out of something you never were in in the first place.' My father said people are always mistaking something for love."

Hope smiles slightly, wiping a tear away.

James turns to stare out the window again. "I think the word has been abused and has lost its importance."

They stare at the horizon in silence until the stars begin to appear in the sky.

"You want to get something to eat?" she asks softly.

"I need to get some sleep."

They stare at one another, both obviously feeling awkward.

"Listen James, I'm not trying to get romantically involved, or into a competition with the past. I just believe we can be friends."

"I'll be out of town for a while. Maybe we can get together when I get back."

She smiles, and James smiles back. It's the first smile he has sincerely felt in a very long time.

*

James lies in bed for hours listening to the rain hit the windowsill before he begins to doze off into a restless sleep. The raindrops tap on the windshield as the wipers streak back and forth. Flashes of light fill his mind, and the sound of metal scraping against rock echoes in his head. A bright white flash appears, and the car begins to roll down an embankment. Another bright flash erases the vision, making his mind blank. The blackness gives way to gray shadows and images. Suddenly, color begins to appear, and red is the predominant color. He stares at Faith's face and the blood leaving her body. He reaches for her, but his extended arm falls inches short. He hears the raspy voice of a man.

"It's your fault, James," the voice says.

A bright flash wakes him, and he sits up in bed. He sits with his head in his hands in the dark, the voice echoing in his mind.

*

    The sun breaks over the horizon, revealing the freshly fallen snow from the night before. The church begins to glow warmly in the morning light as the city streets begin to become active with automobiles.

    In the garden is a single set of footprints. Those footprints belong to Judge Russell, who's sitting on the stone bench, praying for his daily strength, and also asking for his daily forgiveness. After a few moments of silent prayer he leaves the garden. He slowly walks along the sidewalk, heading to work.

    DeMynn steps out from behind a tree in the garden. He lights a cigarette and leaves through the corridor. He disappears into the city streets.

    From a window high above the garden, Greg watches both men leave. He eventually fades from the church window and begins his daily chores.

*

    "Passengers for Flight 211, please begin boarding at gate 12."

    "Good afternoon, sir. Enjoy your flight," the flight attendant says with her permanent smile.

    "Thank you."

    James finds his seat and begins to think back to a happier time in his life. He slowly slips into a daydream.

    "Two wonderful weeks in Europe," Faith says with a joyful expression.

    "That's right, honey. You and I, and the Greek Islands," James says smiling.

    "I can't wait to see the Acropolis and the Parthenon," Faith says, gleaming with anticipation.

    "I'm looking forward to the islands."

    "I've dreamed about this for so long, and it's finally coming true," she says, clutching James' hand.

    "I love you, Faith. More than life itself," he says, staring into her eyes.

    "I love you, too," she says, softly putting her hand on his cheek.

    Remembering her smile and the glow of excitement on her face warms his heart. The pilot's voice over the intercom brings him out of the daydream. A painful longing sets in, and James' eyes begin to glass over. He stares out the window, hoping to fall asleep.

*

"Sir, sir, we have arrived," the flight attendant says, pushing on James' shoulder.

James gathers his belongings and steps out into the warm air of Texas.

A cab drops him off near a dirt road that leads to a ranch. James grabs his bag and throws his coat over his arm and begins walking up the road. A man is walking down the road toward him. He's a large man, wearing a cowboy hat and boots.

"J.R., how in the hell have you been?" the man asks with a smile.

"Good, Joe. How have you been?" James asks, pulling his sunglasses off.

"Better now," Joe says, hugging him. "Damn, I'm so happy to see you, I could just shit myself!"

"Me, too, my friend," James says, smiling.

"Let's get some cold ones," Joe says, putting his arm around him.

"Your place hasn't changed much," James says, sitting on the porch.

"A million years could pass and it wouldn't change. What brings you down here, J.R.?"

"Business," James says dryly.

"You're chasing bad guys down here?"

"Something like that."

"What's going on, James?" Joe asks, sensing something is wrong.

"What are you talking about?"

"Fine. Don't tell me," Joe says, pretending to be upset.

James stares out over the prairie. "I need you to get me something."

"What?" Joe asks, rocking in his chair.

"Explosives," he says with a coolness in his voice.

Joe's head snaps sharply around, and his rocking comes to a halt. He stares at James as if he didn't hear him correctly. "I want to help you, James, but I need to know what's going on."

James stares at the dry horizon, reminiscing about Faith. He remembers the long horseback rides on the ranch and the sunsets they watched from this porch.

"There's a fishery down near Port Issuable. The man that owns it is using it to distribute drugs," James tells him.

"That's not why you want to blow it to kingdom come."

James continues to stare out over the prairie.

"I'm your friend, James."

"He killed Faith," he says, looking down.

"What?"

"He murdered my wife," James says, coldly glancing back at Joe.

"Who?"

James' hands ball into fists, and his eyes reveal vengeance. "Charles Malefic."

"The same guy running for president?."

"That's right."

"Why?"

"She had information on him."

"Is he going to be in the building?" Joe asks.

"No."

"Why not take him out?"

"I can't touch him right now, he's too visible."

"So in the meantime, you're putting a hurting on his business," Joe says smiling.

"It helps pass the time."

"I got some time on my hands," Joe says suggestively.

"You don't need to get involved."

"All or nothing," Joe tells him.

"Joe . . . "

"I don't want to hear it. I lost my wife three years ago. I have nothing to lose. Hell, J.R., the way I see it, I'm on borrowed time. I should have died in that plane crash, too."

They stare at one another, understanding each other's pain.

"Have you been all right?" Joe asks. "I know it's been a messed up year."

"I don't know," James says, bewildered. "It's been a bizarre time. I've experienced some strange things."

"Like what?"

"Strange dreams and visions."

"I went through something like that."

"After Wendy died?"

"Yeah. Like walking along a road toward a bright light . . . the feeling of floating around, things like that. I had a really crazy dream in the hospital."

"What kind of dream?" James asks.

"Did you know I died for twelve minutes and thirty-two seconds?" Joe asks grinning.

"I remember that."

"You want to know what happens to you when you're dead?"

James nods his head and smiles.

"I never told anyone what I'm about to tell you," Joe says.

"You have my undivided attention."

"I went to heaven."

James shakes his head and smiles as he takes a drink of his beer.

"Go ahead and laugh," Joe says, throwing a bottle cap at him.

"I believe you, Joe. I always wondered why you built six churches after the accident."

"I got up to eight," Joe says proudly.

"Unbelievable."

"It was the most incredible experience I've ever had."

"I bet it was," James says amused.

They stare at the horizon and dry landscape in silence.

"I stood before God, James."

James glances over and sees that Joe is serious. James waits for him to continue, but he doesn't. He just stares silently at the horizon.

"What did He look like?" James asks sincerely.

Joe stares solemnly at James and says, "If I tell you, I'll have to kill you."

They burst into hysterics.

"I'll get us another beer," Joe says, wiping the tears from his eyes.

Joe goes into the cabin to retrieve more beer. James sits alone, and his mind flashes back to the murder scene in the alley. 'Why didn't he kill the prostitute? Did she remind him of someone he once knew?' he asks himself.

"Here you go, old buddy." Joe hands him a beer and returns to rocking in his chair. "So, do you want to know?" Joe asks.

"Know what?"

"What God looks like."

James stares at him. He doesn't know if he should take him seriously or not.

"I've thought about it a lot," Joe says, looking out over the ranch. "He looked like He was made of clear crystal, full of water with the sun behind Him. As I stood there, He would slowly transform into the universe . . . then back to the original state He was in. This went on the whole time I was there. Sometimes He would become a beautiful garden or a violent storm. I could never get a good look at His face. There was always a bright light behind Him. I just couldn't focus on Him," he says reflectively. "He sat on what appeared to be a throne. I made the mistake of looking directly at it. You think looking directly into the sun is painful . . . "

James stares attentively, realizing that Joe is very serious . . . and somehow everything he is saying seems familiar. "Did He say anything to you?" he asks.

"'Glorify Me'," Joe says with a peaceful tone.

"What did His voice sound like?"

"Like a million people in harmony," he answers earnestly. "Suddenly, He became as bright as the throne He was sitting on. Then two figures that looked a lot like floating bodies of liquid gold took me by my arms and led me through a beautiful garden. I stood in front of a gorgeous white tunnel that looked like crystal, like if you took a million chandeliers and smashed them to pieces and glued them to the walls, floors, and ceiling. There were two mean-looking guys standing at the entrance. They didn't have wings, but I'm pretty sure they were angels. Before I stepped into the tunnel, I turned around to look back. It was like being on a mountaintop looking across an ocean of clouds under a golden sky. And on the horizon, a majestic sun sat glowing and bright. Then, in one big blinding burst of light, I was hurting real bad. I knew I was back, and so did the doctors."

"Do you remember the ground?" James asks.

"I'll never forget it."

"I remember seeing my feet touching the ground, but I couldn't feel it," James explains.

"You've been there?"

"Yeah, but I didn't die. I keep going back in my dreams. And this large, black, starry thing keeps sending me back before I can go any farther."

"Unfinished business," Joe says.

"A lot of unfinished business. I got this lunatic running around carving messages in people's bodies, and these crazy dreams keeping me awake all night. And, oh yeah, I'm trying to stop Satan from becoming president."

"I know something that can help," Joe says smiling. "My three-step program for stress relief. It worked for me."

"I'll try just about anything right now."

"Step one, go to the refrigerator and get a cold one."

James smiles and takes a sip of his beer. "I like

step one."

"Step two, get into your most comfortable chair and kick back."

"I'm practically stress-free already," James says, closing his eyes and leaning back into his chair.

"Step three, and most important, crack open the Bible."

"What?" James asks, opening his eyes.

"Read the Bible."

"I don't think I'm ready for step three. I'll practice on steps one and two for a while first."

"That book will solve all your problems, James."

James' thoughts wander off as he stares at the horizon, and he begins to think of Faith. She read the Bible every night before she went to sleep. His mind recalls a memory of his grandmother. 'Read the Good Book, James. It will help you', she would always tell him. Then he hears Greg's voice saying, 'All the answers to your questions are in the Bible.' A reflection brings him out of his daydream. It's Joe's crucifix dangling from his neck. He's leaning over the porch railing, also daydreaming.

James and Joe sit quietly in their own worlds. Not much is said between them the rest of the evening.

*

Washington, D.C.

The cold rain falls on the city streets as the temperature drops. The streets will become icy and treacherous before the night ends.

A man in a raincoat with the hood pulled over his head enters the bar. He slowly makes his way toward a table in the corner. There a man sits drinking a cup of coffee. The man in the raincoat stands before the man at the table. Water trickles down the creases of the coat to the floor, forming a puddle around him. With his head tilted down and the poor lighting, it makes it difficult to see his face.

"May I help you?" the man seated at the table asks.

The man in the raincoat lifts his head toward the scarce light available.

"Lazarus, I presume?" the seated man asks, astounded.

"Lazarus died. I did not."

"True. Daniel may be more appropriate. Please, Professor, join me. I must hear how you escaped," DeMynn says, grinning.

132

"I'll leave my escape to your imagination. I'm here to give you notice," Greg says.

"Are you threatening me, Professor?" DeMynn asks, amused.

"Your plan will be destroyed, and you will be vanquished by the One who created you," Greg says, and then turns to leave.

"Does the name James Rood ring a bell?" DeMynn asks.

Greg stops and turns around. His expression reveals nothing, but to DeMynn it tells all.

"I thought so," DeMynn says, grinning.

"He is protected like myself."

"I find that very difficult to believe."

Greg turns and begins to walk away.

"I hope he can swim," DeMynn says loud enough for Greg to hear.

Chapter 39

Texas

James slips out the back door of the fishery. He slowly works his way along the dock. The darkness of predawn prevents him from being noticed as he quietly opens the trunk of his rental car. He slips out of the janitor uniform he's wearing. He climbs into the car and gently closes the door behind him. He reaches down to turn the key in the ignition.

"Hey, J.R.," a voice says cheerfully from the backseat.

"Oh, shit!" James nearly hits his head on the roof of the car. "Damn, Joe, don't do that."

"Sorry, buddy," he says, smiling.

"What are you doing here?"

"Making sure no one sneaks up on you. Did you get the bombs in place?" Joe asks.

"Yeah."

"Don't forget your part of the deal," Joe says earnestly.

James pulls the car up to a phone booth. The sun begins to creep over the horizon.

"Hello, Gulfside Fishery," a man says, answering the phone.

"You have ten minutes to evacuate the building before it blows up." James hangs up the phone and walks over to the car. "Happy?" James asks Joe.

Joe smiles contently.

"Hello, hello," the man says, into the phone. He reaches for the intercom. "Everyone get out of the building! Evacuate the building immediately! There's a bomb in the building!"

Two hundred men scatter across the work floor of the building. They quickly find the exits and reach a safe distance.

James sits on the hood of his car about a half mile away. Joe joins him on the hood of the car. Both of them stare out in the general direction of the fishery.

Joe quietly begins to count, "Three, two, one."

There's a loud, vibrating explosion followed by an orange and yellow cloud mushrooming toward the sky.

"This town is going to smell like fish for a very long time," Joe says smiling, watching the smoke climb into the morning sky.

*

Washington, D.C.

"Good morning. Welcome to News Seven. I'm Cathy Crinsaw. The latest on the explosion at the Gulfside Fishery in Texas. Investigators have not ruled out that it was a bomb, but refuse to comment any further. No deaths or injuries have been reported. We will update you as soon as we receive more."

"Son of a bitch!" Malefic exclaims, and then doubles over from the pain.

"Charles, are you all right?" DeMynn asks, entering the office.

"Someone blew up the fishery in Texas," he says in an aggravated tone.

"Really?"

"Yes, really. Do you know who?"

"Maybe," DeMynn says calmly.

"Who?"

"Don't concern yourself with who. I'll take care of it."

"Does this have something to do with that freak and the RF2 project?"

"I believe so."

"This pisses me off! I'm sick of being a victim."

"I'll take care of the retaliations. You concentrate on your campaign, and becoming president."

"Can I be linked to that building?" Malefic asks nervously.

"No," DeMynn says, making himself and Malefic a drink.

"Was there a shipment in the building?"

"A half of a billion dollars worth," DeMynn says with no concern.

"Jesus Christ!" Malefic exclaims, clutching his painful midsection.

DeMynn shakes his head. "You should really work on your vocabulary," he says, handing Malefic a drink.

Malefic sits in his chair, agonizing.

DeMynn puts on his coat and walks over to the chessboard.

"You don't appear to be upset about it," Malefic says, disturbed.

DeMynn moves his rook and takes the clear-glass

knight. "I'll have my revenge," he says coldly, walking out the door.

*

"Where the hell is Rood?" Captain Ross yells from his office at a group of detectives huddled around a desk.

"He's sick," Tony yells back.

"I want his ass in my office at first sight!" Captain Ross' office door slams shut.

"He's probably hung over somewhere," Detective Ludwig says spitefully.

"Shut the fuck up, Ludwig," Tony says with a sharp and cold stare.

"That's right, cover for your homey."

"Don't you have a KKK meeting to go to?"

"Fuck you, Rodriguez," Ludwig says, walking away.

"What's his problem?" a younger detective asks.

"Him and James came to the department at the same time. James beat him out for the Rookie of the Year honors. He got promoted before him, too. Ludwig blames it on James' color. He says the department hired and promoted him because he's black. James is the best damned detective I have ever met, and color ain't got a damned thing to do with it."

"Ludwig sounds like a racist looking for trouble," the young detective says.

"That ain't the half of it. James crashed his car, and his wife died in the accident. Rumors ran wild about him being drunk. Ludwig and some of his Nazi groupies pushed for his firing. Shit, they tried to get him on manslaughter charges."

"Damn, what a bunch of assholes."

"The blood test disappeared. So no charges were filed. But James got suspended for six weeks for beating the shit out of Ludwig," Tony says, smiling slightly. "I know he had some drinks that night, but he wasn't drunk."

"It's a good thing the blood test disappeared," the young detective says grinning.

"It would have been a damned shame if his career went down the shitter over a couple of drinks," Tony says.

"Man, how did he get through all that shit, while he was dealing with the death of his wife?" the young detective asks, shaking his head.

"He didn't care what happened to him and his career. He didn't care about anything," Tony says, looking down at the floor. "I don't think he wanted to live." Tony glances up. "He lost Faith, and she was everything to him."

"He seems to be better."

Tony stares for a moment. "I think there's hope for him sometimes," he says quietly. "And then there's times I feel there's no tomorrow for him."

The phone on James' desk rings, breaking the silence.

Tony walks over to answer it. "Hello, Homicide . . . he's out." Tony listens for a moment and writes down a message. "Sure, good-bye."

*

Texas

James and Joe relax on the porch with a cooler in between them. The sun beats down on the dry landscape as the wind peacefully blows over the pasture.

"How's Derrick doing?" Joe asks, throwing his feet on the porch railing.

"He's running for president."

"Still in politics."

"Yeah," James says disappointedly.

"That reminds me of a joke. This politician dies and goes to heaven." Joe laughs to himself. "That's funny, a politician goes to heaven. Anyway, this politician dies and goes to heaven. He meets St. Peter at the Pearly Gates. The politician notices there are millions of clocks hanging on a wall. He asks St. Peter about the clocks. St. Peter tells him that they represent people's lives on earth. The politician notices that all the hands on the clocks are spinning at different speeds. He asks St. Peter why this is. St. Peter explains that the hands on the clocks speed up with every lie the person tells. The politician asks which are his fellow congressmen's and the president's clocks. St. Peter laughs and says, 'Oh, the Boss uses them for ceiling fans.'"

They laugh and take turns telling jokes and reminiscing about their college days for the next few hours. But the conversation takes a serious turn as the sun nears the horizon.

"Do you have any explosives left?" James asks.

Joe stares at him for a moment. "No, I don't. We used up all I had left of my Desert Storm souvenirs. Are you thinking about blowing something else up?"

"I can't, no material."

"That's right, we don't have anymore." Joe reaches into the cooler. "Uh-oh, we're out of ammo, too."

"I'll run down to the store," James volunteers.

"No, you're my guest," Joe says, standing. "I'll be back in a flash."

Joe begins walking down the dirt road. James watches him until he disappears around the bend. James goes into the cabin, but there is something different about it. The cabin has become old and dirty. The furniture is covered with a thick dust. The pots and pans they had used last night are filthy and rusty. A chair he had sat in the night before is worn and tattered. The switch for the light over the basement steps doesn't work. He lights a candle and finds the workstation in the basement destroyed. The basement is vacant except for three empty boxes that stored the explosives. The walls are bare, but the night before many pictures hung on them. All that remains are the clean square silhouettes left by the missing pictures. James notices one picture remaining on the back wall. He walks over and pulls it down. It's a picture of him and Joe taken in their senior year of college. He sits on the porch holding the picture in his hand. It's been an hour, and he gets up to go looking for Joe, but a reflection of light stops him. It's Joe's crucifix hanging from a nail on the post. He holds it in his hand. The sun makes the crucifix glow and reflect brilliantly. He begins to think again about how long Joe has been gone. He walks along the dirt road for a few minutes before he runs into the town. He finds the convenience store. It isn't difficult, seeing as there are only three buildings in the entire town. The sign that welcomes you also thanks you for coming.

"I'm sorry, sir, we're getting ready to close," the store owner says.

"I'm looking for someone," James says, glancing around the store.

"Who are you looking for?"

"Joe Clayton."

The man quietly stares at James with a puzzled expression on his face.

"Joe Clayton?" James asks.

"I heard you the first time."

"What's wrong? Does he owe you money or something?"

"Are you a friend of his?" the man asks.

"Yeah."

"Joe's dead . . . for six months now."

James begins to rub the bridge of his nose and then

his temples.

"Are you all right, mister?" the man asks, concerned.

"How?" James asks quietly.

"The doctors never figured that out. They found him on the porch in his rocking chair."

James begins to turn the last twenty-four hours over in his mind. 'What the hell is going on?' he thinks to himself. He looks down at the newspaper stand. The paper has news on the front page concerning the explosion at the fishery.

"You know his wife Wendy is dead also? Plane crash," the man says.

James stares speechlessly at the store owner. His mind is clouded with a myriad of thoughts and questions.

"That's what killed him," the man says knowingly.

"What?" James asks, feeling numb.

"That's what killed him."

"What killed him?"

"His wife dying. He died from a broken heart and loneliness."

*

Washington, D.C.

The night begins to consume the day and with it comes a cold wind. The city reflects itself in the wet pavement of the streets. Like any night in the city, no one should walk the streets alone.

"We're losing her! She's drowning in her blood!" Dr. Wilson's voice hurdles over the EKG and the shrieking oximeter alarms. "Clip her artery and inject 30 cc's of .5% marcaine. Give her another 12 cc's, and bag her." He injects atropine intravenously, followed by ephedrine. He watches the EKG, hoping that the atropine might have a positive effect on the irregular heartbeat, but it doesn't. Dr. Wilson fights for Hope Naples' life. He fights the Angel of Death hanging over his shoulder, waiting. The Angel of Death steps closer. The EKG and oximeter alarms reach unbearable pitches. Her heart stops beating. A nurse heads to the OR desk. "Jesus Christ!" Dr. Wilson yells, "Massage." The nurse compresses Hope's chest. The OR doors swing open. The crash cart arrives along with additional OR nurses. They prepare the defibrillator. Another nurse and anesthetist also arrive. "I'm not getting anything on the EKG!" a nurse yells. "Prepare the paddles," Dr. Wilson exclaims. The nurse takes the defibrillator paddles and applies them to Hope's bare chest. The nurse presses the button. Hope's body jerks. The EKG screen shows no sign of life, and neither does Hope. "Hit her again." The defibrillator paddles are applied once more. Her body jerks again. "Start external cardiac massage! Inject a bolus of epinephrine." Dr. Wilson watches the EKG. There's no change. Dr. Wilson orders the defibrillator to be set at 400 joules. The paddles are applied again. Hope's body jerks severely. The monitor traces a frustrating flat line. Dr. Wilson snaps off his gloves and glances over at the EKG screen. He takes a deep breath, then turns the respirator off. The only sound in the air is the hum of the monitors registering death. The Angel of Death has reached Hope Naples' lips.

*

A woman sits in the dark crying. She hears the front door open. It's her husband, whom she hasn't seen in days. She hurries over and hugs him tightly.

"Anthony," she says in a concerned tone, "Are you all right?"

He pulls away with tears in his eyes. "I've let you down, Beth," he says sorrowfully.

She hugs him again. "We can beat this," she says decisively in his ear. She pulls back and holds his face in her hands. Tears fill her eyes. "You and I, together with the help of God, will beat this."

Beth is a nurse and works at the drug abuse center. She sees the destruction caused by drugs everyday, but she also sees the miraculous recoveries. She has witnessed patients defeating their drug dependence and watched them put their lives back together. That is why she fights and refuses to surrender her family to the addiction.

They sit through the night holding one another in the dark. She silently prays for him.

*

The icy rain rhythmically taps on the dumpster. The sound of small feet pitter-patter across the wet pavement. Coiled in a dark corner sits a figure. He is awakened by a feeling. He senses a soul leaving the physical realm. The feeling is followed by a spiritual command . . . a command of wrath. The figure begins to radiate. Everything surrounding him instantly dries from the radiating heat. He disappears into the glowing sphere, and the sphere disappears into the dark.

"What the fuck?" a man blurts out, startled.

Two men are interrupted during a transaction in an alley by the sudden appearance of a large dark figure. The buyer runs down the alley out of sight. The man remaining pulls out a gun.

"Step out, motherfucker," he demands.

The figure stands ten feet away, but in a tenth of a second he's in the man's face. He stands so close that the gun and half of the man's arm vanish into the body of the figure.

"What the . . .," the man says, stepping back. He realizes the gun is frozen in his hand. He pulls the trigger, and the weapon crumbles to the pavement.

The figure extends his left arm. The man feels a vacuumlike force pulling him. The drugs are pulled from his pockets and are floating above the palm of the figure's hand. The little vials liquefy, leaving the white powdery narcotics revolving above his hand. The figure extends his right arm, pulling the wad of money from the man's coat pocket. The figure now stands before the man with both arms extended, the drugs and money floating above the palms of his hands.

"What the fuck are you?" the man asks in shock.

The figure looks down at the man. "Redemption," he whispers.

"What do you want?"

"You."

"What?"

"I am the crossroad. Choose your path."

"What the hell are you talking about?"

"The path of fire." The figure's hands glow. "Or the path of light." A beautiful, golden beam of light radiates down from the sky onto the figure.

"Fuck this UFO shit," the man says, beginning to back away.

"I am your last chance for God," the figure says with a warm tone.

"Yeah, right."

"Please, renounce the evil one and his tools," the figure implores.

"What the fuck are you talking about?"

"I am the messenger from God," the figure tells him. "Change your life's path. End your greed and stop spreading this poison."

"And if I don't?"

The figure stares down at him. "You shall die," he warns.

The man begins to back away again. "Fuck that, and fuck you!"

The figure begins to sparkle. The drugs and money in his palms are devoured by fire.

"So be it," the figure says with judgment in his voice.

A powerful vacuumlike force begins to pull the man. The clothes on the man start to tear. Piece after piece, the fabric rips off of him, sucked into the figure's body, until the man stands nude.

"What the hell?" the man asks, looking down at himself.

The vacuuming force continues. The flesh begins to rip from his body. The man screams in agony as one layer of skin after another peels off of him. He pleads for the figure to stop, but the torment of the pulling force persists. The veins become exposed. They are ripped and separated from the muscles. A steady stream of blood pours outward, flowing into the figure. The muscles are unraveled from the man's frame until the organs are uncovered. The organs are pulled away and the eyes extracted from their sockets. The man's skeleton remains. One bone at a time is detached until there is no indication of his existence.

The hand of judgment will pass over the city until the night has surrendered to the morning light.

*

James returns to his apartment from the airport in the middle of the night. He throws his travel bag on the floor and goes into the bathroom. He stares into the mirror and realizes why his flight was called a red-eye. He splashes cold water on his face. Joe's crucifix comes out from his shirt as he bends over the sink. He has forgotten he had it on. He sits in his chair, staring at the cross in his hand. He begins to recall the last couple of days, the business he went down to do, and the time spent with Joe. He thinks of how he shook hands with and hugged a man that has been dead for six months. How he spent hours in conversations with someone that wasn't supposed to be there. He thinks about the many strange occurrences that have happened to him, and how he has virtually become accustomed to them. But his experience with Joe has reached a new level of oddness, and it has affected him deeply. He lays the cross on the lamp table and reaches into his travel bag. He grasps a handful of little bottles of whiskey bought on the airplane. He notices a book in the bag. It's a Bible. He opens it and finds the name 'Joseph W. Clayton' printed on the inside cover. Handwritten beneath the name, there's a passage. It says, 'James 1:20'. James turns to the passage and reads it to himself. 'for the wrath of man does not produce the righteousness of God.' He closes it and throws it into the corner of his apartment, adding it to the pile of Bibles already there.

*

    Anthony sits in the dark alone late on Christmas Eve. He stares at the flickering lights on the Christmas tree.
    "I don't know if You exist, but if You do," he whispers, "I want to thank You for Beth and Liz." His eyes begin to tear up and his throat tightens. "I know I don't deserve to ask for anything," he says hesitating, "but please give me the strength to never hurt them again."
    He wipes the tears from his eyes, then sees it . . . a figure standing near the Christmas tree in the shadows. The flickering of light brings the figure's outline clearly into view. Anthony stares fearfully. Suddenly, a box slides out from the darkness and stops in front of his feet.
    "This is for your daughter," the figure says softly.
    Anthony looks down to discover it's the toy his daughter wants. "Who are you?" he asks, tilting his head, attempting to improve his view.
    "I am the proof you seek," the figure says. "Your gift is in Philippians 4:13," the figure says, before fading into the darkness.
    Anthony has learned enough about religion from his wife to realize that Philippians 4:13 is Biblical. He reaches over and picks up Beth's Bible from the lamp table. He turns to the section the figure spoke about. He begins to read the passage out loud to himself. "'I can do all things through Christ who strengthens me.'" He stares at the Christmas tree as the flickering lights reflect in his glassy eyes.

Chapter 40

"Merry Christmas, James," Tony says, smiling and holding a Santa Claus coffee cup.

"Merry Christmas," James responds wearily, stumbling over a box. "What are all these toys doing here?" he asks, looking around.

"It's for the kids at the shelters and hospitals," Tony tells him. "The basement flooded, so we have to store them up here this year."

James notices there are names written on the sides of the boxes. One name continuously appears . . . M. Russell.

"I didn't know Judge Russell was involved with the Toys for Tots Program," James says quietly.

"Oh yeah, the judge does it every year. He nearly runs the whole thing himself," Tony says, sitting down at his desk.

James kneels down and picks up a baseball glove. He holds it carefully in his hand, staring at it as his mind slips into a daydream. He thinks back to the baseball glove he bought for his unborn child. His mind wanders off to a happier time. He and Faith are sitting in a doctor's office. He's holding a sonogram of his little boy. He remembers playfully arguing with Faith about their son playing football or not playing it. The memory begins to fade, and a toy car comes into focus. The toy car's windshield is shattered, reminding James of something uncomfortable. He stands and begins to leave.

"The captain wants to see you," Tony says.

"It's too early for that," James says without turning around and heads for the door.

"Rood! Get your ass in here," Captain Ross yells from his office.

"See ya, buddy," Tony whispers, sneaking away.

"Where in the hell have you been?" Captain Ross barks.

"Merry Christmas," James says.

"Merry Christmas. Where in the hell have you been?"

"I went to a clambake."

"Look at this," Captain Ross says, handing him a photograph.

"Where was this?"

"In the alley."

"The pimp murder?" James asks, glancing up from the picture.

"Yeah."

"He came back and left a clue?"

"Looks that way. This wasn't there before." Captain Ross says.

James stares at the photograph.

The serial killer left another clue. This one was written in blood on the alley wall. It says, 'THE BEGINNING XIIXQUARTER.'

"What's this nut trying to tell us?" Captain Ross asks, frustrated.

"That he's smarter than us," James says under his breath. He walks out of the office staring at the picture.

"Are you all right, James?" Tony asks.

"What?"

"Are you all right?"

"Yeah, sure," he says, throwing the photograph on his desk.

"Some woman called a couple of times for you. She said she had something important to give you. She's going to drop it off today."

"What's her name?" James asks, as his mind wanders off elsewhere.

Tony searches around on James' desk. "Here it is, Hope Naples." he says, handing the piece of paper to James.

"Did you say Hope Naples?" Detective Ludwig asks from across the room.

"That's right," Tony answers.

"I don't think she's going to be dropping anything off today," Ludwig says.

"What are you talking about, Ludwig?"

"She was mugged last night and it got ugly."

"How ugly?" James asks apprehensively.

"Put it this way. I'm working on the case."

James' head hangs down, and his shoulders sag. He shuts his eyes, and his mind begins to flash memories through his head. He remembers her face and the sound of her voice. The pain begins to pound in his head. He pushes away from his desk and walks toward the morgue. He slides out the cold steel drawer. He slowly unzips the plastic bag. The pounding in his head has become deafening, but something keeps telling him that this wasn't a mugging gone wrong. He thinks that she was sought out and murdered for a specific reason. He notices something on the inside of her arm. Inside of the bicep, a few inches from her underarm, a word has been written.

"DeMynn?" James says, puzzled.

James' mind begins to put a picture together. He sees

Hope lying in the street, bleeding to death.

"You knew you were dying," James says quietly to himself, "and you knew I would come and find the name."

He zips the body bag up. "Smart girl," he says, pushing the drawer shut.

*

"I have to tell you something," James says, troubled.

"When did you start wearing a crucifix?" Greg asks.

"What?" James looks down at his chest. It's Joe's crucifix hanging around his neck. He knows he left it at home on the lamp table. "A friend gave it to me. That's what I have to tell you about," he says.

"Your friend?"

"Yeah," James says, hesitating.

"What is it?"

"Something bizarre happened to me. My friend gave me this cross . . . but he has been dead for six months," James says skeptically.

"That doesn't sound bizarre to me," Greg says. "A friend gave you a crucifix. Many people give crucifixes as gifts."

"He gave it to me yesterday."

Greg's eyebrows rise with surprise. "The friend that has been dead for six months gave you the crucifix yesterday?"

"That's right."

Greg sits at his desk, staring contemplatively without speaking.

"What?"

"Why do you think he appeared to you?" Greg asks.

"Wait a minute. I'm not sure if I believe I saw him at all," James says.

"Why not?"

"We're talking about a man that has been dead for six months." James says, as if he were questioning his sanity.

"Maybe it wasn't your friend. Maybe he was an angel made to look like your friend so you would trust him," Greg tells him.

James begins to rub the side of his head.

"Is that easier to believe?" Greg asks.

"I don't know," James says, aggravated.

"Personally, I believe it was your friend."

"So you have no problem believing that I saw my dead

friend? Oh yeah, it must all be part of the plan," James says, annoyed.

"God can do anything."

"I'm starting to see that," James says, staring down at the floor.

"We are speaking about a Creator who spoke the universe into existence. So bringing back the dead would seem elementary," Greg says with no doubt in his mind.

James sits in a chair and leans forward. He puts his face in his hands.

"Did your friend tell you anything?"

"What do you mean?"

"A message, a warning, anything of that nature?"

James stares at his hands. He begins to rub the bridge of his nose. "He told me to read the Bible, that it would solve my problems." He shakes his head with doubt. "A book is going to solve all problems," he says, grinning sarcastically.

"You know how I feel about that statement."

"Yes, I do. You and Joe would get along perfectly."

"I understand you are struggling with all that is occurring, James, but bear with your purpose."

"My purpose!? I have no control over this. It was forced on me!" James exclaims. He stands and walks across the room. "I'm just a puppet, a chesspiece in a game."

"That is one way to view it," Greg says quietly.

"Oh, that's right. I was chosen."

Greg stares, disappointed and frustrated, and James sees it in his eyes.

"I'm sorry, Greg," he says from across the room. "It gets to me sometimes."

"I understand," Greg says, staring down at the scrolls on his desk.

James slowly and quietly climbs the stairs.

*

The winter wind whistles through the bell tower of the church. A loose plank bangs rhythmically on the side of the tower. The banging becomes pounding in the mind of the figure dwelling in the dark corner of the bell tower. The pounding abruptly wakes the figure, ending the nightmare of which he is a prisoner. He begins to glitter and radiate. The bell tower glows warmly. Then, as the figure vanishes into the night air, the tower slowly becomes cold and dark again.

The figure re-forms across town.

"Malefic," a voice says from a dark corner of the room.

Malefic jerks up in bed. "You're keeping late hours," he says drowsily.

"I must speak to you," the figure says in an urgent tone.

Malefic leans over toward the lamp table. The lightswitch clicks a half dozen times. "I forgot," he says. "The lights never seem to work when you're around."

The piercing eyes of the figure have disappeared from the dark corner.

"Where are you?" Malefic asks, searching the corner.

"You must listen to me," the figure says, now directly beside him.

Malefic jerks from the sudden emergence of the figure. "You're going to give me a heart attack," he says, unnerved.

"DeMynn is not a friend."

"He helps me out. Isn't that what friends do?" Malefic asks, grinning.

"Why?"

"Why what?"

"Why does he help you?"

"Because he's a friend," Malefic says.

"Shall I tell you what your friend has done?" the figure asks.

"Are you going to tell me something I don't know?"

"Your friend has murdered for you," the figure says bluntly.

"I don't know if that's true," Malefic responds.

"And if it were true?"

Malefic stares at the figure resentfully.

"DeMynn's sinister deeds benefit you," the figure says. "And your eyes persist in remaining shut."

"I don't tell him what to do," Malefic says with a defensive tone.

"Why would he murder for you?"

"You know everything. Why don't you tell me?"

"You are one and the same."

"What does that mean?" Malefic says with an uncomfortable expression.

"I know your heart, Malefic. I know its darkest appetite, its lust for power, its insatiable greed for money, and its desire for prominence. But as dark as your heart may be, it is virgin white in comparison with DeMynn's," the figure says insightfully.

"You told me he was using me, that he had a hidden agenda. If I become president, how would that benefit him?"

"The project in South America is the beginning of his hidden agenda," the figure says.

"How do you know about the project?" Malefic asks, surprised and fearful.

"He has intensified the addiction potency of the drug manufactured in the rain forest. The crime rate has quadrupled on every level because of his drugs," the figure says, angered.

"This is insane," Malefic says, confused.

"He will attempt to corrupt the entire planet, using his drug in its purest form and integrating it with every other drug known to man."

"What?"

"The drug he has created destroys the conscience. And if you become president, he will legislate a way to coalesce his drug with the drugs that were designed for good," the figure says critically. "Every being will be affected. The repercussion will be a conscienceless society, a world of Sodom and Gomorrah."

"What? Why?"

"Hell on earth."

"I don't understand."

"DeMynn is not a man."

"What are you talking about?"

"He is a fallen angel," the figure says solemnly. "He is attempting to create a world in which he can be God."

Malefic stares, bewildered.

"By the time your presidential term is completed, nearly the entire planet will be his dominion."

"Why is this happening?" Malefic asks, overwhelmed.

"This is the Last Gathering," the figure says.

"Gathering for what?"

"Souls."

"Why is this happening to me?" Malefic asks in confusion.

"There are two souls on earth that can be used for the Last Gathering. But one alone will be in position at the beginning of the Last Gathering before He returns."

"Before who returns?" Malefic asks anxiously.

The figure has vanished into the darkness.

*

"Hey, James."

"Hi, Anna. It's dead in here," James says, glancing around.

"It's the middle of the day."

"Oh yeah, that's right."

"Do you want a drink?"

"The usual."

"The same please," a man says politely.

James glances over at the man sitting a few barstools away.

Anna slides the shots of J.D. toward James and the stranger. They both, simultaneously, shoot down their drinks and slide the empty glasses back to Anna. James and the stranger glance at one another.

"Cool and refreshing," the man blurts out, satisfied. "Anna, another please. How about you James?" the man asks cheerfully.

"Do I know you?" James asks, with an inquisitive expression.

"Perhaps," the man says. "Did you receive my message?"

"What message?" James asks inadvertently.

"I supplied Ms. Naples with a message to deliver to you."

"I never received it," James says with a distant stare.

"Strange, I thought you would have gotten it by now."

"She never made it to my office," James says, staring down at his drink.

"Yes, I read about the tragic incident," the man says sympathetically. "It's an evil world we live in," he whispers, popping a cherry into his mouth.

"What was the message?" James asks impassively.

The man shoots his drink down. "Anna," he says, setting the empty glass on the bar. "Isn't art incredible?" he asks, staring at a painting on the wall of the bar.

James and Anna glance at the painting and look back to the man.

"It is remarkable how individuals can behold a painting and perceive so many different meanings," the man says with wonderment.

James stares at him as he slides his empty glass to Anna.

"For example," the man says, "take this painting here. We have a lamb in a meadow on a somewhat sunny day. There is a storm brewing on the horizon. It appears to be late spring from the appearance of the vibrant green grass and

150

the blooming flowers. Standing alone in the distance is a large bare tree." He stares at the painting, contemplating. "What do you see, James?" he asks, looking over.

James stares at the man curiously. He slowly glances at the painting and back to the man. "A lamb in a field," he says with a candid stare.

"You would be correct," the man says, grinning. He shoots down his drink. "Please, allow me to tell you what I see." His empty glass slides toward Anna. "I see the unblemished lamb and the wooden cross," he says reflectively. "I see the Father on the horizon and a pasture of salvation." He stares at the painting quietly for a moment, disheartened.

James and Anna exchange questioning glances.

"I loathe that painting," the man says bleakly. He stares intensely hypnotized at the painting. "Oh well, no reason to cry over spilt blood," the man says abruptly.

"That's milk," Anna says, correcting him.

"Whatever. Like all works of art, it is signed by the artist," he says. "And only he knows the true message of the art."

James stares into the mirror behind the bar. He shakes his head, thinking to himself, 'this guy is crazy.'

"Do you know what I mean, James?" the man asks, pushing away from the bar. He throws a fifty dollar bill on the counter.

"No, not really," James says, unconcerned.

"Think about it, James," he says. He walks out the front door whistling.

"James, what was that about?" Anna asks, puzzled.

"Hell if I know."

James begins to think about the conversation as he slides his empty glass back and forth between his hands. He remembers the stranger said he had a message for him that he had given to Hope. Suddenly, his eyes enlarge as a thought crosses his mind. He said he gave Hope a message to give to him . . . an artist signs his work.

"Son of a bitch!" he blurts out. He quickly stands and runs to the door. The city streets are congested with people, and the stranger has disappeared into the crowd. James looks out hopelessly into the city streets for a moment before he slowly returns to his barstool.

"What's wrong?" Anna asks.

"Have you ever seen him before?"

"No. Not until today," Anna says, reaching for the fifty dollar bill. "What the . . .," Anna says, quickly dropping the money.

"What?"

She extends her hand to show James. "There's something on the money," she says, wiping her hand off.

James carefully lifts the bill. The name 'DeMynn' has been written on it . . . in blood. His mind flashes a memory of the man's face. He stares into the mirror behind the bar and quietly says, "I got your message."

*

The city's monuments bask in the January sun. The cars sparkle in their tight confinements at the stoplights. The pedestrians quickly rush to their destinations to get out of the winter chill. A small crowd slowly moves along the sidewalk.

"Senator Moore, a question please," a reporter says.

The media swarm comes to a stop along with Derrick.

"Are you answering questions today?" a reporter asks.

"Sure, I have time for one question," Derrick says, smiling.

"Rumors say you put together a plan to stop the drug trafficking in the country," a reporter says.

"That is correct."

"Can you comment on it?"

"I can give you a general description of the plan," Derrick says. "The plan involves America's armed forces and the military reserve personnel. They will monitor and regulate twenty-four hours a day. They will patrol the borders of the country. The plan is set to be activated in seven months," he explains. "Clinics will also be financed and built to support the citizens dependent on the narcotics that will no longer be available to them."

"Great," a reporter says. "But it's been said that the government is responsible for the drugs that get into the country."

"That is and will be investigated. That is all I can say about that issue at the moment, but I promise there will be a report on our findings."

"So how much is the drug trafficking plan going to cost us?" a member of the media asks, grinning.

"Two point eight million dollars."

The reporters begin to shake their heads, displeased.

"Would you like to know how much that means to you a year?" Derrick asks, smiling.

"Why not?" a reporter says with dread.

"There are 250 million people in this country. One hundred and seventy million are taxpayers. Each taxpayer will pay an extra seventeen dollars a year for the plan."

"What? Seventeen dollars?"

"Well, seventeen dollars and some change."

One of the reporters reaches into his pocket and pulls out a twenty dollar bill. "Here you go, Senator. And you can keep the change."

The crowd laughs.

Chapter 41

"Who is DeMynn?" James asks, coming down the stairs. "And how does he fit into all this?" he asks, annoyed.

"What?" Greg asks, looking up from his desk.

"Who is he, Greg? Why is he in my face, and why can't I touch him?"

"I don't understand."

"He killed Hope Naples and he made damned sure I knew he did it." James sits down and stares at the floor. "Hell, he even had a drink with me," he says under his breath.

"She must have gotten too close to Malefic," Greg says quietly.

"I know why she was killed. The problem is, the who?" James says, staring up at Greg. "Among many other titles, I know this guy DeMynn is Malefic's partner. But I can't find anything on him." He shakes his head in frustration. "He doesn't even have fingerprints," he says, staring at a glass of water on the desk.

"He is a very dangerous individual, James," Greg says.

"There isn't any record of him anywhere. No registration in Malefic's computers . . . he owns nothing."

"There is a reason you were unable to locate data on him," Greg says quietly.

"Obviously it's not his real name, but I should be able to find something," James says wearily.

"You won't find DeMynn in the department's computers or on any other database," Greg tells him.

James looks up and waits with a cold stare for Greg to continue.

"If you want information on him, you will find it in the Bible," Greg says, staring back at James.

James' head lowers and he begins to rub his eyes. "What's going on?"

"He isn't like you and me," Greg says. "He isn't human."

"What is he?"

"Evil in its darkest form."

James rubs the bridge of his nose. Then he leans back into the chair. The feeling of anger and frustration are replaced by helplessness. "That's out of my jurisdiction," he says, smiling sarcastically. He stares at the floor with his hands under his chin. "Damn, I know everything, but I can't do a thing about it."

"I'm sorry, James," Greg says, knowing James feels he has to retaliate in some way. "He will not escape judgment," he says assuredly.

"Yes, I know, Greg," James mumbles. "Spiritual justice will be served."

"This battle is being fought on a spiritual field," Greg says. "It will not be won physically."

"Tell that to Hope and Pablo," James says grimly. His face becomes grave. "And my wife."

Greg stares apologetically at James, understanding that words will not relieve the pain.

*

"I never did like winter, too many gray days," Malefic says, staring out of his office window.

DeMynn sits in a black leather chair, examining a notepad in his lap.

"How long have we known one another?" Malefic asks, watching the pigeons fly to a building below.

"Many years," DeMynn says, thumbing through his notes.

"For the life of me, I can't remember the day we became partners . . . or how we even met," Malefic says.

"I seem to recall a convention in London. You had a new fabric circuit wire for telecommunications, and I had an innovative satellite program for development. Our conversation led to a merger of the two products," DeMynn says, flipping a page on his notepad.

"Do you remember Fred Mills?" Malefic asks.

DeMynn looks up from his pad inquisitively.

"What happened to him?" Malefic asks, watching the traffic in the streets below.

"He died in a lab explosion," DeMynn says.

"That's right. The laboratory that we were working in exploded, and he died in the fire. We were celebrating the success of our fabric wire and the partnership with you that day," Malefic says, staring out at the horizon. "How did we get out of there alive?" he asks curiously.

"We were lucky, I guess," DeMynn says, again glancing through his notepad.

"Lucky . . . like the time I came across those documents that informed me of the financial difficulties of every foreign-owned telecommunications corporation located in the States?" Malefic inquires, with suspicion in his tone.

"Charles, what is on your mind?"

Malefic turns to face him. "Who are you?" he asks, uncurtained.

"You have been speaking to our friend again, haven't you?"

"He said you were some sort of fallen angel and that you plan to destroy the world."

DeMynn shakes his head in amusement. "The destruction of the world will come to pass without my assistance," he says, grinning. "I'm no different than you, Charles. We share the same addictions of power and wealth. You choose to feed your addictions and ego through politics, which in time will put us on separate paths."

"What do you mean?"

"Because of the position you will be in, it will be inappropriate for you to have a relationship with me."

"I haven't considered that."

"Our friend is correct in saying that I have a hidden agenda. Securing you the presidency assures a place for me. Of course, I am relying on you to be blind to my dealings when you are in power, unlike one Congressman Moore, who would surely put a stop to my affairs."

"If I don't become president, you lose, too."

"That is why I assist you like I do. I also have a great deal to gain by you becoming president."

"That thing made you out to be satanic or something," Malefic says, relieved.

"It's all about power and wealth, Charles."

*

James sits on the edge of his bed. He takes some pills with a glass of water. He leans over and reaches for the telephone wire. He pulls it out of the wall. The flu has hit him hard and rest is the only thing he can think about. He slowly begins to doze off into a deep sleep.

The sun relentlessly beats down on him in a desolate land. He crawls on his hands and knees. The palms of his hands burn with every attempt to move forward as the sand pushes through his fingers. The smell of death attracts shadows cast from above. They patiently circle around him. Salty sweat stings his blisters, and the sand is pasted onto his body. James sees a man sitting under a small tree, drinking from a canteen in the shade.

"Do you want my help?" the man asks.

James strains to make eye contact. His mouth is

severely blistered and his throat has become raw. He is unable to speak.

"I will help you, but you must give me something in return," the man says, grinning.

"What do you want?" James asks painfully.

The man takes a drink of water and says, "Your soul."

The wind and the falling snow fiercely blow across the frozen tundra, making visibility impossible. James searches for shelter, struggling through two feet of snow. His body shivers uncontrollably and his limbs have become numb. He sees a warm glow coming from an entrance to a cave. He discovers a man sitting beside a fire along with someone else. The man is wearing a wool cloak with a hood over his head. The man seems familiar to James, but the other person has his back toward him.

"Do you want my help?" the man asks.

"Who are you?"

"You know who I am. Come sit with me by the fire," the man says invitingly.

"I've seen you before," James says, rubbing his eyes. "But I can't remember from where."

"Come in, James. You will die out there," the man says. He leans over and picks up one of the many books piled beside him. He throws it into the fire.

James steps closer, getting a better view of the other person. It's a woman. "Who is she?" he asks.

"A poor soul that came out of the cold," the man says, throwing another book into the fire. Sparks fly into the air and a black cloud of smoke rolls to the ceiling of the cave.

James begins to feel strange. A feverish flash and a cold chill run through his body together. "I have to get out of here," James says, wiping his eyes. He begins to turn and leave.

"Don't leave me," the woman says painfully.

The voice of the woman is familiar to James. "What did you say?" he asks.

"Don't leave me," she says again, with her back to him.

The man throws another book into the fire. "Come closer and see," he says eagerly.

James nears the woman. She begins to turn and face him.

"Oh my God!" James cries, falling to his knees. "She can't be with you," he says as his eyes begin to water.

"James, stay with me," the woman says softly.

"Who the fuck are you?" James asks the man, outraged.

"You know who I am. Who are you?" he asks wickedly. He throws another book into the fire, causing a swirling gray cloud of smoke.

James wakes coughing and soaked in sweat. He throws off the covers and turns on the light. He sits on the edge of his bed. He discovers that his entire room is covered with a thin layer of frost. Written on a frosted mirror are the words, 'She is mine'. He finds something strange on the bed beside him. His bed is full of sand. The room has the smell of an extinguished fire. He looks around the room. He locates the source of the smell. In the corner of his room, there's a pile of burned Bibles.

Chapter 42

A tall and lean man walks into Malefic's office. He approaches the desk, but the man in Malefic's chair is facing the large window behind the desk.

"What did you need to talk to me about?" DeMynn asks apathetically, while staring out the window.

"Mr. DeMynn, there's a problem on the street," the man says nervously.

"What kind of problem?" DeMynn asks, spinning the chair around and staring at him coldly.

"We're missing about a hundred men."

"Excuse me?"

"They've disappeared," he says hesitantly.

"Do you know where or why? Have you spoken to the remaining men?" DeMynn asks.

"They said that they quit and that they're not going to sell anymore."

"Did they tell you why?" DeMynn asks, stirring his coffee.

"It appears that a large, black creature gave them an ultimatum . . .
stop selling drugs or die," the man says, with apprehension in his voice.

"Go to the warehouse tonight. After the shipment is delivered, put twenty men on the street from there."

The man turns and quickly exits the office, leaving DeMynn alone.

DeMynn stands and walks over to the chessboard, and stares irefully. One of his tinted bishops has been taken.

*

"I need a drink, Anna," James says, weariness in his voice.

"Sure, James."

"What's this need shit?" a man says from behind him.

"Hey, Mr. Dean," James says, smiling.

Mr. Dean was his father's partner. He helped rise James after his father was killed.

"How are you doing, James?" Mr. Dean asks, hugging him.

"Good. Spring must be around the corner if you're

here."

"Yeah, it's time for us old, black, retired cops to migrate back up north," Mr. Dean says, grinning.

"It's good to see you."

"It's good to see you, too, James. Did you catch that lunatic yet?"

"No."

"Damn, his career is going to outlast yours," Mr. Dean says humorously.

"Looks that way."

Mr. Dean pulls a stool up next to James. "Look at this," he says, pointing at the headline in the paper. "Abortion clinic destroyed in explosion," he reads out loud, shaking his head. "This world is getting more messed up every day."

"More than you know," James says under his breath.

"You have doctors killing babies, and supposed godly people killing doctors," Mr. Dean says, appalled.

"Tell me, Mr. Dean, what's wrong with this world?" Anna asks, instigating.

"I'll tell you, young lady. We spend so much time surrounded by our own creations that we begin to believe we are the Creator," Mr. Dean says, sipping his iced tea.

James and Anna exchange smiles.

"I don't know, Mr. Dean. Do you think that's it?" James asks provocatively.

"There's no appreciation and gratefulness for life today, nor accountability for what we do with it," Mr. Dean says, throwing the paper to the side.

"You're getting deep, Mr. Dean," James says with a grin.

"That's what happens when you have too much time on your hands," Mr. Dean says, standing. "I'll see you around, James. Lay off the booze. See ya, Anna," Mr. Dean says, heading out the door.

"I'm out of here, too, Anna," James says, getting up to leave. "I've got something to take care of."

*

The day has grown old and people begin to search for parking spaces near their favorite restaurants. Four men dressed in black suits, equipped with electrical devices, enter the restaurant. They meticulously walk through the restaurant, scanning the people sitting at the tables. The electrical devices rhythmically beep as they wave them throughout the crowd. They carefully watch the portable screens. Suddenly, one of their scanners emits a high, steady pitch. One of the men dressed in black is standing over a lone man sitting at a table having a drink. The man with the scanner stops dead and stares with his hand tucked in his jacket. The other three men quickly arrive at the table.

"I'll have a steak, medium well," James says, looking up from his menu. "And a hot fudge sundae," he says, holding the menu out toward the men.

The four men continue to stare. The people at the surrounding tables look on nervously. The elevator music in the background keeps the restaurant from being totally silent.

"I sure am getting hungry," James says in a amusing tone.

"Why do you have a weapon?" one of the men asks.

"Why do you ask?"

"It's my job."

James glances around at the staring people seated at their tables, and then at the four men standing in front of him. "My job requires me to carry one," he answers.

"And that would be?" the man asks, with no expression.

"Pest control," James says, entertainingly.

One of the men in black slightly grins, and a woman snickers in the background.

"Why do you carry weapons?" James asks.

"We are employed by the gentleman in the limousine. We are required to ensure the safety of our employer and to remove all firearms from the premises," the man says, sounding rehearsed.

James slowly reaches into his jacket and pulls out his wallet. He flips it open and throws it on the table.

The man glances down at the wallet. "Thank you, Detective Rood," he says politely.

They quickly turn and exit the restaurant. They return through the doors, surrounding Charles Malefic. He sits at a table in the back corner of the restaurant. Two of the men sit with Malefic and the other two position themselves at a table directly in front of him.

A feeling from within James begins to surface. A dark and ugly thought begins to infest his mind, the same thought that has brought him to the restaurant. A bloody memory of Faith's face flashes in his head. The pain and anger rush through his blood. His eyes lock onto Malefic; they burn from not blinking. He slowly reaches into his jacket and holds his gun tightly. The memory of Faith's face flashes again in his head. The image of Hope Naples' body lying on cold steel suddenly emerges in his mind. He slides the gun out and holds it under the table.

James takes a sip from his drink and hears a voice in his head.

"That's right, take another drink," the raspy voice says.

James stares at the ice cubes floating in the golden liquid in his glass.

"Yes, James, drink. Drink from the Great Compromiser," the voice whispers.

His finger begins to itch on the trigger. He begins to raise the gun from beneath the table, but another voice enters his head.

"Make room for wrath, my son. I will repay," the voice says, assertively.

The voice sends a feeling of reassurance through him. The anger and pain slowly begin to leave him. He slides the gun back into his holster, and quietly leaves the restaurant.

*

"Where have you been?" the old chiseler asks, concerned.

"Cleaning and repairing," the figure says.

"I was wondering about something," the old man says curiously. "Where do you go during the day? I mean, I never see you in the daytime."

The figure stares quietly before he eventually speaks. "I know no light," the figure says, reserved. "I follow the night across the land."

"Are you saying that you follow the night around the world?" the old man inquires.

"Yes."

"Why?"

"My conscience has deemed me unworthy of the light," the figure says grievously.

"Your conscience?"

"I did something many years ago, and I can't forgive myself," the figure says, staring at the marble frieze.

"Ask for forgiveness," the old man says, looking up at him.

"It is too late for forgiveness," the figure says, with a mournful tone.

"Why?"

"I am dead," the figure says, lowering his head.

"But you're not dead. You are here so that you can do something for Him. Don't you think you can use this as a chance to ask for forgiveness?" the old man suggests.

The figure turns his head to stare at the old man.

The old man shrugs his shoulders. "Something to think about," he says.

The figure looks back at the marble frieze. A thought enters his mind. He begins to think that his screams from the grave for redemption may have been heard, and that he may truly be alive again. Suddenly he begins to sparkle and radiate. He slowly fades into the darkness.

Malefic sits up in bed reading a book. He hears a sound across the room near the fireplace. The fire begins to burn brighter, casting flickering shadows throughout the room. Malefic stares and waits. Not hearing the noise again, he continues to read.

"What are you reading?" the figure asks, standing in front of the fireplace.

"I knew you were here," Malefic says, looking up from his book.

"I must be losing my touch."

"You certainly are," Malefic says, glancing at the lamp on the table. "The light is still on."

"I can extinguish it if you like," the figure says kindly.

"No, that's all right."

"What are you reading?"

"'Sinner In The Hands Of An Angry God," Malefic says, looking at the cover of the book.

"Interesting . . . which reminds me, have you spoken to DeMynn?"

"Yeah, and I don't think he's who you think he is," Malefic says.

"Have I exaggerated the facts?"

"He's just a guy selling drugs for money and power," he says defensively.

Someone has stepped into the room. Malefic is unaware of the third party.

"I smell brimstone," the figure whispers.

"What?" Malefic asks.

"I smell brimstone," the figure says, sarcastically.

"That is quite humorous," DeMynn says, from the dark side of the room.

"Is that you, DeMynn?" Malefic asks, surprised.

"Yes, Charles." DeMynn walks over to the figure. "I hear you are spreading ugly rumors about me," he says casually.

"Rumors?"

"That I plan to destroy the world," DeMynn says, grinning.

"Have I made you out to be grander than you are?" the figure asks.

"I am a simple businessman," DeMynn says with an innocent expression.

"You are a liar," the figure says calmly. "Why do you keep the importance of the time at hand hidden from him?"

"What's he talking about?" Malefic asks, confused.

"What are you talking about?" DeMynn asks, turning to the figure.

"It is the Last Gathering. That is why I am here, and why you have made a special appearance."

"I can never understand what the two of you are talking about," Malefic says, shaking his head.

"Do you fear that the information will turn him?"

"It is too late for him and you know that. The sphere has reached the bloom," DeMynn says logically.

"Too late for who? What are you talking about?" Malefic asks, flustered.

The figure has materialized beside Malefic. He leans down to stare into his eyes.

"What are you doing?" Malefic asks, attempting to back away.

The figure stares into Malefic's eyes, examining him.

"What's he doing, DeMynn?" Malefic asks uncomfortably.

"Searching."

"For what?"

"The truth."

The figure returns to the other side of the room.

"And the truth will set you free," DeMynn says coldly.

As the words leave DeMynn's mouth, the fire burns hotter and the flames race up the chimney.

"You shall not see me again," the figure says, fading into the shadows.

"What is a sphere and a bloom?" And what do you mean it's too late for me?" Malefic asks, turning to face DeMynn.

DeMynn has vanished into the dark also, leaving Malefic alone with his questions.

Chapter 43

James sits at a table in a restaurant. Malefic sits across the room, enjoying his meal. James' hand slides out from beneath the table with a gun. He fires six shots. The sounds of glass breaking and screams fill the air. People chaotically run for the exit. Malefic's bodyguards lie motionless on the floor with puddles of blood around them. Malefic sits at his table, staring in terror. James reaches into his coat and pulls another gun out. He stretches his arm out, taking aim at Malefic. James' eyes burn with hate and revenge. He fires six shots rhythmically into Malefic's body. Malefic's splattered blood runs down the wall behind him. The room has become smokey from the gunpowder. The scene begins to fade away into a cloudy blur. James reemerges in a dark and tiny room. He is sitting on the edge of a cot in prison. A guard walks up to James' cell and stares at him through the prison bars. James glances up at the guard but is unable to see his face. The guard throws a newspaper into the cell. James continues to stare at the guard.

"I'm sorry, James," the guard says softly.

"Sorry about what?" James asks, with a detached tone.

"Read the headline," he says, looking down at the paper.

James leans down and picks up the paper. The headline reads 'Presidential Candidate Senator Moore Assassinated.' His hands begin to crumple the edges of the paper as his eyes fill with tears.

"You let him down, James," the guard says, in a cold tone.

James looks up and stares painfully at the dark silhouette of the guard.

"I'd like to thank you, James," the guard says.

James stares back down at the headline in the paper. "For what?" he asks, under his breath.

"For removing yourself. It made things so much easier," the guard says with an appreciative grin.

James looks up again. The guard moves closer to the cell, so James can see his face. James stares with disbelief and rage. It's DeMynn dressed as a prison guard.

"You fucked up pretty damn good, James," DeMynn whispers in a cold voice. "And I truly appreciate it. You will always have a special place in my heart," he says, grinning, "That is, if I had one."

James lunges at the bars of the cell. "I got Malefic. I killed your puppet," James says vindictively.

"People like Malefic are a dime a dozen," DeMynn explains. "But a man of God, on the other hand," he says, smiling. "They don't come around too frequently."

James attempts to grab DeMynn through the bars, but he is out of reach. James slides down the bars and kneels on the floor.

"Well, I must be going," DeMynn says with good cheer. "I have some recruiting to do."

James wearily looks up from the floor. "I'll get you."

DeMynn begins to walk away. "I'll see you in twenty-five years, James. That is, if you are a good boy."

James wakes from his nightmare. He lies staring at the ceiling for the rest of the night.

*

Israel

In a small, whitewashed house outside of Jerusalem hides Professor Phault. He sits at a desk interpreting a scroll. The cool, night air blows throughout the room, causing the candlelight to flicker. Phault has developed black circles around his eyes as a result of his recently acquired immunity to sleep.

"Professor," Amsad says, quietly entering the room. "You must leave the country," he nervously insists.

"I will leave soon, Amsad, soon."

"The government will soon be aware of your whereabouts," Amsad says, nervously glancing out the window.

"Yes, I know," Phault says, never looking up from his work.

"They know, Professor. They know of the scroll," he says, again cautiously checking outside the window.

"Go back to your family, my friend," Phault says, looking up for the first time. "I will leave in the morning."

Amsad's expression relaxes for a moment. "Morning, Professor, you leave," he says, relieved.

"Yes," he says, smiling.

Amsad quietly closes the door. Phault continues through the night, searching for the one detail that has eluded him. Then, suddenly, after hours of meticulous scrutinizing of the scroll, he locates it.

"Finally!" Phault exclaims.

The name of the author that wrote the scroll stares hauntingly at him from the parchment.

"Of course, it all makes sense," Phault says. "You were in the middle of it all," he says, with a tone of relief.

A gust of wind rushes through the room, extinguishing the candles. Phault searches for his matches in the dark.

"Thank you, Professor," a voice whispers coldly.

"Who's there?" Phault asks, startled.

"Someone who is going to help you leave this place," the voice whispers.

The sound of neck bones snapping fills the air. Then a deadening thump ensues. The rustling of scrolls being gathered quickly follows. The smell of extinguished candles lingers through the darkness.

*

Washington, D.C.

"Load the truck and get moving!" a heavyset man yells at a group of men standing in the alley.

"Damn, what's the hurry?" one of the workers whispers.

"Really, the druggies ain't going anywhere," a second man says.

"Shut up and load the truck!" the foreman yells.

"Hey, someone's coming down the alley," a worker says in alarm.

"Get up there and turn his ass around," the foreman barks.

"Let me go," one of the men says, beginning to walk down the alley toward the figure.

The cool night air mixes with the warm steam coming from the sewers. The approaching figure fades in and out of the foglike steam. The worker pulls a gun and holds it down by his side. The figure and the man draw nearer to one another. The figure disappears into a thick part of the steam. The man stops walking. He waits for the intruder to reappear. The figure emerges twenty feet away and walks steadily toward the man with his trench coat flowing behind him. The steam drifts toward the worker, limiting his vision to a few feet. Suddenly the figure reappears directly in front of him.

"Oh, shit!" the man exclaims, staring up at the figure. "What in God's name are you?"

"Leave this place and never return," the figure says, looking down at him.

The man points the gun at the figure. "I think *you* should leave this place and never return," the man responds.

The figure quietly stares down at the man. Then he begins to peer down the alley, where the truck is being loaded.

"Hey, hey, are you listening?" the man says waving his hand in the figure's face, attempting to get his attention. "I suggest you get your big ass out of here," the man says, pointing down the alley with his gun.

"I cannot leave. I must destroy the drugs," the figure says in a soft tone, "before they destroy more people."

"Really? Well, I can't let you do that."

"I do not want to hurt you," the figure says.

"Come on, superhero, get out of here before you get hurt."

The figure stares for a moment, then he begins to move forward.

"Sorry, weirdo," the man says, pulling the trigger.

The echo of the gun blast rings through the alley. A group of men begin to run toward the sound of the gunshot. The figure begins to radiate a feverish glow beneath his black bandages.

"Attempt to harm me once more, and vengeance will be mine," the figure warns.

The figure's body is glowing brilliantly, and sparks of light begin to flicker around him. The man with the gun stands motionless, his eyes fixated with astonishment and his arms at his sides, lifeless.

"What the fuck is that?!" one of the other men yells, as they approach.

"Don't shoot!" another man yells.

The man standing in front of the figure turns around. "What the hell are you talking about?" he asks, bewildered.

"I was in Malefic's office when this thing was there. You get one warning before he retaliates," the worker explains. "You can't kill him."

"That's bullshit," the man that shot the figure says. He points the gun and unloads the remaining five shots into the figure's body.

The figure reaches out and grabs the man. He lifts him up off the ground, draws him close to his face, and intensely stares into the man's eyes. "Vengeance is mine," he whispers.

The man ignites into a blazing torch. The figure holds the man out in front of him as the man screams a horrible, suffering shriek. The other men begin to slowly back away. The man has become a charred black form in the figure's grip. The burnt body begins to crumble and blow throughout the alley.

The group of men turn and begin running toward the warehouse.

"What the hell are you guys doing? And who the fuck shot off their gun?" the foreman yells, angered.

"You better get your ass out of here," one of the workers says, running by him.

"What?! What the hell is wrong with you assholes?" the foreman screams. He notices a figure walking toward him. The foreman watches curiously as the figure nears. He draws his gun out from his coat.

"You can't kill him," a worker says.

The foreman glances confusedly at the worker standing next to him.

"He just toasted Frank for trying," the worker explains.

The figure has reached the foreman and the worker. He stands in front of them. The two men stare up at him with rigid expressions. The figure looks down at the foreman's hand holding the gun. The foreman glances down at his gun and then back at the figure. The foreman releases the gun to the alley street and smiles slightly.

"Wise man," the figure says quietly.

The worker standing beside the foreman nods his head agreeably. "Smart move," he whispers.

"What do you want?" the foreman asks.

The figure glances over his shoulder and stares at the truck thirty yards away.

"Drugs? You want drugs?" the foreman asks, surprised.

The figure's head snaps around to look at the two men with a vigorous stare.

"Maybe not," the foreman says apologetically.

The figure quickly glances back at the truck. Suddenly the truck explodes into an orange ball of fire. The flames reach high into the night, and the alley glows with a warm, yellow shade. The blast lifts the two men off the ground. They watch the truck burn to the frame. The fire spreads to the warehouse within seconds. The figure has vanished. The two men watch the blaze engulf the warehouse as sirens draw near.

"I guess he did want the drugs," the worker says satirically.

*

"Hello, Professor. Beautiful day, isn't it?"

"DeMynn . . . I would say it is nice to see you, but it isn't," Greg says, not looking up from his gardening.

"I understand you are a little sore at me for trying to kill you. Please accept my apology. Can we be friends again?" DeMynn asks, grinning.

Greg continues to work on the flowerbed. "What do you want?" he asks, with a candid tone.

"I came across an old manuscript that you may find interesting," DeMynn says. "It speaks briefly about our current situation. It appears no one from either side can be removed physically for a duration."

Greg glances up, smiling knowingly.

"You wouldn't happen to know when the rules will change?" DeMynn asks.

"Have you possibly mistaken this place for the garden of Gethsemane?" Greg asks, staring at DeMynn.

"The day will come, Professor, when you will make a miscalculation, and I will be there," DeMynn says confidently.

"You will lose this battle, DeMynn, and we both know you have already lost the war. Your fate is sealed," Greg says with confidence.

Greg has struck a nerve. DeMynn stares at him, not saying a word. Slowly the uneasiness on DeMynn's face begins to wear off and is replaced with a grin.

"You are a mean individual, Professor," DeMynn says. He takes a deep breath as he glances up at the blue sky. "But, I still like you . . . damn, I just can't help it," he says, kneeling to the ground. "I'm confident that you may know this bit of information, but I'll tell you regardless. There is a large, black guardian angel running around disturbing my operations. But I have found something in the scroll that may eliminate him from my affairs. If he comes calling on you, please inform him that I would like to converse with him." DeMynn stands and stretches his arms as he takes in a breath of fresh air. "You have a beautiful garden, Professor," he says, smiling. "Personally, I have always enjoyed gardens. I got my start in a garden many years ago, but you knew that," he says, grinning down at

Greg. "I must be going. Don't forget to relay my message to our friend if you see him first."

James walks along the corridor, remembering the first time he walked through it, the anxiety he felt because of the appearance of a figure at the end of the corridor. A figure that reminded him of his nightmares. He continues to walk toward the garden to meet Greg. A silhouette appears through the two wooden doors and walks toward him. He feels calm walking toward the figure. The figure draws near.

"How are you, James?" DeMynn asks, smirking.

"What the hell are you doing here?"

"I guess you wouldn't believe praying," DeMynn says, staring coldly.

"What are you doing here?"

"I had a little chat with my friend Greg," DeMynn says, grinning.

James' face hardens with anger and fear.

"Don't worry, he's fine," DeMynn says comfortingly. "Whenever the two of us get together, it is I who gets the worst end of the deal."

James begins to walk away.

"It must be very difficult for you," DeMynn says. "Caught in the middle and unable to follow your natural instinct. I know you want to serve justice. I can see it in your eyes," he whispers.

James lowers his head. The anger begins to boil within him.

"I'm going to disclose a bit of information to you, since you already appear to know what is happening. Charles Malefic didn't kill your wife. He knows nothing of the incident," DeMynn explains.

James stares at him as his mind quickly flashes to the accident. DeMynn's expression becomes serious. "I did it, James," he says coldly.

A cold shiver runs up James' spine and his hands begin to tremble, forcing him to ball them into fists. His eyes begin to form tears of anger. He swallows painfully and clenches his teeth. "I'll get you," he says lividly.

"You don't get it," DeMynn says, smiling. "You don't get me, I get you."

James lowers his head again. He stares at the crucifix around his neck that has found its way out of his shirt.

"Well, I must be going," DeMynn says cheerfully. "I have some misguided people to see in Toronto and Florida, and I must continue to keep it that way," he says, grinning.

James clenches the crucifix with his fist. The anger flows through his body like a poison.

DeMynn begins to walk away. "That piece of metal means nothing if you don't believe in it," he says with a disdainful tone. "To some, it's costume jewelry. Do you know what I mean, James?" he asks, glancing back at him. "I didn't think so."

James wanders into the garden. He quietly sits on a stone bench and watches Greg work in the flower bed.

"James, how long have you been there?" Greg asks.

"I'm getting tired, Greg," James says in a weary voice.

"What's wrong?"

"I saw DeMynn. He said he killed Faith," James says, putting his head in his hands and staring at the ground. "If a man murders your wife, something can be done about it. But my wife is murdered by someone who isn't really here. What am I supposed to do?" he asks, rubbing his eyes. "He's going to torment me with this for the rest of my life. He will dangle it in my face until I put a gun to my head and wipe the memory clean," James says painfully.

"You must not talk that way, James," Greg says, concerned. "I believe deep in my heart that somehow you will serve justice, and he will not be an exception."

"I don't know," James mumbles, staring at the ground.

"I believe God will use you to destroy DeMynn's plan, and that will lead to his destruction."

"I wish I could believe that," James says with doubt in his voice. He stares out into the garden in a daze. "For now, I have to concern myself with a lunatic running around the city," he says quietly. "Today is the first day of spring . . . a new season."

Chapter 44

"Welcome to News Seven. I'm Kathy Webster. We're going live to the Conference Center. Rob, are you there?"

The news program flashes to a live shot of a reporter standing in a crowded room.

"Yes, Kathy, I can hear you. We're waiting for Senator Moore to arrive," Rob says, adjusting the receiver in his ear.

"How is the atmosphere there?" Kathy asks.

"There is definitely electricity in the air tonight and a great deal of curiosity."

"Has anyone revealed what the senator has planned for tonight?" she asks.

"There are rumors about the senator stepping down from the presidential race," Rob says, "but the strangest rumor I've heard is that Senator Moore is going to make a public prediction. About what, no one knows. We are simply going to have to wait."

"What do you think he's up to, DeMynn?" Malefic asks, watching the newscast in his office.

"I don't know," DeMynn says, sitting on the leather couch.

"Why would he arrange a special conference?" Malefic asks curiously. "I know I'm not lucky enough to have him drop out of the race."

"Kathy, Senator Moore has arrived," Rob announces. "He is making his way to the platform."

The sounds of the cameras flashing and the excitement of the media have made the conference room deafening. Derrick quickly reaches the podium, closely surrounded by Secret Service agents. Derrick stands quietly, staring out over the sea of media.

"The senator appears much more serious than usual, Rob," Kathy observes from the news studio.

"He appears to have something of great importance on his mind," Rob says.

Slowly the camera flashes come to a stop and the noise from the crowd tapers off to a dead silence.

"What I have to say tonight will be said once," Derrick says directly. "I will not repeat it, nor will I answer questions concerning the subject. I believe it will be self-explanatory."

The reporters' heads repeatedly bob up and down as they jot down Derrick's quotes.

"I have been chosen by God to lead this country," Derrick says ingenuously.

The headbobbing of the reporters has come to a sudden halt. All eyes in the crowd have locked onto Derrick.

"Through me, the church and the country will be reformed," Derrick says, with a decisive stare. "The Lord will provide a sign proving that I am speaking the truth. In the month of April, there will be a duration in which there will be no birth and no death in the universe. Only one death and one birth will be witnessed. If the sign does not appear, I will step down from the presidential race. Thank you for your time. God bless."

Derrick steps off the platform and is immediately surrounded by additional Secret Service men. He is escorted through the crowd to a waiting limousine. He enters the backseat and the limousine quickly disappears into the night. As the shock begins to wear off the media personnel, they begin to murmur among themselves. Most stand with bewildered expressions on their faces, and others shake their heads in astonishment.

"What was that?" one reporter says to the other.

"Shit if I know."

"I'm glad I was recording it. I stopped writing somewhere in the middle of that craziness."

"Rob, are you there? What did you get out of that speech?" Kathy asks, amazed.

"It appears that the senator believes he was chosen by God to lead this country," Rob explains. "And I would say, whatever that sign is, if it doesn't materialize, we lose a good candidate for president."

DeMynn stares at the television screen but isn't watching anything. His mind is elsewhere.

"What was that?" Malefic asks, dumbfounded.

DeMynn continues to stare at the screen in a daze.

"DeMynn . . . hey, what's wrong?" Malefic asks, waving his hand in front of the television screen.

"What?"

"What's wrong with you?" Malefic asks, turning off the television.

"Nothing," DeMynn says quietly.

"What was he talking about?"

"I don't know," DeMynn says with a faraway look in his eyes.

"You're not worried about this, are you?"

"What?"

"Are you worried about Moore's speech?"

"No," DeMynn says, standing and walking over to the chessboard. He notices that his tinted king is in check.

"Do you think it's a publicity stunt?" Malefic asks.

"Maybe," DeMynn answers, fixing himself a drink.

"People are going to think he's crazy. No one is going to vote for him now," Malefic says, pleased. "He has blown any chance he had with that nonsense tonight."

"If the prophecy doesn't come true," DeMynn says under his breath, staring out the window.

"What?"

DeMynn turns around. "Moore has made it much easier on us," he says apathetically. "We shall indubitably win the election now."

"Well, I'm going home," Malefic says, with satisfaction in his tone. "I need some sleep."

"Good night, Charles," DeMynn says, watching him leave the room.

DeMynn turns to stare out into the night. He stands there quietly, contemplating the events of the night. He thinks about Derrick's prophecy and the ramifications it may have. His mind arrives at a conclusive thought.

"I need a volunteer," he says with a cold whisper.

Chapter 45

James walks along the sidewalk, remembering the walks he took with Faith. She loved the Smithsonian and all the monuments in the city. He remembers how she would drag him around sightseeing every year. She would get excited every time, as if it were the first time. He stands and watches the flags that encircle the Washington Monument wave and flap in the wind. He checks his watch as he waits for the crossing light to change.

A few feet away, standing near the bus stop, is a man with ragged clothes and a shabby beard.

"Be afraid, children. The battle for souls is all around us," the man says, with warning in his tone. His blue eyes stare out from beneath the gray strands of hair hanging in his face. "And it is becoming bloody."

A man in a business suit standing next to James shakes his head. "Poor, crazy fool," the man in the suit says.

James glances over at the man who spoke. "The crazy part is that he's right," he mumbles, beginning to walk across the street.

*

"Hey, James. Where've you been?"

"How have you been, Pop?" James says, entering the barbershop.

"Good, real good," Pop says, brushing off the chair. "Come on over and have a seat," he says, smiling.

"How's business?"

"OK," Pop says. "Reggie, wake up. Look who's here," he says, hitting the other barber in the head with a comb.

"You better stop hitting me on my damned head, old man," Reggie says, annoyed. "James, what's up?" he asks drowsily.

"Not much. How about you?"

"I'm all right. James, let me ask you something," Reggie says with a thoughtful expression. "How many years would I get for killing an old man?" he asks, glancing at Pop.

James grins. "I don't think they put you in jail anymore for killing old men. I believe you get a tax break because you're saving the government money. That's one less Social Security check going out."

"I know one thing," Pop says with a warning stare. "The unemployment line is about to get one person longer."

"What are you guys laughing about?" Mr. Dean asks, entering the barbershop.

"Hey, Mr. Dean. When did you get in town?" Reggie asks, surprised to see him.

"A few days ago," Mr. Dean says, rubbing James head as he passes him.

"I can't believe this," Pop says happily. "James and Dean on the same day, just like the old days."

"Back then you had to bribe James with a lollipop to sit still," Mr. Dean says, grinning.

"He still has to," James says with a serious expression.

"I have something for you, James," Mr. Dean says, pulling a small box from his coat.

"What is it?" James asks.

"Open it."

James opens the box and quietly stares at the object. Pop and Reggie grin contentedly with Mr. Dean. James lifts the silver badge from the box.

"Your dad wanted you to have it," Mr. Dean says meaningfully. "He told me to give it to you when I thought you may need it."

James tearfully stares up at Mr. Dean.

"He would be very proud of you, James," Mr. Dean says in a confident tone.

"That's for sure," Pop says decisively.

"We all are," Reggie says.

"Thank you," James whispers, looking down at the badge.

"All right now, I need a haircut, Reggie," Mr. Dean says, jumping in the chair. "This is how I want it, Reg. I want this side over here to be longer than this side over here," he says, instructively pointing to his hair. "And I want the back to be uneven and this sideburn to be higher than this one."

James and Pop stare at Mr. Dean with strange looks on their faces.

"I can't cut it like that, Mr. Dean," Reggie says, confused.

"Why not?" Mr. Dean asks, grinning. "That's how you cut it last time."

*

Greg sits at his desk in the cellar of the church. The candles burn warmly throughout the room. He's holding a photograph of himself, his wife, and child. His eyes well with tears. He weeps and smiles with every passing memory. Greg is unaware that James has walked into the room.

"Greg," James says with concern in his voice.

Greg glances up from the photograph with a bittersweet expression.

"Are you all right?" James asks.

"I'm fine," he says, wiping the tears from his eyes.

"What are you looking at?"

Greg hands him the picture.

"Is this you?" James asks, smiling.

"Many years ago," Greg says, grinning.

James stares inquisitively at the badly damaged photograph. He runs his finger along the burnt edges. "This is your family," he says, looking up at Greg. "You were the one who lost his family in that fire. You were the one who donated the land to the church."

"I am that man," Greg says quietly.

James stares down at the floor. "I'm sorry, Greg. I never put it together."

"And you call yourself a detective," Greg says, smiling.

James hands the photograph back to Greg. "The limp should have clued me in," he says with a grin.

"You had a great deal of anger and pain then. You understandably weren't very receptive at the time," Greg says.

"How did you get through the years?" James asks, staring down at his hands.

"After the accident, I journeyed to the Middle East, which in turn, led me to discover the ancient scrolls that I possess today . . . the same scrolls that I believe will help you," Greg explains. "I have perpetually believed that those scrolls were my reason for surviving the accident, that it was all part of His plan."

"Don't you hurt?" James asks, looking up at Greg.

"Sometimes," Greg says, glancing at the photograph. "Through the years I found comfort in doing God's work and waiting for the day His plan would be revealed to me. But now the waiting is over," he says optimistically. "I was asking the same questions thirty-five years ago that you have been asking yourself this past year. But you didn't have to wait thirty-five years for the answers."

"I wouldn't have made it that long," James says with a weary tone.

"I believe you could have."

"No, that's why I'm here. I came to tell you that I have to get out of here. I need to get away from all of this," James says with a desperate look in his eyes.

"You can't. It is essential that you protect Derrick. It is a crucial time," Greg says urgently.

"He will be fine without me."

"Would he have been fine without you when someone took those scandalous photographs of him or the time someone attempted to stab him in the park and you stopped the madman before he got there? And what about the crazy guy you tracked down that was sending death threats? His apartment was full of weapons and pictures of Derrick with targets painted on them. Would Derrick have been fine all those times without you?"

"Derrick is well protected now," James says quietly. "He has Secret Service all over him."

"That isn't enough."

"I can't be around forever."

"Your responsibility is to get him to the presidency. After that has occurred, your obligation is completed."

James sits down and puts his head in his hands. He begins to rub the sides of his head as if he were attempting to rub a headache away.

"What is going on, James?" Greg asks perceptively.

"What do you mean?"

"I mean why has the pressure suddenly gotten to you?"

James continues to rub his temples.

"What happened?"

James stops rubbing his head and leans back into the chair. "DeMynn keeps getting into my dreams. He keeps showing me the accident. He keeps showing me Faith with him," he says with a painful stare.

"He's using an illusion to deceive you. He will also use your guilt and anger against you," Greg explains.

"She seems so real," James says painfully.

"He doesn't have her, James," Greg assures him.

James closes his eyes and leans further back into the chair. "Is it all right with you if I catch a little sleep here?" he asks, closing his eyes.

"Sure, James. I'll wake you in a couple of hours," Greg says, covering him with a blanket.

Greg sits back down at his desk and begins deciphering the scrolls.

*

DeMynn sits at his desk examining an ancient manuscript. The sun begins to climb into the sky and the city streets below begin to awaken. A knock at the door breaks his concentration.

"Enter."

"Excuse me, Mr. DeMynn, but I have to tell you something," the man says apprehensively.

"Bad news, I presume," DeMynn says, staring at the man.

"Yes, sir," the man mumbles. Beads of sweat begin to form at his hairline.

"What is it?"

"The truck and the warehouse blew up last night and burned to the ground," he says nervously. One of the beads of sweat rolls down his forehead.

DeMynn leans back into the chair. He stares at the manuscript on his desk.

"There was nothing we could do, Mr. DeMynn," the man says, with a defensive tone.

DeMynn looks up at the man with a slight grin. "So tell me, Mr. Jenkins, how did I lose forty million dollars worth of merchandise?"

"This big black thing came . . . "

"I know the story," DeMynn interrupts. He leans forward, rests his elbows on the desk and locks his hands together in front of his face. He stares at the large diamond ring on his finger. "Any problems with the authorities?" he asks in a calm tone.

"No, they were ours."

DeMynn looks up from his hands and stares at the man. "Have you seen the new shark exhibit?" he asks, grinning.

"No, sir," Mr. Jenkins answers with a puzzled expression.

"I must show it to you sometime soon," DeMynn says, smiling. "We'll invite all your coworkers. We'll make a day of it."

Mr. Jenkins stands with a confused grin on his face.

"Good-bye, Mr. Jenkins," DeMynn says, spinning his chair around to face the large office window. He hears the door quietly close as he stares out into the city. "I know who you are," he whispers coldly.

Chapter 46

James and Derrick sit at a table tucked away in the corner of a restaurant. Men equipped with ear receivers, which lead to transmitters hidden in their coats, patrol the restaurant area. The crowd begins to grow as the workday ends.

"Thanks, James, for hiding Jane. She was freaked out over the death threat," Derrick says appreciatively.

"No problem. She'll be safe while my guys finish securing the house."

"Did you see the newscast?"

"Yeah, I did," James says, smirking.

"What did you think?"

James smiles. "You came across like," he hesitates for a moment, "like a religious nut."

"Good," Derrick says, smiling. "I wouldn't want to be misunderstood."

"You have the whole world talking."

"There's a special report coming on tonight. A committee was assembled in an attempt to interpret the prophecy."

"They'll come up with something crazier than the speech itself," James says jokingly.

People begin to steadily enter the bar, looking for their happy hour-fix. One at a time they enter through the door, passing Secret Service agents that are waving metal detectors around them. A man sits on a stool at the end of the bar. He loosens his tie, pulls off his glasses, and begins to rub his eyes. He appears to have had a long day at work. He lights a cigarette as a strong drink is handed to him. He watches the crowd walk by behind him in the mirror. A couple of drinks later, he pushes away from the bar and approaches a man with an ear receiver and asks him something. The Secret Service agent points the man in the general direction of the restrooms. The man begins walking toward the restrooms. He enters the men's room, passing a janitor that is on his way out. He steps into one of the stalls. He locks the door and pulls his wallet out. He stares at a photograph of his family. He turns and lifts the lid off the back of the toilet. He sticks his hand into the water and retrieves a gun that is sealed in a plastic bag. He begins walking back to the bar but unexpectedly makes a quick turn toward the table where James and Derrick are sitting. He swiftly maneuvers through the tables. Two

Secret Service agents race toward the man. The man is a few
yards away, directly in front of their table. James stands
to approach the intruder. The man drops the pen and paper
he was carrying to the floor. He reaches into his jacket
and pulls out a gun. More Secret Service agents close in
on the gunman. The man carefully takes aim at Derrick's
heart as the Secret Service agents rush at him. James
quickly positions himself between the gunman and Derrick as
he reaches for his gun in his holster. The man fires off a
round. Heads turn, others duck from fear. The crowd begins
to move in a chaotic manner. Screams and breaking glass
fill the air. The bullet cuts through the smokey atmosphere
as sparks and gunpowder smoke exit the barrel of the
intruder's pistol. The bullet's path ends in James'
shoulder, shattering his collarbone and ripping a hole
through the back of his shoulder. The blood splatters onto
the wall and Derrick. James' lower back rests against the
table, preventing him from falling. He pulls his weapon out
and fires off two rounds into the intruder's chest. The
Secret Service agents tackle the bloodstained gunman, but he
squeezes the trigger as he falls to the floor. The bullet
slices through the air and pierces James' body. The bullet
smashes his ribcage and punctures the lower part of his lung
before exiting from the side of his body, ending its
destruction in the bloodstained wall. James lies on his
back across the table. The white tablecloth becomes soaked
with a dark red shade and small puddles of blood begin to
form beneath the table.
   "He's dead," a Secret Service agent says quietly,
leaning over the gunman.
   Derrick presses blood-soaked napkins against James'
bullet wounds. He stares painfully, in shock, as he waits
for help to arrive.

*

   "We interrupt our regular broadcast to bring you this
special report. Good evening, I'm Kathy Webster live at the
United Nations Building. We are about to hear from a
council committee that was assembled to decipher and
interpret Senator Moore's speech. It appears Walter Turner,
a professor of theology, has reached the platform. We would
also like to welcome the thirty-two other countries tuned in
to the broadcast this evening. The remainder of the
committee has joined Professor Turner on the platform.
Susan Anderson, a climatologist, and Timothy Brandon, an

astronomer, are seated to the right. Scientists Gary Tompton of Heidelberg University and Ronald Doth of France are seated to the left. Directly behind Professor Turner is Michael Isatal of Jerusalem's Hebrew University. The group has been behind closed doors for days. They announced the conference late last night."

"May I have your attention please," Professor Turner says, attempting to quiet the large audience in the conference room. "If the prophecy is reality, we believe it will begin the first Friday after the first full moon after the Jewish Passover, following the spring equinox. We believe April eleventh at twelve midnight Israeli time will be the precise starting time, if it begins at all," Turner explains skeptically.

"How did you come to this conclusion?" a reporter asks.

"We believe Senator Moore's statement about one death and one birth being witnessed parallels the crucifixion and the resurrection of Jesus Christ. We believe it will follow the oldest known tradition of this custom: the Eastern Orthodox practice of calculating the date of Easter," Turner explains.

"What about the no birth and no death in the universe prediction?" another reporter asks.

Professor Turner stands for a moment, staring out at the crowd. Reluctantly, he says, "We assume that Senator Moore means precisely what he states."

The crowd begins to murmur, and the sound of equipment moving fills the air.

"Are you saying that nothing in the universe is going to die or be born during Easter?" the reporter asks dubiously.

"Yes, we believe that is what Senator Moore means by that particular statement," Turner answers quietly.

The murmur becomes louder and the media people seem entertained by the thought.

"How will we know?" a reporter inquires with a smile.

"We have established an information-gathering center in Washington, D.C.," Turner explains. "Every hospital in the United States is connected to the computer system. If there is a death or a birth in the United States, we will be informed through the computer immediately. Thirty-two countries around the world will also participate in the information-gathering process. They will be linked directly to our computers. Thank you and goodnight," Turner says, quickly turning and leaving. The rest of the committee follows him.

"Weirdest thing I ever heard," one reporter says to the other.

"Yeah, it's weirder than the speech itself."

"Senator screwed up pretty damned bad," the reporter says, shaking her head.

"I liked him, too."

"I can see the headlines now, 'World Keeps Dying, Along With Moore's Presidency,'" she says, smiling.

"What if it happens?" one of the reporters asks, grinning. "'World Stands Still For God's Man;'" the reporter suggests.

"Yeah, I like that. How about, 'No Death, No Birth, No Malefic.'" The reporters continue back and forth with potential headlines as they walk through the parking lot to their cars.

*

"We interrupt our regular broadcast for this special news break. An assassination attempt on Senator Moore has left one man dead and another in critical condition. Senator Derrick Moore and homicide detective, James Rood, the senator's brother-in-law, were having dinner at Hogates Restaurant on the waterfront. Witnesses say that an unidentified man approached the senator's table with a gun. Four shots were reportedly fired. Witnesses state that Detective Rood stepped in between the gunman and Senator Moore, leaving the detective in critical condition. However, Detective Rood was able to draw his weapon and return fire. The gunman was pronounced dead on the scene. The senator did not sustain any injuries. This makes the second attempt on the senator's life."

DeMynn stares at the television screen with a satisfied expression. He presses a small button on the armrest of the chair and the television screen becomes black. He spins his chair around to face the large window behind him.

"You are quite good at concealing your presence," DeMynn says, noticing a figure in the dark.

"Thank you," the figure says, stepping out of the shadows.

The city lights filter through the horizonal blinds, outlining the figure.

"I thought you were from the Doubting Thomas era, not the Peeping Tom generation," DeMynn says with a grin.

The figure's eyes peer out from the dark silhouette at DeMynn.

"What can I do for you?" DeMynn asks, walking over to the chessboard. "Or are you here to give me a lecture on tonight's activities?"

"No," the figure says quietly.

"No lecture, no retaliation, no threats?" DeMynn asks, surprised.

"Why would I?" the figure inquires from the dark.

"I suspect you do not watch the news," DeMynn says, standing over the chessboard. He traps the clear queen with one of his pieces.

"Do you believe you had something to do with what occurred this evening?" the figure asks.

"I had everything to do with what took place tonight," DeMynn says coldly, turning around.

"You can believe that if you like."

DeMynn stares at the figure inquiringly. His eyebrows pull down, contemplating a thought.

"Your plan was merely a part of a grander plan," the figure explains.

"I don't believe you," DeMynn says with a suspicious tone.

"I do not require you to believe me," the figure says.

DeMynn begins to walk about the room. "He used me," he says, aggravated. He stands in front of the fireplace, staring into the flames. The flames ascend higher into the chimney, and the coals burn hotter in his presence. "But why?" he asks himself quietly.

"Only He comprehends His plan," the figure says. "But be assured, it is a notice to you."

"What are you talking about?"

"It is a reminder," the figure says, staring from the dark. "Remember who you are. You may be the most intelligent creature in this world, but you will eternally be second in the universe," the figure says candidly.

DeMynn stares intensely into the eyes of the figure. The flames begin to descend behind him. A piece of blistering coal pops out onto the floor beside DeMynn's feet. He squats down and stares at the orange glowing coal in front of him. He reaches out with his index finger and thumb and carefully picks up the golf ball-size piece of coal. He turns the scalding coal with his fingers in front of his face like a diamond cutter examining a precious stone.

"I know who you are," DeMynn says quietly, staring at

the radiating piece of coal. "You belong to me, soldier boy," he says sinisterly.

"Not anymore," the figure says with insecurity in his voice.

A blinding white flash of light bursts into the mind of the figure, followed by a memory. A hammer slamming down onto the head of a spike and blood splattering into the air flash through the figure's mind. Another white flash erases the memory.

DeMynn continues to stare at the orange glow of the burning coal. He allows the piece of coal to fall into his palm. His fingers draw together into a fist. His fist glows as if it were the piece of coal itself. The burning glow begins to dim and his fist returns to its customary color. He opens his hand, revealing a gray ash in his palm. He draws his hand close to his face and blows the ash into the air. He stands and wipes his hand clean. "Shall we test that theory?" DeMynn asks, coldly staring at the figure. An ancient hammer appears in his hand. He grins wickedly as a spike appears in the other hand. "Look familiar?" he asks scornfully.

"What are you doing?" the figure asks apprehensively.

"It wasn't a very kind day for either one of us, was it?" DeMynn asks, grinning.

"I do not belong to you," the figure says in a weak tone.

DeMynn begins to rap the head of the spike with the hammer. "Does this disturb you?" he asks sarcastically. "If it does, I'll be delighted to stop."

The figure's eyes stare painfully out from the dark bandages around his face.

DeMynn's expression becomes grim and evil. "How does it feel to carry the blood of God on your hands for two thousand years?" he asks chidingly.

A white flash explodes in the figure's mind. He stares down at his hands. They're covered with blood. The figure stands over a man with spikes nailed through his wrists and feet. The man stares up at him with forgiveness in his eyes. A white flash brings the figure back to the present. His head hangs down and he closes his eyes tightly. "Dear Lord, help me," he pleads.

"Step forward and kneel before me," DeMynn demands, sending a shiver through the figure's soul and a tremble beneath his feet.

The figure lifts his head to look at DeMynn, but an outline of another figure in the shadows of the room draws his attention. DeMynn quickly glances across the room. A man wearing a dark robelike garment with a beard and hair resting on his shoulders stands silent and motionless in the shadows. The crackling of wood in the fireplace provides the only sound. The figure and DeMynn stare at the man. The tapping of raindrops on the window has joined the crackling of the wood. The flames burn brighter behind DeMynn, but the yellowish glow of the fire stops before the man's sandals. DeMynn tilts his head slightly to obtain a better view. A thunderclap rumbles in the distance and a burst of lightning follows. The man's identity is revealed to DeMynn by the strobelike flickering of the lightning.

"Get him out of my sight," DeMynn says demandingly to the man.

DeMynn glances over to the figure, but he has vanished. He looks over to the man, but He also has disappeared. He stares into the flames in the fireplace. A piece of burning coal pops out before his feet. He crushes it beneath his shoe.

Chapter 47

"I hate hospitals. I hate the way they smell, the sanitized atmosphere," Mr. Dean says, staring down at his hands. "No matter how clean or pure, there's that strong image of death around every corner, on every floor, in every room. Every bed is stained with pain, so much pain," he says fearfully.

"He's going to be fine, Mr. Dean. He will make it through," Greg says with a determined stare.

Greg and Mr. Dean have been sitting in the waiting area, staring at the swinging doors of the operating room for hours, battling grave thoughts from entering their minds. Time in a waiting room can strengthen a person or destroy him. The OR doors swing open and a man wearing a white smock covered in blood walks out. It's the doctor, and he appears to have been fighting with the Angel of Death himself. He slowly approaches the two men. His facial expression and a slight shaking of his head suggest bad news.

"What's going on, doc?" Mr. Dean asks impatiently.

"He's in a coma," the doctor says quietly.

Greg sits down on the sofa, and Mr. Dean walks over to the window and stares out into the dark.

*

"James, listen to me. You have to hold on," Derrick says desperately, leaning against the bed holding James' hand. "You can't go out like this," he says, laying his head down on the bed. "Dear Lord, please don't take him now. I need him," Derrick prays. He lifts his head and stares at James and at the half dozen tubes entering his body. The monitors hum and beep, and James continues to lie motionless in this world.

"Hey, J.R."

"Joe?" James asks, turning around.

"How are you doing, old buddy?" Joe asks joyfully.

"Great, I think," James answers, examining his own body.

"Good. Let's take a walk."

"Where are we going?"

"To see someone," Joe says.

James realizes they are walking along a beach. "What's going on, Joe?" he asks curiously, looking around.

The waves quietly break onto the sand, and the water gently washes around their feet.

"You were shot, and you fell into a coma," Joe says casually.

"Am I going to die?"

"I don't know," Joe answers.

They continue to walk along the wet sand. The sun rests on the horizon, radiating an orange glow, and a warm breeze blows softly across the shore.

"I was told to meet you and take you to a specific place," Joe says.

"Who told you to meet me?" James asks, looking around inquisitively.

"God," Joe says, smiling.

James stops walking, but Joe walks ahead a few feet before realizing that James has stopped.

"Is there something wrong?" Joe asks, turning around.

"Am I in heaven?" James asks quietly.

Joe smiles as the sound of surf begins to fade.

"I am going to die?" James asks with a glance.

"I don't know, James."

"Then, why am I here?"

"We'll find out, if we ever get there," Joe says jokingly. He begins walking ahead. "At this pace, I'll miss the Second Coming," he mumbles to himself.

The beach has transformed into a valley surrounded by majestic snowcapped mountains. They begin walking through a beautiful green field. The lush grass feels like a soft sponge beneath their feet. The air is filled with the abundance of wildlife sounds.

"Were you at the ranch?" James asks.

"Yes, I was," Joe answers, grinning.

"Why?"

"To help you."

"Help me blow up a building?" James inquires with a stare.

"That's right."

"God let you do that?"

"Who do you think sent me?" Joe asks, smiling.

They come to a glorious garden. Every tree and plant radiates its perfection. The sound of birds singing and the rhythmic flow of waterfalls creates a peaceful atmosphere. Thousands of flowers thicken the air with fragrances. The mixture of aromas provides a scent never encountered in the worldly dominion since the beginning of time. Creatures that human eyes have never seen roam the garden.

"Am I meeting God?" James asks, glancing around the garden.

"I don't know."

"You don't know much, Joe."

"I know who I am."

"What does that mean?" James asks, a little irritated.

"Why do you conceal your true heart?" Joe asks directly.

"What?"

"Let go of your life. I know you believe, but you continue to push it down deep into your soul. Let go and become the righteousness of justice," Joe says urgently.

The winds begin to gust through the trees in the garden. The trees sway and rustle before coming to a quiet rest. A presence is felt in the garden.

"Be still, and know that I am God," a voice says with divine might. The voice permeates the garden with a comforting assurance.

A peacefulness falls over the garden.

James glances around the garden, waiting for something to happen. "Why am I here?" he asks firmly but respectfully.

A path develops across from him. A figure wearing a brilliant white robe begins walking toward them. James and Joe watch the luminous figure draw near. The figure is a woman, and she is carrying something. James recognizes her. His eyes begin to tear and his throat constricts.

"Hello, James," the woman says softly.

James stares as tears trickle down his cheek.

"Hello, Daddy," the small child says from Faith's arms.

"James, I'd like you to meet our son," Faith says joyfully.

James' eyes well with tears as the child reaches out for him. They stare at one another for a moment before the child leans forward and hugs him. His son kisses him on the cheek. "I love you, Daddy," he says sweetly.

"I love you, too," James says, glancing up inquisitively at Faith.

"James," she answers.

James smiles slightly. "I love you, too, James," he says, touching the child's cheek.

Faith takes the child and gently lays her hand on James' cheek. "I love you," she says.

"I love you, too, Faith."

"Now you know the truth," she says, backing away.

"Finish what you have started. We will be waiting for you," she says peacefully.

Her face glows with peace and contentment as the path closes in behind her.

Chapter 48

"Welcome to News Seven, I'm Bradley Hunt. Our top story tonight, Senator Moore's prophecy. It officially started five hours ago in Israel. We are moments away from the beginning of Senator Moore's "no death, no birth" prediction here in the States. We have received no data concerning the Middle East from the council committee at the information-gathering headquarters. Let us go live to Israel where News Seven's Thomas Weathers has been stationed the last twenty-eight hours."

The newscast switches to a live broadcast from Israel, near Jerusalem.

"Thanks, Brad. It's a little after five a.m. here, and we are already beginning to witness strange occurrences. Thirty-eight farmers and livestock owners in the surrounding areas have reported all of their livestock missing. With every passing minute, a new report is registered. As for the hospitals, there have been no births nor has there been a single death reported in the last five hours. But the locals here, right outside of Jerusalem, say it isn't rare for a day to pass without a birth or a death in the region."

"How do the people there feel about the prophecy?" the anchorman asks from the studio.

"The people here are taking the prophecy very seriously and are being more than cooperative," the field reporter says. "Many of the townspeople that I have spoken to are convinced that the prophecy will come true. I have discovered that many strange events have taken place throughout the Middle East over the last seven months. I was told that burning hail fell from the sky in the desert. It has also been said that an earthquake destroyed an archaeological site, splitting open an ancient tomb, where the people believe an Angel of Death was released."

The newscast switches back to the studio in Washington, D.C.

"We have received a report from the council committee that there will be a twenty-four-hour waiting period before information will be released concerning the prophecy. We will keep you updated."

*

"Hey, Ron," Gary says, entering the information-gathering headquarters.

"How was dinner, Gary?" Ron asks, looking up from his book.

"Good, here's your sub. What's up with the Middle East?" Gary asks eagerly.

"Check out the prints," Ron says casually, preparing his meal.

Gary reaches down and lifts an armful of computer printouts. He rips the last few sections off and glances through them. "This is unbelievable," Gary says, sliding the papers through his fingers. "It's all blank," he says, glancing at Ron.

"That's seventeen countries," Ron mumbles, mayonnaise dripping onto his chin. "And in fifteen minutes we'll be joining them," he says, smiling.

"I cannot believe no one has been born or has died in nearly seven hours over there," Gary says suspiciously. "We're talking over two billion people."

"You want to check the computer again?" Ron asks, grinning.

"I don't trust the link between our computers and theirs. We'll see what happens in this country before I get too excited," Gary says skeptically.

*

"Elsewhere in the news, the beef industry has reached its sixth day of the strike, driving beef prices to an all-time high. Both sides appear far from a resolution. The beef industry took its second major blow yesterday, when test results revealed a cattle disease that may be hazardous to human health, bringing all cattle distribution to a halt internationally. The poultry industry has also been affected by the virus. The latest report puts the financial losses in the billions," the anchorman reports, as a piece of paper is slipped in front of him. "This just in. Inspection officials at the USDA fear that the virus has spread to all livestock. An international alert has been put into effect. All distribution of meat products is to stop immediately," the anchorman announces with urgency.

*

"Thirty seconds," Ron says, staring at the clock.

All the members of the council committee stand eagerly watching the computer screens. There are eighteen computers monitoring every birth and death in the United States. The screens are entirely full of births and deaths. The computers' screens continue registering with every passing second. Computers one through six attract the committee's complete attention. They are the computers observing the East Coast, the first to experience the senator's prediction. Monitors one through three register every birth on the east coast, and four through six track every death pronouncement.

"Look at all those people dying as we sit here," Gary says, amazed.

"Thousands of babies were born as you spoke that sentence," Michael says.

"Showtime," Ron says, smiling.

The births and deaths continue to register after midnight. The computers are informed minutes after a birth or death has occurred.

"Time?" Professor Turner asks earnestly.

"One minute, thirty-two," Ron says.

The committee members stare at the screens, watching the hundreds of names, dates, and times scroll down them.

"I knew this was bullshit," Gary says, shaking his head arrogantly.

"Patience, Gary," Michael says, grinning. "Let the computers catch up."

"Time?" Turner asks.

"Two minutes, two seconds."

"We wasted the taxpayers a lot of money," Gary says, balling up a piece of paper and shooting it into the trashcan.

As the balled-up paper bounces off the rim of the trashcan and hits the floor, monitors one and four become blank.

"Check it," Professor Turner says insistently.

"It's functioning properly," Gary says from the keyboard.

Monitors two and five run out of names and display blank blue screens.

"The computer is working!" one of the committee members yells from behind the large computer board.

The screens of numbers three and six have joined the others and the international monitors. The members of the committee stand staring speechlessly at six blank monitor screens.

*

Washington, D.C., General Hospital 1:00 a.m.

"What in God's name is keeping this guy alive?" the doctor says quietly.

The nurse glances at the clock hanging on the emergency room wall. "It's after midnight," she says.

The rest of the medical personnel look over at the clock.

The doctor takes a quick glance and continues to dislodge bullets from a man's chest. "Well then," he says, smiling under his mask, "I guess it's his lucky day."

*

Southern California, The Fishery Enterprise 7:00 p.m.

"You guys are about two hours early, aren't you?" the supervisor says with a displeased expression.

The captain of the charter boats stares at him, perplexed. "We were out there for ten hours and we didn't catch a single thing, and I'm talking all twenty-two boats," he says.

"What?"

"Didn't you hear what I said, not a thing," the captain exclaims. "Then this crazy storm came out of nowhere and wiped out two of our charters," he says, removing his hat and scratching his head.

"This is bullshit!" the supervisor says, aggravated.

"You think so?" the captain says seriously. "One of my crew showed me this article in the paper about that guy Moore saying nothing in the universe is going to die or be born," he says, handing the article to the supervisor. "It's supposed to be a sign from God. I've been in this business for forty-one years, and I've never seen the likes of today," he says, turning to leave. "It was time to get off the water."

"Where the hell are you going?" the supervisor yells.

"I'll see you in a couple of days," the captain says, waving without turning around.

*

Arizona, Science Center Laboratories

"Larry, come over here for a second," Wayne says, motioning with his hand excitedly while he looks in a microscope.

Scientist Wayne Bowen is the head researcher on the West Coast for the United States government. He was confidentially advised to observe the prophecy.

"What's up?" Larry asks.

"Take a look," Wayne says, smiling.

Larry leans down and places his eye against the microscope. "Yeah, so, it's a freshly cut piece of grass," he says, unimpressed.

"I cut it twenty hours ago," Wayne says earnestly.

Larry stares for a moment, contemplating what he just heard. He quickly sits down and gazes into the microscope again. "There's no deterioration," he says with astonishment.

"I know," Wayne says, grinning.

Larry stands and stares with a confused look on his face. "It's not decomposing," he says, insinuating there must be a mistake.

"See that rat over there in the cage?" Wayne asks. "I gave it enough poison to put an elephant to sleep forever over ten hours ago."

Both stand speechless, staring at the rat moving about the cage, healthy and unaffected.

Chapter 49

The information-gathering headquarters

"What the hell is going on?" Gary asks, staring at the blank computer printouts.

"It appears that no one is being born and no one is dying in the world at the moment," Ron says, grinning sarcastically.

"This is impossible!" Professor Turner declares.

"There's nothing wrong with the equipment," Michael objects.

"There must be a malfunction somewhere," Gary says.

"The only malfunction is in your heart and soul," Ron mumbles, smiling.

"What?" Gary snaps.

"Knock it off," Professor Turner says. "Susan, Timothy, what do you think?" he asks.

"It seems that something extraordinary is happening," Susan says, astonished. "But I can't officially commit to having proof that nothing in the universe has died or been born."

"If we come out with a report declaring that the prophecy has been fulfilled and some sort of evidence surfaces conflicting with our report, we will look like fools," Timothy warns.

"Our reputations are on the line," Susan adds.

"They'll believe whatever we tell them to believe," Gary says with an arrogant tone.

"I can't believe you people. We have the most advanced equipment in the world telling us that it's happening, but you stand here denying the facts that are right in front of your faces," Michael says, with an annoyed expression.

Professor Turner rubs his eyes and sits down. "We'll check the system again and go from there," he says in a tired and frustrated voice.

"I have a better idea," Ron says, smiling and picking up the telephone. "Let's call all the hospitals in the United States."

*

The sun breaks over the Blue Ridge Mountains of West Virginia. The golden rays streak through the evergreens and the morning mist. The dew sparkles and the cool ground begins to warm. A man rises from his bed and throws on a shabby coat. He stands on a ragged porch, stretching his arms and yawning. He jerks an ax out of a log. The man walks around to the side of the house with the ax thrown over his shoulder. He approaches a broken-down chickenhouse. He disappears into the chicken coop and quickly comes out with a chicken in his grasp. He holds the chicken down on a tree stump with one of his feet. He lifts the ax over his head into a striking position. The ax begins falling quickly, gaining speed as it nears the chicken's neck. Suddenly, the head of the ax shatters into hundreds of pieces. The man stumbles backward as the chicken scurries back to the coop. He stares mystified at the hundreds of fragments of what was once the head of the ax. He lifts the handle of the ax to his face and shakes his head with astonishment.

*

The waiting room at the hospital has become crowded. The media caught wind of Derrick's presence at the hospital. Greg and Mr. Dean walk out of James' room and attempt to push through the waiting area.

"Hey, do you know the senator?" the reporter asks.

Mr. Dean turns and sees a young, ambitious reporter standing in his face. "Don't you have some pencils to sharpen?" he asks.

"Who are you?" the reporter asks impudently.

"None of your business," Mr. Dean says, turning away.

"Hey, how about you? Do you know the senator?"

"Beat it, kid. Leave the professor alone," Mr. Dean tells him.

"Professor of what?" the reporter asks.

"What is it that you want, young man?" Greg asks quietly.

"What's going on? I need to write a story."

"Have you heard about the senator's prophecy?" Greg asks.

"Yeah," the reporter says, disinterest in his voice.

"It is being fulfilled," Greg says softly.

"That's your story," Mr. Dean says, grinning from behind Greg.

*

"It's time to go back, James," Joe says.

"Back where?"

"Back," Joe says obviously.

"I don't want to go back."

"You have unfinished business," Joe says with importance in his tone.

James stops walking along the shore. He quietly stares at the whitecaps of the breaking waves. "Is Hope here?" he asks.

Joe nods his head with a smile.

They begin walking again. After a few moments Joe disappears, but James doesn't notice. He has fallen into a daydream.

"Hold on to him, James."

"I got him, Dad."

"He's a big one, son."

"Wow! Look at him."

"He's a beauty," James' father says, leaning over the side of the boat and sticking his thumb into the bass' mouth. "He's got some weight on him."

"Let me hold him," James says joyfully.

"He's an easy three pounder."

"Wow! He's heavy!"

"I'm very proud of you, James. I want you to know that."

The fish jerks out of James' hand and falls harmlessly into the sparkling lake. James and his father begin to laugh, watching the ripples on the surface of the lake.

Slowly the daydream slips away into another one.

"James, honey, come here for a second," James' mother says softly.

James sits in a chair with his feet dangling above the floor.

"I have to tell you something," she says, hesitating.

"What is it, Mom?" James asks, noticing tears in his mother's eyes. "Are you all right?" he asks, concerned.

"Remember when Grandma was telling you about heaven?" she asks.

James nods his head.

His mother reaches out for his hand. "Well, honey," she says as the tears begin to well in her eyes, "Your daddy has gone to heaven."

James' eyes begin to water. "When is he coming back?" he asks.

"He's not coming back, honey," she says softly.

He lowers his head to stare at the wooden floor.

"One day we will see him again, when we go to heaven," she says comfortingly.

"When can we go?" he asks painfully.

"When we are finished doing God's work here on earth," she says, smiling.

As James continues to walk along the shore, his mind flashes to his father's funeral. He remembers staring at a large, closed casket. There were numerous men in uniforms standing behind him. His mother stood by his side crying, held by two of his aunts. The sound of sorrow filled the room. The room felt dark and dismal, despite the large accumulation of flowers. He remembers stepping out of the funeral home into the sunshine. His eyes slowly adjusted to the bright day. The warmth of the sun on his face gave him a feeling of peace. The late-summer breeze felt as if it were blowing through him, easing his mind from the pounding questions in his head. As his eyes began to fully adjust, he saw his grandmother. He ran to her and hugged her tightly. In her arms, he felt warm and secure. He looked up at her smiling face.

"Everything is going to be fine, James," she said lovingly.

Chapter 50

"Rejoice, rejoice!" an old man with a long gray beard yells. He stands on the street corner, waving his arms with a grin. "The resurrection of the world is upon us!" he exclaims.

People pass quickly, attempting to ignore the old man.

"A spiritually dead world will be alive again," the old man says to a young couple passing by on the sidewalk. "Rejoice, rejoice, the old, evil world is dying!"

A few blocks away around the corner, the dinner crowd slowly begins to retire. A few romantic couples remain in the corners of a restaurant. The flickering candlelight fills the room. The fragrance of fresh flowers permeates the air along with the aroma of Italian meals. An unlikely couple sits in one of the darker corners of the restaurant.

"I must say. I'm very disappointed."

"I'm sorry, Mr. DeMynn," the man says, pulling a cigarette out of a fresh pack. "They want nothing to do with it."

The cigarette mysteriously lights before he ignites his lighter. The man stares at the cigarette in his hand oddly.

"So, Ronald and Michael won't cooperate," DeMynn says, running his finger around the rim of the wineglass.

The shimmering candlelight reflects in DeMynn's eyes. The circling of his finger on the wineglass creates a musical pitch. The sound slowly transforms into a quiet symphony.

"It was a rudimentary plan," DeMynn says, dissatisfied.

"Yes, but I can't alter the prophecy report without the agreement of the entire committee," the man says nervously.

"They refused the money?" DeMynn asks, amazed. "Unique occurrence for these times."

"We can't let the report go out as is," the man says, concerned.

"Yes, that would put a damper on my plans," DeMynn says, pulling his finger away from the rim of the wineglass.

The music pauses as he takes a sip of wine. He sets the glass on the table and interlocks his hands under his chin.

"And, of course, it will do wonders for your book," DeMynn says sarcastically. "What was the name of your book again?" he asks coldly.

The man glances down at the table. "'Who Made Whom?'" he says quietly.

"That's right. Who made whom?" DeMynn asks, smiling. "Did God make man, or did man make God?" he asks with an amused expression. "It appears I squandered a great deal of money publishing your book, Professor Turner," he says, staring at him coldly.

"If you talk to them, maybe they'll change their minds," Professor Turner says desperately.

"It is not their minds that need to be changed," DeMynn says.

"What can we do?"

DeMynn stares intensely into Turner's eyes. "Do Mr. Doth and Mr. Isatal have families?" he asks grimly.

Chapter 51

"Good morning, I'm Coral Jones. Welcome to 'Eye on America'. We continue to wait for the council committee to present the official report on Senator Moore's prophecy. No word has left the information-gathering building. Rumors continue to spread across the world via the Internet. We have been surveying the Internet, and the latest poll of sixty million computer owners suggests that a phenomenal occurrence has transpired over the last three days. Not one account of a birth or a death has been reported. Of course, that is unofficial. We have also queried seventy-nine hospitals across the country. The results are identical to the Internet survey. There have been no births, nor have there been any deaths in the last three days. That also is unofficial," the newsperson says, smiling sarcastically. "We will update you as any new information arrives. Please stay tuned."

*

The hospital room hums with monitors. The equipment surrounding James' bed blinks a dull white flash in the darkness. The blinds allow the city lights to filter through the window, casting streaks across the room. A woman wearing a white uniform enters the room. She examines the monitors and checks a chart. The nurse walks across the room to inspect a screen. James' eyes flicker beneath his eyelids. His fingers begin to twitch. Suddenly his eyes open. He stares at the ceiling, collecting his thoughts. His mind flashes back to the restaurant. He realizes he was shot, but he can't recall what happened to Derrick. Movement across the room draws his attention. He focuses on an outline of a figure, a figure of a woman. She approaches James and sits beside him on the bed. He thinks to himself that she is beautiful. She has straight, long black hair, light green eyes, and the golden tan complexion of a Native American. James stares at her green eyes as the feeling returns to his body. She smiles down at him. Her smile complements her beauty. She crosses her legs, and the uniform tightens around her thighs. She runs her long fingernails down the center of his chest. She uses her index finger to make circles around his bullet wounds.

"Personally, I have never been shot, but it appears to be quite painful," the nurse says.

James' eyebrows pull down to a vengeful stare. The voice coming from the woman reveals that the nurse is actually DeMynn.

"Was it painful, James?" DeMynn asks, grinning.

James continues to stare intensely. His hands are clenched into fists.

"Well, I'll see you around, James. I just wanted to see how you were doing, and to welcome you back," DeMynn says, standing and adjusting his uniform. He walks out of the room singing, "If I Was Your Girlfriend" by Prince.

*

"Where have you been?" the old chiseler asks, lighting candles.

The figure quietly stares at the marble frieze.

"Hey, are you all right?" the old man asks, preparing his polishing cloth. "You're awful quiet, more than usual anyhow," he says, staring up at him.

The figure stands tightly wrapped in his trench coat, staring at the frieze. He removes one of his gloves, revealing his hand. The figure's hand is glossy black with stars floating within it. He reaches out and touches the marble frieze. He slowly runs his hand across the smoothly polished, sculptured figures. His hand caresses the deep chiseled curves and design of the work. The candles reflect their golden glow onto his hand. The figure's hand searchingly slides along the cool marble frieze. His hand stops suddenly beneath Jesus Christ. He stares painfully as he slowly draws his hand back to his side.

"You have done well," the figure says in a quiet voice. "It is more beautiful than I imagined," he says, gazing at the frieze.

"Thank you. You're my number one fan," the old man says, smiling.

A breeze sweeps through the church, extinguishing the candles. The scent lingers in the air.

"What was that?" the old man asks, fumbling through his pockets, searching for matches.

"This shall be the last time we will speak," the figure says softly.

The old man strikes a match. "Why?" he asks with disappointment in his voice.

"The time is at hand," the figure says.

"What does that mean? Ouch!" he says, throwing the match on the ground.

"My time here is ending."

All the candles in the church ignite once more.

"Where are you going?" the old man asks.

The figure lowers his head. He stares at the marble floor. "I do not know," he says.

"You did what you were supposed to do, didn't you?"

"I obeyed His commands faithfully," the figure says quietly.

"Then, you should be OK," the old man says with optimism.

"I sense incompleteness."

"I'm sure you're going to be fine."

"Your faith is strong."

"Your faith should be strong, too," the old man says. "You, of all people."

"Yes," the figure says, glancing down at him, "but I know."

"Know what?"

"What it is like to be away from His presence," the figure says with a distant stare.

An explosion of blinding white light consumes the mind of the figure, sending him back to the summit of a hill. He stands staring at a man hanging from a wooden cross. The sky is dark, and the ground is rumbling.

"Truly, this man was the Son of God," the figure says regretfully.

A second flash of light sends him to a different place. He is standing in front of a large wooden door. He knocks. Inside, an old man with long gray hair and a beard sits immersed in his work. "Enter," he says sternly.

The figure enters the dimly lit room. The only source of light is a single candle burning on the table in front of the old man. "Are you the one they call 'Paul'?" the figure asks in a desperate voice.

"I am."

The figure falls to his knees. "Please help me," he says, with tears filling his eyes.

Paul stands and hurries over to the figure. He kneels down on the dirt floor and places his hand on the figure's shoulder. "What happened?" he asks.

"I have done something unforgivable," the figure says, looking down.

"Ask the Lord for forgiveness, and He shall forgive," Paul says confidently.

"I cannot," the figure says faintly, staring downward.

"He forgives all that believe in Him," Paul says.

The figure looks up at Paul with tears and pain in his eyes. "I can't forgive myself," he says in anguish. The room begins to darken. Another brilliant white flash fills the figure's mind, returning him to the man hanging from the wooden cross. The figure stares up at the man.

The man peacefully gazes down from the cross at the figure. "Father, forgive them, for they do not know what they do," He says with a beseeching tone.

The memory begins to fade into darkness. Slowly the golden glow of the candles in the church begins coming back into focus. The figure stares at the marble frieze with glassy eyes.

"Hey, hey, are you all right?" the old chiseler asks.

The figure looks down at the old man. "Good-bye my friend," he says, beginning to glitter. He slowly fades away, leaving small particles sparkling in the air.

*

Malefic sits at his desk with papers spread out in front of him. The National Presidential Debate looms in the near future, and he is ardently preparing himself. The debate between himself and Derrick will be a crucial point in the presidential race. It will propel one of the two to the forefront, and Malefic is entirely aware of this fact.

Hours have passed and his eyelids begin to weigh heavy. He leans back into his chair, pushing a button on the armrest. The lights go out, leaving the small desk lamp as the sole source of light. He begins to doze off into an exhausted slumber.

"Malefic," a serene voice says from behind him.

"Oh, shit," he says, jerking forward and making a groaning sound. He spins his chair around, holding his stomach. His facial expression says what he can't. "What are you doing here?" he asks, aggravated.

The large silhouette stands wrapped in his trench coat in front of the window. His eyes pierce out from his dark face. "I must speak to you," he says quietly.

"Sure," Malefic says, shaking his head and rolling his eyes. "Can I get you some tea perhaps?" he asks sarcastically.

One of the studio lights hanging from the ceiling comes on and shines directly on the figure. He removes the hood and the trench coat from his body, allowing them to fall to the floor. The figure removes the black bandages from his face and body. The glossy, black surface of the figure's physique glitters under the light.

"What are you?" Malefic asks astoundingly.

"Your redemption," the figure whispers.

"I thought you were going to leave me alone?" Malefic says, irritated.

"DeMynn lied. It isn't too late for you," the figure says.

"You're both crazy," Malefic says with a wearied expression.

"You must see the truth," the figure says with urgency.

Malefic stares into the figure's body, seeing his reflection perfectly. He runs his fingers through his hair. "Why didn't you tell me my hair was a mess?" he says humorously.

"Look closer at yourself," the figure says with an intense stare.

"Yeah, so, I need some sleep," Malefic says, seeing the bags under his eyes.

The image of himself begins to distort and fade. A face of a young child appears. He looks to be six years of age. The child is playing in his parents' room. In the background through the hallway his mother sits in the kitchen on the telephone. His father is mowing the lawn. The little boy finds a small wooden box. He opens the box and discovers packets of white powder. He also finds a small mirror and a skinny glass tube. He pours one of the packets onto the mirror, spilling most of the drug on the carpet. The child holds the glass tube up to his nose and imitates his parents. Malefic's eyes expand into a painful stare. The drug shoots through the little boy's nostrils, burning a destructive path to the child's brain. A sudden jolt puts the little boy on his back. He stares at the ceiling, as tears trickle down the side of his face. His stomach rises and falls dramatically in short breaths. His heart races and his skin color becomes pale white. The child's stomach rises and falls for the last time. His eyes stare at the ceiling. Malefic stares with anguish on his face. The figure's body flashes a bright white light, causing Malefic to squint. Pictures begin to flash in the figure's body. One scene after the another appears in between bright flashes. First, a woman in a nightclub purchasing drugs. Next, two men standing in an alley; then a group of men standing in front of a warehouse appears. A dock scene follows. Finally, the chain of events ends at a building in a rain forest, a building Malefic recognizes immediately.

Malefic's head slumps. He begins to rub his eyes and the bridge of his nose. "It's not my fault," he says painfully. "I didn't kill him."

"No?" the figure asks, angered.

"No. It's not my project," Malefic says defensively.

"It is DeMynn's project. The two of you have become one and the same."

"I'm not like him."

"He lives through you, Malefic," the figure whispers.

Malefic stares down at his hands, rubbing them together as if he were attempting to cleanse them. "It's not my fault," he mumbles. Malefic lifts his head and discovers he is alone.

Chapter 52

"Hey, James, welcome back!" Derrick says, entering the hospital room.

"Are you all right?" James asks Derrick.

"Do you believe this guy?" Derrick asks, amazed. "He gets shot and he asks me if I'm all right."

Greg and Mr. Dean laugh as they maneuver over to the other side of the bed.

"You didn't get shot?" James asks.

"No, I didn't. Thanks to you," Derrick says appreciatively.

"So you think you're a big hero now," Mr. Dean says jokingly. "Jumping in the line of fire like that."

"I was trying to get out of the way," James says, grinning.

"How do you feel, James?" Greg asks.

"Good, better than I did before the shooting," he says, with a peaceful smile. "But I did have some strange dreams."

"Well, you're back now, Dorothy." Mr. Dean says, smiling.

"That's right, Auntie Em."

"I have a joke for you," Mr. Dean says with a slight grin. "A burglar breaks into this house. As he is sneaking around, he hears a voice that says, 'Jesus is watching you.' The burglar freezes and looks around, but he doesn't see nothing. He continues to sneak around the house. Then he hears the voice again saying, 'Jesus is watching you.' He stops and looks around again, but sees nothing. He walks through the house a little further and again he hears the voice saying, 'Jesus is watching you.' He looks in the corner of the room and sees a parrot in a cage. The burglar approaches the parrot and asks the bird if he said that. The parrot says, 'yes.' The burglar asks the parrot his name. The parrot says, 'Ernie.' The burglar smiles and asks what idiot would name his parrot Ernie? The parrot says, 'The same idiot that would name that Rottweiler over there Jesus,'" Mr. Dean says, beginning to laugh. "Here, I saved this for you," he says, throwing a newspaper on James' lap.

"What's this?" James asks, turning the paper around. The headline reads, 'Detective Rood Saves Senator Moore's Life.' "Do you think Oprah will call?" he asks, grinning sarcastically.

"Sure she will," Derrick says, with a doubtful expression.

James observes another headline. "What's going on with the prophecy?" he asks.

"The official report is being delayed by the council committee," Derrick says suspiciously.

James and Greg exchange glances, both knowing who is the cause of the delay.

"Regardless of the committee's postponement of the report, the world is slowly beginning to realize it is actually happening," Derrick says in a optimistic tone.

"What's this?" James asks, staring down at a small caption in the paper.

"The National Debate," Derrick says. "It's being held at the Convention Center."

"Who's Bert Wilkins?"

"Some big political talk-show host," Mr. Dean says, unimpressed.

"They're turning it into a circus," Derrick says with a daunted stare.

"They're setting up the stage to look like a late-night talk show," Mr. Dean says, shaking his head with disapproval.

James stares down at the newspaper for a moment, thinking about the security headache. "How many people?" he asks.

"Around two thousand," Derrick answers.

James and Greg glance at one another again. "Do you have to do this?" James asks.

"I have to," Derrick says, constrained.

"This should be your last public appearance before the election," James says with an insistent stare.

"I believe it would be for the best," Greg agrees.

"At least get into office before you let another psycho take a potshot at you," Mr. Dean says from across the room.

A woman in her late fifties enters the room. She has short gray hair, a healthy complexion, and stands no more than five feet tall. "All right, gentlemen, get out," she says jokingly.

"Hey, Grace, how are you this evening?" Mr. Dean asks, smiling.

"Fine, thank you. Now, get out," Grace says, motioning them out like children.

"James, I'd like you to meet your surgeon, Grace

Harper," Derrick says.

"Hello, and thank you," James says, smiling. He recognizes her voice. She had read to him while he was in a coma.

"Nice to meet you again, James," Grace says, smiling. "Maybe the conversations won't be so one-sided now."

"I don't know about that," Greg says. "He doesn't say a great deal when he's awake."

"All kidding aside, gentlemen, I need him to myself, and the rest won't hurt him," she says.

"We'll see you later, James."

Grace pulls his chart from the foot of the bed. "Looks like you're going to get out of here soon," she says cheerfully. "You made a remarkable recovery."

"Good," he says, throwing the newspaper on the chair.

"How do you like being a hero?" Grace asks.

"I don't," James says, glancing down at the bandages and tubes on his body. "Too painful."

"I'm sure," she says, checking the monitors. "You may be out of here as soon as tomorrow." The intercom in the room pages her. "I'll be back in a moment," she says, walking out of the room.

James reaches for the telephone. "Tony."

"Hey, buddy, how do you feel?" Tony asks.

"Good."

"Where are you?"

"The hospital."

"When are you getting out?" Tony asks, with anxiousness in his voice.

"Tomorrow, I hope. Do me a favor. I need the Evil Dog file out of my desk," James says urgently.

"Sure."

"Tonight," James tells him.

"Tonight?" Tony asks, as if he misunderstood.

"Tonight. Thanks, buddy," James says, hanging up the telephone.

*

A familiar scene takes place after the sun has set, and the cover of night blankets the city streets. Hundreds of thousands of dollars are exchanged in the darkness of the alleys. With every transaction, another soul falls deeper into bondage.

"I need some. You got it?" a wreck of a man in a business suit asks nervously.

"Take it easy, buddy. I got it right here," the dealer says with a calm grin.

The exchange is made. The buyer hurries away with his head tucked low in between his shoulders.

The dealer leans against the wall, counting his money. He hears a rustling sound. He looks down to the dark end of the alley. "Who's there?" he asks, gripping his gun stuffed in the front of his pants.

"How much?" a soothing voice asks.

"How much do you want?" the dealer asks casually.

"How much do you have?" the voice asks quietly.

"Listen man, I don't got time for games."

"This is no game," the voice says, deepening. "Five thousand dollars worth."

"Sure, buddy, whatever you want," the dealer says with a cynical tone.

"The money is beside the dumpster," the voice instructs.

The dealer begins walking over to the dumpster. His gun is by his side. He bends down and spreads the money out with the point of his gun. His eyes widen with disbelief. The dealer quickly gathers the five thousand dollars. He stands to examine it in the streetlight filtering down the alley. A dark figure appears behind the dealer.

The dealer smiles, discovering the money isn't counterfeit. "I'll be damned," he says, pleased.

"How true," the voice says, becoming raspy.

*

James sits in his room with the contents of the file spread across his bed. He leans over to retrieve the Bible from a table beside his bed. Grace enters the room.

"You were the one reading to me while I was in the coma," James says.

Grace smiles, standing at the foot of the bed with the chart.

"But I heard another voice," James says, confused. "A man's voice."

Grace reaches into her pocket. She pulls out Biblical audiotapes. She glances at the radio beside James' bed. She walks over and sets the tapes on the table. She looks at the crime-scene photographs on the bed. "Ugly business," she says quietly.

"It's amazing what we do to one another," James says.

"Yes, I know what you mean," she says, glancing down

at his wounds.

James flips through the Bible. "I want to thank you," he says with appreciation.

"For what?"

"You gave me an idea," James says, continuing to flip through the pages. "You randomly selected places in the book to read. You read the chapter number and passage number sometimes before you read a section."

"That's right."

"The tapes state the title of the sections," he says, pointing to the large letters in the beginning of a section.

James reaches for a note left behind with one of the victims. He holds it beside the Bible.

"'BESIDE THE GREEK GODDESS AN OLD CITY OF ANCIENT GREECE 1 tOXV,'" he reads the clue out loud. He turns to the Bible. "The Greek goddess is Athens and the old city is Corinth, which existed in ancient times in Greece. The 'tO' is the number two and the 'XV' is fifteen. The serial killer wants me to go to Corinthians 1, chapter two, verse fifteen," James says, looking up at Grace. "He uses chapters and verses from the Bible as clues," he explains.

"Will you be able to catch the killer now?" she asks with hope in her voice.

"Once I figure out what the passages mean," James says, grinning.

"I'm sure you will," she says optimistically. Grace stands and begins walking out of the room. "Try to get some rest soon. Tomorrow we'll run some tests. You may be out of here by lunch."

James stares at the photographs, the notes, and the Bible. Images and words flash through his mind. His memories carry him through segments of his life. He thinks about the time without Faith, and how it seems like a lifetime has passed. He thinks about the walls that he has built to protect himself, from exactly what he can't recall. The walls were too high and too wide for anyone to get through to him, but the walls have finally fallen. He will keep the ruins in the back of his mind as a reminder to never build them again.

Hours have passed, but James hasn't noticed. He holds the clue he read to Grace in his hand. He knows, 'BESIDE THE GREEK GODDESS AN OLD CITY OF ANCIENT GREECE 1 tOXV' means, Corinthians 1, chapter two, verse fifteen.

"'But he who is spiritual judges all things, yet he himself is rightly judged by no one,'" James reads the verse to himself. He stares at the verse, waiting for something to click.

James looks at a close-up photograph of evidence. A clue carved into a drug dealer's abdomen. The carved markings state 'NTH9XXVII.' James realizes the 'NT' of 'NTH' represents the New Testament. The only section in the New Testament that begins with "H" is Hebrews. The number "9" is chapter nine of Hebrews, and 'XXVII' is verse twenty-seven.

"'And as it is appointed for man to die once, but after this the judgment,'" he reads out loud to himself.

James closes his eyes for a moment to allow his mind to absorb the passage. He stares at another photograph of a victim. The abdomen of a young girl. The killer carved the image of a half-drawn heart and the words 'Warm Water' into her stomach. James concludes that the killer wanted him to look at the book known as Luke, because the words warm water and halfhearted can be defined as lukewarm. The markings 'XVIIIto' direct him to chapter eighteen, verse two.

"'There was in a certain city a judge who did not fear God nor regard man,'" he reads quietly from the Bible.

He pulls two other photographs out of the file. The abdomen of the victims had 'EVIL DOG' carved in it. The other victim has a similar marking. This victim has 'Z3VI1 DO6' on his abdomen. Two clues that remain dead ends. He continues to stare at the evidence as his mind attempts to piece the clues together. A memory surfaces, the memory of an elderly woman living across the street from one of the murder scenes. "'Open your eyes and mind, you must look at it from all perspectives,'" she said to him. The phrase rolls through his head. Suddenly a thought crosses his mind. A thought that sickens him. A gold-plated plaque flashes through his mind, the same gold-plated plaque found in a man's office he has visited many times. He reaches for a pencil. He places the two photographs beside one another. He stares at the photographs of the abdomens that have 'EVIL DOG' and 'Z3VI1 DO6' written on them. He begins to spell out EVIL DOG backwards. He adds the letter 'S' that he now believes was mistaken for a 'Z'. He stares, nauseated, at the words 'GOD LIVES.' He begins to slump into the bed. His mind continues to put the pieces together. He thinks of the dozen clues he has deciphered and the one thing that ties them together. The word 'judge' appears in all of the passages in one form or another. The murders started six years ago, a year after that man lost his family to the streets. Things have become painfully clear to James. Suddenly he feels the need to close his eyes and not to think about it anymore.

Chapter 53

James carefully walks down the stairs leading to the cellar of the church. He is meeting with a man he has come to respect and regard as a friend. As he steps down the staircase, he thinks of the unique bond formed between them, a bond formed from two lives that appeared entirely different on the surface. One in a chaotic struggle, searching for answers, and the other possessing answers, but with no questions to apply them to. Two lives intersected and constituted a reason for their existence. Together they have discovered understanding, and together they will feel a sense of certainty.

Greg sits at the table analyzing scrolls with a single candle burning. He is deep in thought and unaware of James' presence.

"What are you doing, Greg?"

"James," he says, jerking up. "You startled me."

"Sorry."

Greg pushes papers beneath the scrolls. "The hospital released you?" he asks, surprised.

"Yeah, I got on their nerves," James says quietly.

"How do you feel?"

"Great," James says, sitting down and leaning back into the chair.

"Are you concerned about the debate?" Greg asks.

"I checked the security today. It seems I have nothing to worry about."

"But you are."

"Is there anything in those scrolls about the debate?" James asks jokingly.

A passing expression of concern crosses Greg's face.

"I guess there is," James says, grinning, "And it appears to be bad news. What's going on, Greg? Now is not the time to keep things from me."

"The scrolls say there will be a clash of the spheres and that blood will be shed." Greg hesitates for a moment. "Blood of the righteous and blood of the forgiven will run together," he says quietly. "But it doesn't signify in any way that the debate is the clash."

"But you think it is."

Greg stares down at the scrolls.

"Which one am I, the forgiven or the righteous?" James asks, unaffected.

"The righteous," Greg says, looking up from the

scrolls.

James leans forward and sits on the edge of the chair. "Greg, it's all right," he says, smiling with a peaceful glint in his eyes. "I'll be fine, no matter what happens."

"I know, James," Greg says quietly.

"But, just in case I don't see you again," James says jokingly, "thanks for everything." He stands.

"I'd like to thank you, too, James," Greg says gratefully.

James and Greg shake hands. They stare at one another with appreciation in their eyes.

"I'll see you around, Greg," he says, slightly smiling.

"Where are you going?"

"To look in the mirror," James says quietly, "to see who I might have been."

*

It's late in the day and many have gone home to their loved ones, but some have nowhere to go.

James walks slowly down the corridor of the courthouse. He can hear his own heart beating. Obscure emotions run through his head. His mind turns over a single thought continuously. He thinks to himself how close he stood to the edge of insanity. The man in the office could have easily been him. He stands staring at the door. The music of Beethoven quietly filters through it. He knocks gently and a voice instructs him to enter. He stands in the doorway, thinking he understands the madness and the suffering that dwell in this man's mind, the endless vengeance driving him. James understands the man's motives of justice, but he is unable to accept or ignore them.

Judge Russell stares at James. The expression on James' face proclaims the purpose of his visit.

"Congratulations, James," Judge Russell says soothingly.

James stares at the judge with an emotionless expression.

"I know you understand," the judge says.

James glances at the gold-plated plaque hanging on the wall with the words "GOD LIVES" engraved on it.

Tears begin to form in Judge Russell's eyes. He looks upward. "It's over," he says, relieved. He closes his eyes as he lowers his head. "Thank God it's over."

Judge Russell begins to neatly put his papers away.

He carefully hangs his robe on the coat rack. He stares out the window, watching the last rays of sunlight color the sky an orangish red.

"May I request a favor?" the judge asks softly, staring out the window.

James waits, staring quietly.

Judge Russell turns around. "May I turn myself in tonight?" he asks.

James and the man he has been pursuing for the last six years stare at one another. James turns and walks out the door, alone.

*

James walks through the department toward Captain Ross' office. He stops and stares at the large city map hanging on the wall. The map that has red tacks stuck to it for every murder that Judge Russell has committed. He now notices that the red tacks are placed in a way that creates a cross, and where the cross would intersect is where the courthouse is located.

James walks into Captain Ross' office and throws a thick file onto his desk.

"What's this?" Captain Ross asks.

"The Evil Dog file."

"What? Are you giving up?"

"The case is closed," James says, turning to leave.

"What?"

"The name of the killer is in the report."

Captain Ross opens the file. "Are you crazy?" he exclaims.

"He's turning himself in tonight."

"What?"

"He wanted me to let him turn himself in."

"Do you really think he's going to turn himself in?" Captain Ross asks incredulously.

"No," he says quietly, beginning to leave.

"Do you think he's going to run?" Captain Ross asks, looking up from the file.

James turns before he exits the room. "I think he's going to face his judgement," he says, walking out the door.

*

A man enters the bar and finds a stool near the corner. Another man follows closely and sits next to the first man.

"Hey, Phil," the bartender says, handing him a beer. "You want a burger today?"

"Hi, Frank," Phil says, smiling. "Yeah, thanks."

Frank turns to the man sitting beside Phil. "What can I get you?" he asks politely.

The man stares at Frank with an evil expression. "Privacy," he says coldly.

Frank walks away with a look of contempt on his face.

The man turns to face Phil. "Excuse me," he says, smiling.

"Are you Phil Gram, the Secret Service agent?"

Phil looks at him curiously. "Yes, I am."

"Wonderful," the man says delightedly. "I require a favor."

Phil takes a sip of his beer and stares with an inquiring expression.

The man leans inward. "I want Senator Moore to have an accident tomorrow night," he says, grinning. "A fatal one."

Phil's face strikes a bewildered expression, which quickly converts to anger. "I could have you arrested," he says with a stare.

"You very well could," the man says, pausing for a moment to smile caustically, "but you won't."

"Oh, really?"

He stares into Phil's eyes. His expression becomes sinister. "You have a nice family, Phil," he whispers.

"What the fuck does that mean?"

"Now, you don't use that sort of language around your daughter, do you, Phil?" the man asks with a grin.

The bartender walks over with a telephone. The man glances over at Phil. "It's for you," he says, smiling.

Phil lifts the receiver to his ear. "Hello," he says quietly. His eyes begin to water and veins in his forehead begin to show clearly. "Do as they say. Everything will be fine," he says. He listens for a moment as the anger causes his face to harden. "I'll take care of it. I love you. Tell K.C. I love her," he says, slowly hanging the telephone up. "What do you want?" Phil asks with an angry stare.

"I believe I made that quite clear," the man says.

"How in the hell am I supposed to do it?" Phil asks with discourage in his voice.

"You alone are in charge of security on the upper balcony. There is a rifle hidden in the floorboards under seat two in Section D," the man says.

219

Phil lowers his head and stares at the floor.

"Moore dies, your family lives. Moore lives . . . " the man says, pushing away from the bar. "I believe you grasp the concept," he says coldly. "Have a nice day," he says, throwing a photograph of Phil's family on the bar before he walks away.

Chapter 54

"Good evening, I'm Arthur Hunt. We are minutes away from commencing the National Presidential Debate between self-made billionaire, Charles Malefic, and Senator Derrick Moore. A crowd of about two thousand guests, including the media, continue to enter the Conference Center at a slow pace due to the tight security. We're entering the fourth hour, but we believe we have reached the point where they are not allowing anyone else into the building," the newscaster says, standing in front of the sea of people.

The placement of the host's desk and candidates' chairs on the stage resembles a late-night talk show. The black marble desk trimmed with ivory stone, displaying the presidential seal, is in the center of the stage, flanked by two large black leather chairs. An enormous facsimile of Washington, D.C., hangs suspended in the background. Written in red, white, and blue across the facsimile are the words, 'Presidential Debate.' The American flag is positioned behind the host's desk with a light fixed on it from the base of the flagpole. The flags representing the individual states of the nation are located across the back of the stage, hanging from the rafters, a small spotlight shining directly on each. On the floor in front of the desk and the chairs is a large light-simulated American flag being projected from above. Running the length of the stage and ten feet in height is a clear bulletproof shield. On both sides of the stage are large viewing screens. The assembly will be seated solely in the floor area. The seats are red, white, and blue and gradually ascend from the front of the stage to the back of the Conference Center to a five-foot platform. All photographers and camera personnel are restricted to the general seating area. The remaining seating areas are sealed off with barricades and hundreds of police officers and Secret Service agents that are patrolling the perimeter. A human barrier of armed government officers stands between the stage and the crowd.

"The latest poll shows Senator Moore's points climbing every day," the newscaster says, adjusting his ear receiver. "Some say his increased popularity is due to the prophecy. Others in the political arena say the prophecy has no bearing on his favorable acceptance with the American people. The same sources say the prophecy, if anything, is a negative factor on the senator's campaign. 'A bold boast that remains unofficial,' one Congressman was quoted.

Charles Malefic was quoted earlier in the day. When asked about the prophecy being embraced by the world and the actuality of its occurrence, he said that 'The senator's prophecy is simply a myth embraced by the imaginations of a spiritually starving world.' Other politicians find it difficult to ignore the millions of accounts and testimonies around the world as easily as Mr. Malefic and some of his peers. Many have taken the position to remain undecided until the mysterious council committee report is released. One congressman was asked to comment on the resistance to the prophecy in Congress. He was quoted saying, 'Jesus Christ Himself couldn't influence them,'" the newscaster says, grinning.

The assembly begins applauding and the cameras rhythmically flash. The host, Bert Wilkins, has taken his place behind the desk. Malefic and Derrick remain in the wings, surrounded by Secret Service agents.

"The debate appears to be getting under way," the newscaster says, glancing toward the stage. "It's a very important night for both men, but this may be Charles Malefic's final chance to regain the presidential lead. I have just received the latest National Opinion Poll. Senator Derrick Moore has taken a slight lead. Something dramatic must occur for Charles Malefic to contend with the senator's climbing numbers."

*

DeMynn stares at the television. "Something dramatic . . . I agree," he says coldly, sitting comfortably in his office, sipping a drink.

Seated beside DeMynn are the Secret Service agent's wife and daughter. Standing behind them are two men wearing black suits.

"Why?" Mrs. Gram asks quietly.

"It's a hobby," DeMynn says, sipping his wine. He glances over at the little girl. "Your daddy is my hero. Did you know that, K.C.?" he asks, grinning.

The little four-year-old looks at him with frightened eyes. "You're a bad man," she says softly.

DeMynn stares heartlessly. "That's only half true, honey," he whispers.

"He won't do it," Mrs. Gram says.

DeMynn glances at the television and takes a sip of his drink. "Let me tell you something, Mrs. Gram," he says, staring coldly at her. "Your husband, with absolutely no doubt, would kill Moore for you and K.C. And I believe you know that." He takes another sip of his wine and stares at the television. "But your husband will not assassinate Moore," he says with a slight grin.

Mrs. Gram stares at him with a puzzled expression. "I don't understand," she says quietly.

"Please allow me to explain," he says. "Do you know what a fall guy is? He is the one that endures the blame. That, my dear, is your loving husband. You see, I have a young disciple among the crowd. He will join your husband on the balcony, and he is equipped with a marvelous sedative. Your husband will take a short nap, seven minutes to be exact. He'll regain consciousness as his colleagues arrive, and my pupil will have rejoined the chaos on the floor of the center by that time. He escapes, and Mr. Phil Gram becomes famous," he says, raising his glass in a toasting manner.

"And us?"

DeMynn stares at the television contemplatively. "That depends on my mood," he says coldly.

*

Derrick and Malefic begin walking out onto the stage, greeted by steady, resonant applause. The sea of camera flashes resembles strobe lights. A man dressed in a black suit with a Secret Service ID attached to his blazer begins working his way through the crowd away from the stage. He quietly and inconspicuously disappears into a stairwell. He reaches the balcony and stands unnoticed behind Phil. Phil is squatting between the seats and the wall with a rifle in his lap. The man reaches into his pocket. He holds a syringe filled with a clear liquid. He injects it into the back of Phil's neck. The burning liquid quickly works its way to his brain. Within seconds, Phil is quietly lying on his side. The man takes Phil's position. He inspects the weapon and surveys the crowd. He wraps the weapon's strap around his forearm and rests the rifle on the wall. He places his eye on the scope. Slowly, he scans the floor and the stage but suddenly stops. He recognizes James standing on the edge of the stage. He lays the rifle down and pulls some papers out of his jacket. The papers are newspaper clippings of Derrick, and written on them are prejudiced comments and death threats. He crams the papers into Phil's coat. He resumes his position and places his eye on the scope again. The cross hairs lie steady on Derrick's heart.

The shooter's heart slows down and a coolness begins spreading through his veins. His finger releases the safety. His finger carefully slides onto the trigger. He waits for his watch to beep.

*

DeMynn pulls a timepiece from his pocket. The gold chain sways as he glances down at the time. "The time is at hand," he says, glancing at the television screen. "I feel the scales tilting."

*

James scans the crowd as if Derrick's life depended on it. The wires of a radio transmitter stretch from his side to his mouth. He carefully listens to the information registering in his ear receiver.

The shooter's finger softly lies on the trigger, waiting.

Malefic glances into the crowd as Derrick answers a question. He begins to stare into space, daydreaming. His mind flashes pictures of children playing at a playground on a sunny day. Within seconds, black and gray clouds rush in overhead. Lightning splits the sky and thunder rumbles from above. Malefic sees DeMynn grinning at him, standing in the middle of the children on the playground. Suddenly tombstones begin punching out of the ground as the children get sucked into the earth. A flash from a camera erases the scene from his mind.

He slowly returns his attention to Derrick and Bert Wilkins, but a glossy black, tubelike object catches his eye. He squints slightly, attempting to shield the bright lights. His eyes focus and his mind rapidly searches to identify the familiar object. Suddenly a thought enters his mind, and his eyes expand into a panic. He leaps from his chair. "Nooooo!" Malefic screams, running toward Derrick.

The shooter's watch beeps. His finger squeezes gently. The shot is deadened by the silencer. The bullet travels through the air, cutting through the cameras' flashes.

Derrick looks at Malefic with confusion, as Malefic frantically rushes at him.

Bert Wilkins watches Malefic rush at Derrick.

The shooter looks on.

Malefic lunges across Derrick's body. The bullet

pierces Malefic's breastbone, striking his spine, then exits out his back and enters Derrick's thigh.

The gunman observes through the scope. He fires a second shot. The bullet hurls its way toward Derrick's head.

James leaps onto Derrick. They both plunge to the floor, followed by the chair. James lies motionless on Derrick.

Phil begins to regain consciousness. The gunman quietly vanishes into the darkness of the stairwell.

Derrick slides himself up to a sitting position, holding James' head in his lap. Blood oozes from beneath James, rapidly flowing across the stage, mixing with Malefic's blood, which is leaving his chest at a fatal pace.

Malefic lies motionlessly staring at Derrick as he bleeds to death. Derrick glances over at him. They lock eyes. Malefic smiles as his eyes slowly close.

*

Somewhere in a bell tower of a church, a soul finds forgiveness. The dark cloths and bandages fall away from his body. The black shimmering skin of the figure begins to crack and chip away. A man appears from beneath the darkness of guilt. The hammer and spike he has carried throughout the centuries fall to the ground, shattering into pieces. The pieces transform into white doves that fly out into the moonlight. A warm, golden beam of light shines down on him. He slowly ascends upward through the sparkling rays and fades into the open arms of the warm light. Rest awaits his arrival.

*

DeMynn sits on the couch, staring at the white static on the television screen. The broadcast disappeared from the air immediately after the first rifle shot. DeMynn looks on unaware of what has developed at the debate. He doesn't know if Derrick is alive or not. He stands and walks over to the chessboard.

"Take the woman and child home," DeMynn says quietly.

The two men in black suits instantaneously escort them out of the room.

As DeMynn stares at the chessboard, he discovers he is now in checkmate. He now knows that Derrick is still alive. He slowly reaches out and lays the tinted king down. He turns and walks away.

Chapter 55

A small crowd dressed mostly in black slowly returns to their automobiles. The cars depart one at a time, leaving a lone man standing by a fresh grave. A summer breeze blows gently beneath the gray overcast sky, rustling the leaves on the trees.

Greg stands peacefully staring at James' and Faith's headstones. "Well done, James," Greg says proudly. "Well done."

"Yes," a voice says from behind Greg. "I agree."

Greg doesn't turn around to see who it is, knowing it is DeMynn. A few heavy raindrops begin to fall.

"I must confess. I underestimated him," DeMynn says with a regretful tone.

"Yes, you did," Greg says quietly.

DeMynn steps up beside him and throws a black rose in the grave. "I believe the man with character got the girl," he says, referring to the earlier conversation. "I'll linger around for the wedding and see how long the honeymoon lasts," DeMynn says, grinning and staring at the horizon.

Greg glances over at DeMynn apprehensively.

"Don't worry about Senator Moore, Professor," DeMynn says. "I made an arrangement." He looks out over the cemetery grounds. "I leave the imminent President Moore alone, and in turn He keeps His hand, or should I say His fist, out of my affairs."

Greg senses that DeMynn had no choice in the arrangement but is attempting to keep his pride intact. Greg stares at the horizon contentedly. The rain begins to taper off.

"I found dealing with Senator Moore quite tiresome," DeMynn says quietly.

Greg glances over. "And unhealthy for your reputation," he says.

DeMynn smiles. "It was more work than it was worth," he says with a defensive tone.

"I understand," Greg says patronizingly. "Plus you made an arrangement."

"This will allow me to go abroad," DeMynn says with a grin. "There's a gentleman with potential in the Middle East that I need to spend time with."

The rain has stopped. Greg doesn't hear DeMynn's words anymore. He stands with contentment in his heart and a feeling of peace within himself for the first time in his life.

Like a jigsaw puzzle, pieces of the blue sky begin to appear through the breaking white clouds. The sun's rays streak down to the ground, and a rainbow appears in the distance.

Greg glances up at the sky. "It appears to be clearing up," he says, smiling and standing alone.

The End